Made Woman

S. Perez

ISBN: 9798771928692

Cover design by: Canva
Library of Congress Control Number: 2018675309
Printed in the United States of America

Made Woman

Losing her mother was the final blow for Nova Corzo, blaming her life troubles on mobster Daniel Crespo. She decides that to kill a boss you have to think like one. Nova decides to get the help of three notorious mobsters Ero, Shot, and Bash Dominic. The problem is they can't trust the other, hopefully, they either learn to get along or kill each other before they get a chance to kill Crespo.

Or will she be caught up in these mobsters who dare show her what it means to be a **_Made Woman_**.

Contents

Chapter 1

Nova
Three Months Ago

I sit in my tiny one-bedroom and watch the news reports of Daniel Crespo's trial. The evidence was stacked up against him, he was going to jail. I had to wait for this moment my entire life. This low-life mob boss was finally going to get his just desserts. My heart pounds as I wait for the results. "Daniel Crespo found not guilty of all charges!" The reporter announces. My heart sinks, tears fall from my eyes onto my legs. He beat me again...

Present

The strip club is full tonight, I'm tending the bar and the tips are rolling in. "Babe, are you okay? Let me know if you need a break?" Yara, the manager of the club asked.

"Nah, I'm good. I love nights like these. "

She smiles sheepishly. "Ok. I'll be back in an hour to check on you again. I know you have school."

Oh yeah.... school. Law school got put on the back burner after Daniel Crespo outsmarted the system.

Just thinking about it all, makes me angry all over again. I want him to bleed, I want that old man to lose everything. His wife, his boys, his power.... everything.

I have people coming at me, and the new girl, left and

right. "Busy bar." Says a man. I haven't looked up because I'm mixing drinks. "Yeah, it's just one of those nights." I look and see a gorgeous man in front of me. He is tall, his black hair was slicked back, and he was in a suit. I could also see the tattoos on his neck hiding behind his suit.

He doesn't take a seat and continues to stand, "When do you get off?" He flashes a small smile that was more of a smirk. It stirs something in me.

I continue to mix the next drink, "An hour from now." I answer.

He nods, "Sounds good. I'll wait, I got some business here, I should be done by the time you get off." The guy was smoking and honestly, I needed a stress reliever.

I continue work until the hour runs out. I look for the guy I met, and I went to the back booth to see him sitting there talking to a bunch of other men. "I'm off if you wanted to leave now," I say to him. He looks at me confused as if he had no idea what I was talking about. Something is strange about him; his suit had an assorted color to it. Did he change his clothes?

He gets up from his seat and grabs my hand. "Let's get out of here." A fancy black SUV pulls up and we step inside. Looking at him better now, he was still beautiful to look at. His eyes were a nice shade of hazel. I sit right next to him, and my heart is going off the charts. His eyes pierce into mine. "Nervous?" He asks. I am, of course, I am. I have never just gone home with a guy without finding out his name.

To pretend I wasn't nervous, I pressed my lips to his. He pulled me in closer pushing me down on the seat of the car, a spacious car it was, and dragged his fingers down my chest, refusing to break eye contact with me. He leans down into the crook of my neck and nibbles at it. A moan escapes my mouth.

He snickers at my reaction. My pussy soaked at this point, I have an urge to ride him here and now. He takes his jacket off, to get rid of his restriction. His hand reaches under my skirt, and he can feel how wet I am.

"All this for me?" He taunts. He rubs slightly which makes my hips buck wanting more. Slipping two fingers, "You look so pretty dripping on my fingers." The car suddenly stops, and he grabs my hand and helps me out of the car all gentlemen as we make it into an elevator that takes me up to the last floor. When it opens, I realize it's a penthouse, it is so spacious and beautifully decorated. He leads me down the hall into a room. It was a modern room, not much decoration. Everything was black and white. He sits me on his bed.

"Nice room," I comment.

His smirk returns, "Thank you." He undoes the bottoms on his shirt, showing off his body, which was perfectly sculpted. I run my hand down his body in appreciation. "Turn around and lean against the bed." He orders. I do as commanded, my ass in the air. He takes his thumb and presses it against my warm opening.

"Stop the fucking teasing please." I moan. This makes him snicker.

He moves his thumb and enters three new fingers, which made my hips buck, "Be good for me, or I'll have to fill that mouth first." His taunting continues. I wouldn't mind him filling my mouth. He takes off my shirt and panties, leaving me in just my skirt. He fists my curls and yanks me back so that my back is resting on his chest. I could feel his bulge through his dress pants. "You, see? You're not the only one suffering." He refers to his obvious hard-on.

With his hand still gripping my hair, he pulls me into a kiss, while slipping fingers in once again. I can feel myself wanting to cum. "Bad girl, what did I just say."

STEPHANIE PEREZ

"Let me cum, please." I plead. Letting go of my hair, I turn around and he looks into my helpless eyes and kisses me.

He unbuckles his pants and he kicks them to the side revealing his impressive cock. I realize our height difference even more as his cock pokes my stomach. He picks me up to lay me down on the bed once again. One of his hands on my hip and the other holding his weight. Before I can prepare for his penetration, he slams into me harshly. I scream from the intensity, but it doesn't hurt...much, it feels good.

"Go ahead." He whispers into my ear. Like a switch I fall apart and cum with a loud moan, digging my nails in his back. "So beautifully obedient." He continues to pump into me until he finally reaches his climax. He withdrawals himself and cums on my stomach. The worst part, this makes me horny all over again. We go another three rounds before going to sleep.

When I wake, he is gone and I'm left in the bed feeling the chill of the room. I put my clothes back on and take my leave.

"Hey!" I hear behind me before going into the elevator. It was him, in a more casual leather jacket type clothing. "Why are you here?"

"This is embarrassing I was just trying to leave. I thought you left."

He looks at me confused again, just like last night. "What happened to last night, I came back to get you and you were gone." Does this man have memory loss or something? What the fuck is he talking about. I decide not to try and figure out and leave.

"I don't understand what's going on so I'm going to head out."

Before I leave, he smiles as if he knows something I don't.

4

After a couple of hours later in the day, I get back to the strip club to get ready for my shift. "Nova, the owner is coming back again today just a heads up," Yara announced.

I look at her confused, "Again?"

"Yeah, they were here yesterday you have probably missed them when you were working it was a busy night but today should be more relaxed. Only one of them will be here today."

My best friend, Jia Li Feng, who works as a stripper here walks up to me. "Hey J.L, you're here early," I comment hugging her.

She sighs, pulling away from the hug, "Girl, medical school is killing me, and my son's father is being difficult. So lucky my mom was able to take him today."

"How is Bo?"

"He's getting big." I smile, J. L's son was such a cutie. He was a little gentleman; he is going to be a good guy when he gets older. "So, the boss is visiting today?" She revisits.

"Yeah, supposedly they were here last night but I didn't see anyone."

"You know who the boss is, right?" She gets closer, her voice a whisper. "This club is owned by the mob boss of the *Casa Rossa*. I've never seen what he looks like but that's what they say."

My eyes widen, I heard about them when I was a child. They have been rivals with Daniel Crespo's *La Fiamma*. "Really, oh shit." I was a bit surprised that I hadn't realized that.

Not even a second later, the guy from last night and this

morning are back but his hair had been cut. He now had an undercut and an all-black suit. I do not know what I should do, why is this guy showing up at my job. I walk up to him and put my hand against his chest, "What are you doing? I thought it was a one-time thing, you can't just show up at my job." I explain.

He looks at my hand and grabs it tightly, making me wince. "Who the hell are you?" He asks glaring. This is the third time he has looked at me like this. It's like he has short-term memory loss.

"Why do you keep forgetting me? Do you have short-term memory loss or something?" I growl. He lets go of my hand.

He was about to answer me when Yara comes, "Mr. Dominic, this is our bartender Nova Corzo."

"Nova, this is the owner, Romero Dominic." She introduced. So that's his name. This is the boss of *Casa Rossa*? Did I sleep with the boss of *Casa Rossa*? Romero walks with Yara to the back room.

I didn't see Romero come out of the back room for hours. The club started to pick up and I was hounded by people ordering drinks. Out of the corner of my eye, I see Romero look at me coldly and then leave.

At the end of the night, I went out to mom and I's favorite restaurant. Today is the anniversary of her death. I sit by myself and drink mom's favorite wine. As I sit, I realize how empty the restaurant is. I look around and see some men standing at the entrance and the surrounding walls. I recognize the faces of the men. Without a doubt, he is here, Daniel Crespo the bastard himself.

"You know my father always said humanity's greatest

weakness was patterns." He quotes sitting down in the empty chair in front of me. "People love routines. Routines get you killed." He continues.

I glare up at him, "What do you want? Why are you here?" I growl trying to keep my composure.

He links his fingers together and leans over resting his elbows on the table. "I'm sorry about your mother." His eyes seem to soften slightly but go back to his cold stare.

I bring the wine glass to my mouth and close my eyes as I set it back onto the table, " A little late for that...about a couple years too late."

"Nevertheless, I'm sorry. She was a sweet girl." He smiled. "I remember when she was sixteen and wanted to be a pilot. She would-"

I start laughing almost maniacally, "Are you serious? Are you sitting there trying to bond with me old man?" I get up from my seat.

He flares "I know your mother didn't raise such a disrespectful brat. A punishment would do you some good."

I stop in my tracks, not out of fear but to give him my parting words, "Was she not enough?" I whisper to him.
The arrogance of this piece of shit, I want him gone. He needs to die.

Later that night, I went back to work, I was called in because the new girl just was not hacking it. During my shift, I noticed Romero was still here and went into the back room. I waited till my break to speak to him. What I was about to do was the dumbest thing you should ever do when dealing with the Mafia. I walked over to the back room and opened the door. All eyes watched me, I knew someone of the faces and many I did not know. Then it hit me. I was seeing three Romero's. "Everyone leave." One of the Romero's spoke, but I didn't know which one was the actual Romero. The rest leave quickly, responding to his order.

"My obedient girl, you're back." Another Romero said.

"Really Bash?" The third Romero scoffed.

Are they triplets? "There's three of you? Which one of you is which?" My voice frantic with so much confusion.

One the Romero's smiled sweetly, "I'm Jameson, but everyone calls me 'Shot.' I was the one who was waiting for you to get off work, Sebastian my brother was the one who took you home, and you ran into Romero today."

"Stop talking." Romero orders. Jameson sighs heavily and leans in his chair. "You must be fearless or moronic to come in here."

I was fearless, but stupid as well. "I want to talk to you Romero, you're the boss, right?" I gulp. Romero glares at me. He doesn't find my barging in here charming. Coming in here was extremely disrespectful. "I want to make a deal."

The three stares at me, Sebastian smirking at me, Jameson looking confused, and Romero's eyes keeping an icy stare. "Speak," Romero ordered.

I take a breath, "I need to kill Daniel Crespo, lucky for me the *Casa Rossa* has been at war since I was a child."

Sebastian sighs, then speaks, "Why would we go to war with that relic for you, sweet? I mean after last night, I could see why, but even this is too far." He snickers, looking me up and down.

I narrow my eyes at his jokes, "I'm not asking you to go to war. I'll kill him myself, but I need help getting there. I can't take him down alone. When he is gone you will be able to take his territories, without any looks from the other families." I explain. "I'll take the blame."

"No," Romero replies.

Jameson looks like he wants to say something but Romero has already spoken. "Ero, this might not be a bad idea, she kills the decaying dickhead and we reap the benefits." Sebastian offers.

Romero looks over at his doppelgänger, "Don't be blinded by your dick."

"Fuck you Ero." He growls.

Jameson again is silent; he sits with pondering eyes. As if he was trying to think the situation through. "It works." Jameson finally speaks up. "Daniel Crespo isn't liked by many already anyone could kill him, but someone who is not a part of the families will have no blowback. His territory would be fair game."

Romero still is not convinced, "And how do we know she won't betray us?"

"I won't. I want this more than you do." I state clearly.

Sebastian cocks his head to the side, "We could always keep her, making sure she is being watched at all times. That she is always in dicks reach."

Jameson again wanting to make a statement, but Sebastian just smiles and gazes at me.

"Fine." Romero accepts. Bringing wide grins to Jameson and Sebastian's faces. "Make no mistake, if this goes wrong for any reason...well you get the idea." I could tell it wasn't a threat but a promise.

I nod showing him I understand and make my way out of the room.

Chapter 2

Jameson

This girl truly is one gutsy bartender. She is so nice to look at. Her curly hair stops at the middle of her back. She is not that tall, about five feet, but she is determined. Ero being Ero still is suspicious of her. He is not a trusting person to begin with.

"We need to keep an eye on her. She could be playing us." Ero states. His paranoia in full swing today.

I sigh, "Ero we can't keep tabs on her 24 hours." He rolls his eyes at my statement.

Sebastian runs his fingers through his hair, "Well, technically we could if she lived with us."

My eyes widen at the idea of having her with us. I was still annoyed that Bash slept with her. My brothers are some serious bastards sometimes. "No." Ero votes.

"Why are you so irritated Ero? Sexual frustration? It felt really good being inside her if you're wondering." Sebastian teases. It was my turn to roll my eyes, she was supposed to be in my bed that night. "I don't know why you're getting so bent out of shape, if she proves to be a problem, we kill her."

My brothers can sometimes lack basic human emotions except for pleasure and power. I mean I'm no saint, but I don't think I'd want to kill her. Unless she truly was playing us, then maybe, but even then, I would have to think deeply about it. Ero and Bash do not need to think about anything when they feel betrayed, they are extremely impulsive, mainly Bash. If emotions are not involved Ero can think something through. After our father died and Ero became the new boss of the family he has been on edge, wanting to live up to dad's legacy. Before Ero became the boss he was more fun to be around.

Nova

I did not think they would work with me. Romero seems like he is going to be difficult to deal with. Jameson seems a thousand times relaxed. He has an almost child-like niceness to him. On the other hand, he is still a Made Man, I would not put it past him if he were truly as cold as his brother appears. Then, Sebastian, my head is still spinning about our night together. I know I really shouldn't even be thinking about this but fuck that was a good night. Sebastian is a cocky bastard who takes pleasure in watching people squirm. I'll have to be careful around him.

"*Oye tienes tostadas y café con leche*? [**Hey, do you have toasted Cuban bread and coffee with milk?**]" I ask the server at my favorite Cuban restaurant.

"*Si amor, como lo quier?* [**Yes love, how do you want it?**]" Asks the server.

"*Clarita con azúcar.* [**Light with sugar.**] "I answer.

I then go ahead and order for J.L. "At some point, I need to learn some Spanish." J.L laughs.

I laugh in return, "Teach me some Mandarin and I got you with the Spanish."

"Your Mandarin is already pretty good." She praised me, but my mandarin was only at a 67% level I would say. Growing up my mother spoke many languages, she loved learning about diverse cultures. She taught me to speak Spanish, Italian, and a few other languages here and there. My mother was originally from Cuba and came to the states at twelve. She was a true beauty, ebony skin with light brown eyes and beautiful curls. She also had long legs, which irritates me because of the fact that I'm such a pip-squeak.

"Aunt Nova?" I almost forget Bo is sitting on my lap coloring.

I look down at him, his big brown eyes shine back at me, "Yes babe?"

"Does this look like a cat?" He points to his drawing.

I narrow my eyes, "Kinda looks like a cat/bunny."

He nods and continues to draw. Bo really was such a cute kid.

Several days passed and I didn't hear anything from the *Casa Rossa* triplets. I haven't even seen any of them at the club. Did they decide to back out? Damn, this means I'll have to find another angle in hurting Daniel. "Fuck." I say aloud to myself. I take a shower and wash the day off me and continue to think of a plan. Nothing even comes to mind; it is like my strategic mind went blank. What if what I do is not enough? What if I can't take him down? Fuck, this is stressful.

A knock came on my door after my shower. It was pretty late, I try to dry off and hurry and put some clothes on, my hair was still wet, and it was dripping into my clothes. I answered the door and saw Jameson. Now realizing that they were triplets I noticed that Jameson's hair was slightly not as put together as his brothers and his eyes with a lighter green. His smile could make anyone smile. "Hey, glad to see you're up." He greeted. I looked at him a bit confused. "So...we have been thinking you should stay at the penthouse with us." He offers, but in the back of my mind, I feel like it's not a request.

"I can't I already live here and what's the point in moving in?" I ask.

He sighs, "In all fairness, we don't know much about you and what we are doing is a pretty serious declaration. We all need to be on the same page. Living with us will make us all be able to better trust each other in this process." Jameson putting it as nicely as possible.

I narrow my eyes, "In other words, Romero doesn't trust me and wants to keep a close eye on me." I bluntly spell it out. He nods, with a sheepish smile.

I realize that without their help I can't get my revenge, but I'm not just going to do whatever they say either. "I have a lease I can't move out," I explain.

"We bought the building. We have been trying to get into real-estate, maybe it's fate, sweet." Sebastian says coming up the steps from the first floor. Great he gave me a new nickname, I guess it's better than 'obedient girl.'

My eyes are wide. Are they insane? Who buys a building just because? Fucking mafia men and their endless supply of illegal money.

Romero

Something about this woman feels familiar. Have I slept with her before? No, from the way Sebastian spoke I would remember. This shit is driving me fucking insane. For now, I'll have to put it to the side and just keep her in arm's reach. I need to know if she is an enemy I can't remember. I have such a great memory; it is not like me to forget a face. I even remember the girls I fuck from time to time, not names, but faces. Every time I think of her, it sends a chill down my spine that I can't pinpoint.

I hear the elevator open and the voices of my brothers. "I would give you a tour but I'm sure you remember your way around." Sebastian's voice echoes through the hall. I hear an annoying female groan. The voice sounding familiar, and I realize who it is. Did these bastards really bring her here? I got up from my desk and walk downstairs into the living room. I see Shot, Bash, and Nova.

Shot looks at me frantically, then looks at Bash. Almost accusing him of bringing Nova. "Someone explain," I growl.

Bash sports his signature devilish smile, "Ero, I'm doing this for you. With her here you have peace of mind that she is down for the cause as much as she says she is."

I scoff at the bullshit coming out of Bash's mouth. "How sweet of my big brother and little brother to disobey my orders."

"Exactly little bro, you get it. It must be that triplet bond." Bash sarcastically gleamed.

My eyes now focused on Shot. "What about you?" I interrogated.

Shot clears his throat, "I just want to say that I'm just an innocent bystander. Bash told me we were going to Antonio's to get pizza. I would never disobey you, boss." Shot can be such a lying suck-up.

I breathed in, then out, "Fine. You guys want her here? You both will oversee her. If she slips up, your deaths will follow."

Nova

"Can you guys stop talking like I'm not here," I growl? "Look, I agreed to come here as a peace offering. So, let's just act like adults and get the job done."

Romero walks up to me and looks down at me. All these guys were a foot taller than me. "Watch your fucking mouth. Remember who you're talking to. Show some respect, before I figure out a way to teach you some manners."

I look at him with a blank stare. He doesn't scare me, But I do not say anything because I need this asshole's help. "Now Ero, that's no way to speak to a lady, well not unless you're balls deep in her." Sebastian steps in, pulling me back into his chest.

Jameson grabs my hand, "Hey, I'll show Nova to her room." He pulls me from Sebastian's grip and past Romero into a hallway.

He opens the door with a key and then hands it to me. "This is the guest room, but it's your room for the time being. So do whatever you like to it."

Jameson was about to walk away when I grabbed his hand. "Hey," I stop him. "Thank you. You've been sweet to me ever since we met. I appreciate it."

He smiles at me wholeheartedly and pushes my hair behind my ear. "No problem, *tesoro*." Treasure is what he called me. Was he this sweet or just as manipulative as his brothers? For a moment, his eyes narrow at me, "Can I ask you something?"

I blink, "Sure."

"Why do you want to kill Crespo?" He asks, his light green eyes tracing for an answer in my facial expressions.

I lean against the door frame. "He killed my mother." I

simply say. "When I was younger my mother had involved herself with *La Fiamma*. She had just come from Cuba at twelve with her seventeen-year-old sister. It was hard getting by, so my aunt basically pimped herself out to *La Fiamma* in exchange for protection and shelter. My mother stopped talking to her after she got involved with them and distanced herself. When I was nine, she saw the news that my aunts' body had been found. My mother knew it was *La Fiamma*. The boss at the time was Cedro Crespo. My mother went to speak to him, she didn't come back that day. A neighbor had been watching me, but hours turned into days."

Jameson looked at me empathetic. "But how do you know it was Daniel Crespo?"

"My mother. She told me stories of her life being around *La Fiamma* for two years before she distanced herself from my aunt. They used to talk about Cedro all the time. He was not very respected by his men. He could never get his hands dirty he always sent his son to finish loose ends."

"Daniel Crespo." The realization sets in for Jameson. Now understanding the complete picture.

"What about you guys? *Casa Rossa* and *La Fiamma* have been enemies since I was a kid, but if I remember correctly the families were fine before.

Jameson pushes me lightly into the room and closes the door behind him, I guess he did not want anyone to overhear. "To be honest, I don't know where it started. I have a feeling my brothers do, but they won't talk."

"Oh." Was all that came out of my mouth.

Jameson walks over to the bed and sits in front of it on the floor. He taps the ground next to him, urging me to sit. I follow suit and sit down next to him. "Taking down Crespo is going to be a while, so tell me what you like to eat, hobbies, etc."

"You first." I challenged my eyes squinted, causing Jameson to laugh.

He crosses his arms playfully, "Let's see...my hobbies include threatening local businesses that don't pay up the loans they owe." He started. My eyes widen at his response. I guess looks can be deceiving, he's an enforcer. "I like Thai food, specifically Tom Yum soup." He finished.

I look up to the ceiling trying to think, "I like Mac and cheese and chicken tenders. No matter how expensive the restaurant I will ask for either. I basically have the pallet of a five-year-old." I confess. Jameson snorts a laugh. "Or if I'm at a Cuban restaurant, I always get pork with a side of white rice and plantains. Hobby...would be learning about laws and culture."

His laughter quiets, "Can I ask you another question?"

I cock my head to the side, "Go ahead."

"Have you ever killed anyone?" His tone did not seem accusing but curious. His twinkly green gaze set upon me.

I inhale softly before asking, "Why?"

Jameson's eyes look up to the ceiling as looking in deep thought, "You want to kill an active boss with our help, I just need to know you will deliver the blow. If you can't this ends up bad for all of us."

I hold out my pinky and wrap it with his. "I promise, I'll do it. If I don't, I owe you guys for life or you guys get to kill me I suppose. Either way you guys have the better end of the deal."

His laugher comes through once again, as he shakes my

pinky. "I guess we do..." His voice trails off and he detaches his pinky and grips mine between his fingers. A sweet warm feeling that seems familiar.

Sebastian

"Shot has been gone for a while..." I growl. He would not dare touch her, knowing I'm not done playing with her yet.

Ero glares and smacks the back of my head lightly. "Don't get distracted." He growls back. It does not quiet my irritation. Once Ero has gone back to his office for the day, I go to the room Nova is staying in and as I reach the door, I hear laughter.

"I'm telling you cheesy puffs are better stale." Nova's laughter echoes through the door.

Shot's laughter follows as well after her. "There's no way." He snorts. Since when is he so damn cheerful? Shot is usually silent and observant.

"No, I swear. I don't know why but they are better. Oh, and if you get cheese ruffles and dip them into cookies and cream ice-cream is really good to." She claims.

"You need a new tongue your taste buds are all fucked up." He jokes. I hear a small smack; she must have playfully hit him.

"Why is he in her room?" I think to myself. My childish side gets the best of me, and I knock on the door. This causes both to fall silent. "Let's go Shot, did you forget the meeting with Matanza."

I hear them say their goodbyes and he open the door bumping into me on purpose. "The fuck is your problem?" I bark in a whisper tone.

"Jealous prick." He scoffs and walks down the hall. The balls on this brat...

Nova

Several days passed and I started to notice the difference between the triplets. Jameson is slightly slimmer than Sebastian and Romero and his hair was a bit wavier, slightly curly even. He is also sweeter and nurturing. Sebastian had way more tattoos out of the three of them. He is a smooth talker, but he can be brash. Romero was easy, his hair was long on top with an undercut, cold and distant. That was it. Jameson was basically the parent of the family; he cooks every meal. I'm pretty sure because they do not trust others to make their food.

Sebastian and Jameson were out today again. Leaving me with the "cold and distant" brother. Romero and I have the most awkward encounters. For instance, this morning for breakfast he sat across from me, trying to put as much distance as he could, and drank his coffee, while he dabbled in his laptop. He would not make eye contact with me for one second. It was so quiet in the room you could hear low AC pressure. The silence was driving me insane. The good thing was that Jameson was around to lighten the mood.

There was a housekeeper here who would do our laundry. It was extremely weird the last person to do my laundry was my mom and I was nine. Looking through my clothes I realize that my socks might have been misplaced. Of course, "cold and distant" is the only one home. I go and knock on his door. I get no answer. I guess he left for the day, I decided to just check quickly and walk inside and check in a drawer and see if my missing socks. His room was not that much different from Sebastian's room it just had more blue stuff to accent the black.

"What are you doing?" An irritated voice says from behind me.

I freeze for a minute, but I get up and turn around. "Lucy, put my socks in your drawer by accident. I thought you left so I was going to grab them before you came back." I explain.

His eyes seemed darker, or maybe they always were. I don't think I have ever been this close to him. "You really do have bad manners..." He comes close to me taking off his suit jacket and tossing it. He then loses his tie. "I think it's about time I teach you some. "

Chapter 3

Nova

Goosebumps run across my body, a reaction to his cold words. "Excuse me?" is all I manage to spit out. What is this cold doppelgänger thinking?

"Sit." He orders. I don't move an inch, playing this game of chicken was going to be risky. "And here I was told you were obedient." A devilish smile spreads on his face. Even with that evil smile I still found him desirable. They all were, just perfect to look at. My knees felt weak, and I thought I would fall from the weight of my arousal.

Romero suddenly picks me up and sets me on the bed. He puts a knee on my leg to keep me still, while he ties my hands with his tie. "What the hell are you doing?" I whisper, as if I were scared to be heard more than what might take place.

He ignores my words and leaves me tied up on the bed. Walking over to his nightstand, he takes a sip of his water before returning his attention to me. "Have you ever heard of B.F Skinner? "

I minored in Psych in college, so I know all about it, but I indulge his ego. "Pray tell, cold one, please inform me." I mock.

"From your tone, I'm guessing you already know what I'm getting at. He believed rewards and punishments were the keys to conditioning. Let's see if I can do the same with you." He explains with a blank expression.

"Ha, I'd love to see you try. "I scoff. He returns my scoff with a smile.

His long fingers slide down my thighs. I try to hold in my gasp, but my lips fail me. He snickers at my lousily attempt. His eyes are only focused on my face. Searching for any weakness I can offer him, but I try to stay as strong as possible. He may be a dick, but I still can't deny him physically. He leans down to my eye level to get closer. I narrow my eyes, trying to figure out the wolf's next move. "It's okay to moan, it's your body's natural reaction to me."

I pick at my restraints in annoyance. "What is this boring foreplay? If you want to fuck me, just get it out of your system, and then let's go back to barely speaking-" Before I could finish the sentence his lips crashed into mine, I thought it would be harsh and brash, but it was sweet and soft. I kissed him back not being able to stop such a sweet kiss. He tasted like coffee and toothpaste, such a weird combination but I somehow enjoyed it.

Then he bit my lip *hard*. I pull back, "What is your problem, fuck!" I growl.

I can taste my blood. I also see some of my blood on his lips, but he just licks it clean. His smile remains, "Reward and Punishment..." He pauses, wiping his thumb against my bleeding lip. "I *will* teach you well."

A humph comes from me as I left my hands, "You had your fun. Untie me."

He snickers once more, "Did you put up this much of a fight with my brother? How did it feel? Do you scream when you cum?" His tone didn't give away the motive I was looking for. Before now, Romero barely spoke to me, now all he is doing is talking. "Bash gave it up too easy, which is probably why you have already assumed that I would fuck you today." I try to get up, but his hands hold my waist to the bed.

I notice the bulge in his pants, it makes me giggle. He raises a brow at me. "You're the one giving it up too easy," I say rubbing his bulge with my barefoot. He exhales, in a hushed moan. I push my head against his chest trying to feel his beating

STEPHANIE PEREZ

heart. I'm surprised he let me rest my head on him. Maybe this cold personality is all an act? Maybe I just need to keep pushing. "I'd say you want me. Want me *badly*...I just hope you make it as fun as your brother did." I say trying to instigate a reaction from him. A window of weakness is all I need to beat him.

He laughs...like full-on laughing. It honestly shocked me. He has a bit of a raspy laugh. It soothes me as he continues. "You are...a terrible actress." He stops himself. I lift my head from his chest. The dark green gaze holding me in place. It was his turn to rest his head on my chest, his hair tickled the gap in my shirt that exposed my chest. "Your heart is speeding up." He says as he moves his head back and pulls down my shirt, exposing my pointed breasts.

I twitch from side to side. "Romero-" Before I can finish, soft lips cover my breasts. His tongue swirls around my left nipple, while he rubs the right one with his thumb. I bite my lip, "Tease." The words barely making it past my lips. He shifts gears and uses his right hand to pull off my shorts. Leaving me my black thong.

With one long finger, he pressed against the damp fabric, "It seems *you* want *me* badly. Look how honest your body is being with me? It's practically yelling for me to fuck that cunt of yours." He purred. He parts the fabric pushing it to the side to slip a finger in. "I might drown in this cunt..." He takes out his finger and starts licking me brutally. He doesn't even warm up to his pace. The strong sensation has me bucking, but he keeps me still.

My breath escapes me, "S-S-Stop...it's too much." I beg.

He ignores my plea and continues his fierce attack on my pussy. "I will decide when you've had enough. Didn't I tell you already? Is it time for a punishment?" He growls into me, just feeding the sweet vibrations of my body.

I can feel myself getting closer and closer to my climax...but then he just stops. He stares at me as he licks his lips

24

of...well *me*. He stands up releasing me from his grip and unites my hand. "Why did you stop?" I scowled.

His emotionless face, stretches into a smirk, "You think I would reward your unruly behavior?"

I close my eyes and breathe in deeply, "Can I leave?" I ask.

His thumb brushes against my cheek, "Of course. Thank you for asking. You're learning. I'm already teaching you to be polite."

I pull my face away from his touch and walk past him and pick up my clothes. Quickly dressing I get ready for work and make my way to the bar.

J.L was doing amazing today and made so much cash. I wasn't doing too bad either, the tips were pouring in tonight. Before I knew it, it was three in the morning, when we finished our shifts and went to a 24hr breakfast place called *Siempre*. It was so good, nothing better than some bomb Caribbean food in the morning after a long shift.

"My hair needs a trim starting this weekend, you wanna come?" J.L asks.

I look at the curly mess on my head, "Yeah I need a trim. Do you think Mya or Dani will be able to do my hair though? I refuse to go to anyone else; I swear these so-called 'Hairdressers' don't even know how to do hair. Like if you can't do all types of hair how you can call yourself a hairdresser."

I notice for the past hour a man has been watching us. "Hey, don't look but I swear this guy has been looking over at us for a while," I whisper.

Picking up my spoon I angle it in a way that J.L can see the reflection. "It's giving very much Ted Bundy." She sneered and rolled her eyes.

The wonderful thing about working at a bar with a massive number of drunk idiots clawing at you, is you learn to carry a butterfly knife in your sneakers. Rubio, our friend who always makes fun of our drunk asses when we are in here, comes to the table with a vanilla and chocolate shake in hand and sits with us. Well, his name is actually Felipe, but we call him Rubio because he died his hair blond-haired person once in middle school and it was horrible, so we kept calling him that. "Finally on break, these are for you guys." He said pushing the shakes towards us.

"Damn he wanna give us a sugar high." I say, pinching his cheek, but he swats it away laughing along with J.L.

"Speaking of sugar highs, I gotta pick up Bo from my mom and take him to school in two hours so I'm gonna head out. You scrubs good?" She teases.

"She must be talking to you." Rubio and I say in unison. We squint at her and reply, "We good here."

Seconds later she leaves, "So, you got into Columbia Law School." Jealousy foaming at my mouth.

"I still can't believe it. This is crazy man." I pat him on the head, "Good shit man." It does sting a bit. I put Law School on the back burner for this. Seeing his excitement, makes me rethink my plan of revenge. Only for a second though, I'm still going to kill that bastard.

"What about you? I mean you're the poster child for Law School. You graduated first in our class. I'm surprised you haven't accepted Columbia's offer yet."

"Yeah..."

"I mean if you want to give yourself some time, I understand. School was like your life for a long time. You could use a break."

This is the year I'll either be in jail or dead. The system left me no choice. I can't wait for them to keep letting him get away with what he did. He is a Made Man; therefore, I must become a "Made Woman" to beat him.

Jameson: What are you doing?

Nova: Breakfast, long workday.

Jameson: Be right there. We got business. See you soon.

Nova: Ok.

Right, where? How does he know where I am? Not soon after a big black SUV parks in front of the restaurant. Are these triplets tracking me?

A man steps out of the car that doesn't look familiar; he looks like a secret service agent. "They are ready to leave Ms. Corzo. Please follow me to the car."

Rubio looks at me bewildered, "Um…" He trails off.

What the fuck do I even say. I think quickly, "Oh shit, I started dating this guy, he said he was gonna pick me up. Sorry, it slipped my mind." I lie.

Rubio is skeptical but doesn't give it too much thought. He hugs me goodbye, and I step inside into the car to see all three triplets. Yet, there is nowhere to sit in the SUV, I'm guessing the bodyguards are taking up space.

Sebastian throws me his idea of a charming smile and pulls me into his lap. "You can sit here, sweet." He coos, wrapping his arms around me. I finally get comfortable sitting on him, but then I feel something poking me, which makes my body boil with heat. "Look what you're doing to me, I haven't had you since that first night. Should I fuck you here? Let my brothers understand who you want most." He whispers in my ear. So, close I could feel his breath on my neck as he pushes a curl away.

Romero and Jameson sat across from us and can't hear what he is saying, but they can guess as they study my face and body. "W-Where are we going?" I asked still a bit flushed by my seating arrangement.

"Eleno "Matanza" Sosa Jr. is a drug trafficker from Cuba. His father was the last head, but now that he is dead Matanza took over. He has been going back and forth on supplying *La Fiamma* and *Casa Rosa* for years but since we no longer hold ties with *La Fiamma*, he decided to side with them after our father died. So, we are paying him a visit in Queens." Romero explained.

"*Il miglior motivatore è la paura...* [**The best motivator is fear...**]" Sebastian says in Italian, I don't need to turn around to see that Cheshire smile behind me. I didn't even realize he spoke Italian I wonder if they all do.

"Think before you speak. Matanza is old-fashioned, he lives by a code. If he feels even the slightest aggression, he will not work with us. This man is not moved by fear. Our father respected this man." Romero snapped.

Sebastian huffs and rests his head into my curls, pulling me in tighter. Jameson is extremely quiet in front of his brothers, I noticed. When we are alone, we can talk all night but here he is reserved. He isn't making much eye contact with me either. I started to notice this trend whenever we were all together.

I give him a few glances, hoping he will look my way, when he does, he smiles quickly before looking back outside the window. It makes me smile right back. When I make eye contact with Romero, he glares at me, which means he's back to normal, I guess. The mood swings on this guy I tell ya.

The drive was long and at some point, I just fell asleep.

About an hour later, I feel Sebastian rubbing my head slightly. "Wake up, sweet." Sebastian cooed. I ignore his words and just snuggled up into the crook of his neck. It was almost instinctual, which was starting to worry me.

The smell of his cologne filled my nose, it smelled fresh, but a bit sweet. A flick to the side of my forehead wakes me. "Get up." Romero's stern voice rings in my ears. I open my eyes glaring at him, while Sebastian snickered.

I get out of the car and walk alongside Jameson. We were

in front of an old-looking run-down warehouse. It was insanely creepy and under kept. "This isn't sketchy at all." I laugh nervously.

No one said anything and we continued to walk inside. I was surprised to see it was a beautifully decorated underground casino. I could hear loud laughs and dominos slamming against the tables.

"*Hijo de la gran puta!* [**Son of a bitch!**]" Yelled one of the men. He slammed another domino on the table. "*Mamita, ponte a trabajar y tráeme un trago.* [**Baby, get to work and get me a drink.**]" He barks at the woman on his lap. He looks over at us and smiles.

"Good to see you Matanza." Romero greets Sebastian and Jameson nods in accordance.

"Excuse the festivities. I'm feeling generous tonight, so I won't take these fools' money. Take a seat to play a few rounds with us."

Romero smirks, "Of course." He agrees. The other men get up and Sebastian and Romero take their place. Jameson stands beside me; his eyes look over the casino like a watchdog.

"Matanza..back to business. We need your product. I understand our clash with *La Fiamma* is causing some pushback, but we have been in business for over sixty years. You are the best producer we have ever worked with. What can we do to get back to business?" Romero starts.

Matanza sits up in his chair and sighs, "Romero, listen my issue is not with *La Fiamma* I could give fuck about how they feel. You know me and I'm all about numbers and no disrespect, but your father was a beast and how do I know you have that same drive. I can't afford to fuck up with these fucking feds breathing down my neck. I'm sure your father raised you in his image, but you haven't put in the years yet. So why should I gamble on you?"

Before Romero opens his mouth, I step in, " *Señor Matanza, veo que le gusta jugar al dominó. Yo también juego. Me preguntaba si le gustaría hacer una apuesta* **[Mister Matanza, I see that you like to play dominos. I also play as well. I was wondering if you would like to make a bet.].**" I suggest. I could feel Romero's hard glare. Now he must have wanted to kill me for butting in.

Matanza looks at me intrigued, "That's a Cuban accent I hear?" He chuckles, "*¿qué estás pensando?* **[What are you thinking?]**

"*Yo jugaré contigo. Si gano, trabajarás con los Dominics.* **[I'll play you. If I win, you work with the Dominics.]**

"*¿Y si yo gano...?* **[And If I win...?]**" He trails. He looks down and then back to me.

All stares were on me, the triplets, Matanza and his men. I breathe out softly, "Name your price." I answered.

"Name my price? Damn you sound like you got nothing to lose *niña*." He laughs.

"I don't," I answer a bit coldly.

He smiles wildly then chuckles, "You know what? Fuck it, you caught me in a good mood. If you can beat me, I'll back the Dominics. *Pero*, if I win...you work for me." He states.

I raise a brow, "How so?"

"You're pretty, nice curves and those lips are beautifully plump. You would do well in my whorehouse." My eyes widen at the fact that was his offer. "*This fucker really has it coming...*" I thought to myself. I look over at Jameson and he puts a protective hand on my back. I then look over at Sebastian who is twirling his gun under the table as if he were itching to shoot someone. Romero did not show a hint of interest and just laid back in his seat, arms crossed, and eyes closed.

"But of course, you don't have to accept the offer- "

"I'll do it." I interrupt.

The game began and the dominos were passed around. My mother loved playing dominos, it's basically a sport to Cubans. I remember my mom playing with the neighborhood elders all the time while I sat on her lap. Many people say dominos is only a game of chance, but it is a game of skill and chance.

The dominos were mixed by the woman next to Matanza. Matanza went first since he had the highest double. From there we went around the table and continued to play. My mom always said doubles were used to defense, not to attack. If you knew someone did not have a certain number, doubles were great to block a turn.

The game went on for a while, Sebastian and Romero were already behind. This game truly was Me vs. Matanza. I did not let my guard down or get overconfident that I might win because skill can only go so far in this game.

We were down to our last dominos, and I can't lie and say I wasn't nervous. It was my turn, and I couldn't play my hand. I froze in shock and fear. I looked up to Matanza who smiled at me. Did he win? He skips his turn and we run out of dominos. Now we are at a block. In this situation, we show the last domino, and the one with the lowest number of numbers wins. His last domino had four, and mine had two. I had won the game.

Matanza belts out a laugh. "What the fuck! Damn, you were not fucking around. I almost beat you. I fucking salute you."

I breathe out, "Fuck that was close..." I whisper to myself.

"I guess we are back in business. The Dominics sure got themselves one lucky girl." He commented.

Romero opened his eyes and uncrossed his arms. "Great to hear we will be working together again. I'm sure we will be hearing from each other." Was all that Romero said before getting up.

"Yes, we will," Matanza replied. Sebastian and Romero stood up and I took that as a sign to follow suit. "Come and play again with me some time *niña*." He flirts. I nod politely and Sebastian leads me with his hand at the small of my back. Romero and Jameson walk behind Sebastian and me. We make it to the car, and everyone is silent. The entire ride back to the penthouse was a continuous silence. I wonder if I fucked up by challenging Matanza like that in front of Romero. Again, I am the reason they got the plug back so really, they should be thanking me.

Once we made it back, we all sat together for lunch at the dining table. I kept looking at Romero, waiting for him to say something. He took a sip of his water and cleared his throat, "So, you *are* useful." He comments. I feel like he believes that's a compliment.

I don't say anything, just keep eating. "Seriously, who knew you were good at the game. What else are you good at, sweet?" Sebastian taunts, pinching my cheek. I swat him away and take a drink of water.

I clear my throat, "My mom taught me to play when I was little. I grew up playing lots of games like that. Dominos, spades, blackjack, poker...etc. It was how we passed the time."

"Lucky your foolish outburst saved us. Next time think before you act. This is not your world." Romero added. I scoff a laugh at his ungrateful ass. He looks over at me, "What's funny?"

"I came here to work with you, not for you. You know this world better than me and I understand that but stop treating me like a pest. What is your problem with me? Like I genuinely want to know. Matanza didn't even want to work with you, and I risked selling myself to help you and you can't even say 'Thank you.' Then you try to school me on manners." I rant. I got up from the table, "Thanks for lunch. I'm going to bed; I have been up for twenty-nine hours. Excuse me." With that, I walked to my room and took a nice shower. I was knocked out after that.

Chapter 4

Nova

The next day I wake up at three in the afternoon. I'm completely sluggish and it's hard to get out of bed. I jump in the shower to wake myself up. Shortly after my shower I go down the hall and into the kitchen. A smell penetrated my nose, I could smell Cuban coffee from a mile away. Jameson was standing by the island in the kitchen. "Good afternoon." He greets with a warm smile. "I made you your favorite coffee. My way of saying sorry for yesterday."

I blinked a couple of times and ran over to him. "No! I'm so sorry. I wasn't mad at you, just Romero. I should have made that clear. Thank you. You're so sweet."

"No problem. My brother is really caring I swear. He just doesn't know how to express it. I'm sure what he was trying to say is that you should be careful about who you speak to and challenge. Matanza's family has been around for a long time. They are ruthless, if Matanza wasn't in a good mood it could have gone very wrong. We would have been forced to protect you against them, if something happened and to be honest, the last thing we need is problems with him."

I nod my head getting a better understanding of what he meant. I took a sip of my coffee it was perfect, mostly milk and sugar.

"Nova, come with me." Romero's sudden voice is heard coming from the elevator.

I glare, "Am I coming back?" I ask honestly. After my outburst at lunch, he just might have my head.

"Don't worry, if I decide to kill you, you'll know." He answers truthfully. It brings a slight chill down my spine.

I put on a hoodie, sneakers, and jeans. I then follow Romero down in the elevator to a car. It was a fancy Rolls Royce. I sat in the passenger seat quietly trying not to make eye contact with Romero. He was talking on the phone through the car in Italian. Something about closing a place. To be fair, my understanding of Italian is at like a solid 40%.

The drive was not that long which was good. The silence again was stressing me out. The car stopped at a boutique. Romero got out of the car, and I followed suit. "Where are we?" I asked as we walked through the door.

"A luxury shop that is owned by a friend of mine," He takes off the jacket piece to his suit and sets it on a nearby couch. I don't think I have ever seen Romero in regular clothes, it's always suits with this guy.

"Hey Ero, I never thought I'd see you in my store." Says a woman walking toward us. She was exceptionally beautiful. She had olive skin, long black hair, blue eyes, and long legs. She looked like an actual goddess. I was definitely blushing and in awe of her beauty.

She kissed Romero on both sides of his cheeks. "Nova, this is Camilla Sartori. Cami, this is Nova. She needs a renovation." Romero explains.

I glare, "I'm not a building." She comes up to me and hugs me, we exchange cheek kisses. "Nice to meet you."

"Like wise." She looks over at Romero, "This must be important. The last time Romero was in this shop, we were kids, and my mom was the owner." She giggled. She had a cute laugh. So, she and Romero had been friends since childhood.

Romero ignores her and checks his watch. "I'll be back I have a meeting to get to. I am leaving Nova to you. I trust you will fix her attire. I will also need you to give me a list of what you have available for the new season. Email it to me, please."

"I got her. Don't worry she is well cared for." She says putting both hands on my shoulders.

Romero glared at her, "Try to keep your hands to yourself." He warned, before walking out of the store.

"God, he so grouchy." She rolled her eyes, "Anyways, so what's your style? Do you like skirts, pants, or dresses? All of the above?" Her eyes gleamed with her questions.

I smiled, "I like dresses, shorts, and pants, skirts are okay, but I don't wear them much. Rompers are cool. I love heels, but I can't walk in them, but I can walk in wedges. I usually wear athletic comfortable sneakers, but I don't run or do any athletics, so it doesn't make much sense. Unless you think tending a bar for thirteen hours is a sport.

"Honestly, it should. Do not worry today is about you. I won't put you in anything you do not like or are not comfortable in." I don't know why but Camilla gave off a nice big sister vibe about her. J.L would love her.

For a couple of hours, we tried a million dresses. I had only seen clothes like this in fashion magazines and award shows. "These clothes have to cost thousands..." I say touching the fabric.

"Of course, only the best. Don't worry, Romero texted me to go big." She squealed. "We have a beach collection that is not coming out, but I'm going to add some swimsuits to your new wardrobe. Think of it as a gift, I mean Romero coming here is special."

"Why?" I ask inquisitively.

She looks down and crossed her arms, "His mother came here a lot for clothes. Our mothers were best friends. After she died, he had no reason to be here. I also think he just did not want to be reminded of her. Those boys were such mama's boys for sure. She was such an elegant woman, she had dark curly hair and light green eyes. They look just like her."

I never see any photos around the penthouse, not even in their rooms. I mean I didn't get a good look at Sebastian's room because the last time I was in there was the day we met, and I couldn't really concentrate with him blowing my back out.

They are all so closed off. They never talk about themselves. Jameson tells me things here and there but nothing ever too personal. "And their father what was he like?" I pry.

"He was born in Italy. His hair and eyes were light brown. He didn't like the states much. He stayed for his wife. He was not much of a family-oriented person. I never saw him being an affectionate father to any of them. Their mother was always the one showering them with love."

"*Great so they have daddy issues?*" I thought to myself.

"But they grew up always smiling and laughing. After she died it seemed like she took everything with her."

I know the feeling. This made me see them differently a bit. It's hard to lose a mother, any parents for that matter. My mother was my partner in crime. We always slept in the same bed, talked to each other about our days, went to the salon together. She really was my best friend. Then, she didn't come home that day, and time stopped for me.

Camilla tried to switch the subject to a lighter topic since she could see the distress in my face. We talked clothes for the remainder of the time.

Romero soon came back from his meeting. "I trust you found everything you wanted?" His eyes focused on me as he asked his question.

"Of course, she did. I have already put in an order for her clothes to be delivered." Camilla answered. She turns to me and gives me a slip of paper. "Here take my number. If you ever need any new clothes, I'm your girl."

"Definitely." I smiled, taking the paper from her, and putting it into my pocket.

She waved us goodbye, and I waved back. The black SUV was waiting for us outside. Romero opened my door, and I went in first. He slides in across from me. The dark green gaze was back and stronger than ever.

I looked back at him not breaking from his gaze, "Why the new clothes?"

"You want to be part of our world; you need to look the part. No one will respect you in this world wearing hoodies and shorts. Especially in our line of work. You want to bring down Crespo? Then act like it. No more bartending it takes too much of your time. Your manners still need work. You want to beat a Made Man, and so I'll have to turn you into somewhat of a Made...Woman."

"Don't I have to be Italian for that?"

He sighed, "Obviously, there is no such thing. Therefore, there are no rules for a Made Woman."

"Is this your version of an apology?" I huff.

He smiles at me dangerously. "What do I have to apologize for?" He challenged.

"For being a psychopathic dick who could care less about the cordial things someone does for them. If you think clothes is the equivalent of me almost selling myself for your sake, then you are sadly mistaken."

His smile disappeared, but his strong gaze didn't waver. I waited for his response to my words, but nothing came out. *"Did I strike a nerve?"* I gloated internally. Before I could finish my little mental happy dance. Romero pins me down on the seat. "This feels familiar..." I think aloud. Sebastian did the same thing our first night.

He glared at my words, his grip tightening on my wrists.

Again, he didn't say anything. Suddenly, that devilish smile returned, and he picked me up and set me on his lap instead. I shifted uncomfortably. "Sit still." He ordered. His strong hands holding me in place, so that I was facing him.

"What are you doing?" I barked.

He exhales, closing his eyes, "I think it's time for a punishment." One of his hands held my wrists behind my back together and the other pulled my hoodie up. I wiggled around, but his grip only became firmer. My breasts were on full display for him.

With one swift movement his mouth was covering my nipple. His tongue glided sweetly. The sensation was over whelming. I tried to break my hands free, but it was no use. I wanted to touch him back. To be in control of my own pleasure, but he won't let me. That was my punishment. "Please." I beg.

To my surprise, he immediately let my hands go. It was my turn to tease this bastard. I grabbed onto his hair pulling him closer to me. His hands begin to wander, as do mine. I touch the buttons on his shirt. Chuckle's rumble through his body, lips leaving my breasts. "Not used to taking clothes off men?" He teased.

I roll my eyes in response. I quickly unbutton his shirt; it reveals a masterpiece of tattoos. Sebastian had more, they all had the same neck tattoo, but the rest of the tattoos were different. I brought my lips to his neck, licking and sucking like I was trying to make the longest lasting hickey.

He groaned at the touch of my lips. "Such sweet lips." His whisper into my ear. I could feel his hands running up and down my back. I pull back, licking the bottom of my lip. His other hand wrapped around the back of my neck, rubbing it ever so softly. I leaned in close and crash my lips into his soft ones hungrily. "Fuck this." His voice almost animalistic. He rips off my shorts, leaving me in my hoodie and panties.

"If you're going to just tease me again, we should stop, because I won't be able to." I say in between kisses.

He grabs my ass harshly, making me jump, breaking our kiss. "Who says I'm stopping?" He growled back. Romero lifted me up slightly and thrusts his fingers into me. As much as I try, a loud moan still escapes my mouth and straight into his ear. "If you want to hide your moans, suck me off. I'm sure my cock could block those sweet noises you make." Romero words made my pussy drip with anticipation.

"Fuck you." I was still mad at him for the other day. Sex wasn't going to change that.

He smiles kissing me roughly, "No, I'll be doing the fucking. I'll fuck that bad attitude out of your system." He removed his fingers from me. His fingers were dripping, coated in my hot liquid. I watched as Romero licked me off his fingers. Slowly, like he was trying to savor the taste of me. "Take my cock out." He ordered. I was a bit shocked by his words but did it anyway.

I decided to stare at him while I rub him up and down. I loved seeing him at *my* mercy. "I think it's time for a punishment." Throwing his words back at him, I rub my pussy against his hard member. His breathing became louder, which made me smirk with glee. Although, this punishment was a double-edged sword. The more I teased him, the more I was teasing myself.

Romero's hands stopped at my waist and pulled me down on him. He was now fully inside me. My eyes almost rolled back from the overwhelming pleasure, my head now resting on his.

"Against me, you will lose." I didn't need to look up to see the smirk on his face as he said it.

For a moment we were still as if he wanted me to get used to his size. I lifted my head from his shoulder, that was all the approval he needed to slam into me once more. "Fuck!" I yell, my eyes shutting almost immediately.

"Open your fucking eyes." Romero growled in between his pants. "Look at me when I fuck you. I will not let you think of anyone else. I will engrave myself in you."

I tried my best to keep my eyes open, as did he. We both continued to look into each other's eyes as he continued to slam into me. He didn't care that I was getting sore, he wanted to destroy me.

I leaned in for a kiss, I had to close my eyes for that. Luckily, he didn't fight me on it but leaned in as well. The mixed of tongue kisses and his cock pounding into me was magic. "So... good." I moaned finally reaching my expected climax.

He chuckles, "Good? Good sex doesn't make your sweet cum ruin a good pair of expensive Italian dress pants." His cock continued to pound into me before I mouth off. His breathing indicated that he was close. Slowly but surely, he lifted me up just before he came with a roar. Then let me fall back into his lap.

Once I was able to catch my breath, I retort back, "It's your fault."

"No, it's *your* fault for those bratty little words, you spew at me." This man was such a narcissist, does he have a moral compass?

Even with his nonchalant attitude, his arms were still wrapped around me, his fingers rubbing my back. The calmness of it all made me fall asleep.

Romero

My head fell back against the seat. Fuck, she is amazing. Why I didn't do this sooner, I will never know. Her curls had puffed up due to the sweat. Her breathing began to calm, and I realize she fell asleep. "Tired already?" I chuckled. I noticed that she either sleeps too much or too little.

"Boss?" I forgot that the driver was waiting on me.

"Go ahead." I ordered.

My eyes went back to the small sleeping puff ball who was nuzzled into my arms. She was so warm; I want to hold her

40

closer. She was beautiful to look at, once you get past her cheap sense of style. She suddenly moved, almost like she had been able to read my thoughts.

Arriving home, I carried her back inside. "Did you go and marry her behind our backs brother?" Sebastian's mocked. He had the personality of a horny teenage boy and so I tried to ignore him if I could. I put Nova in her bed and came back out to the living room.

Bash was watching something. It looked like old home movies. "What is that?" I asked.

"*Mira mami, se me cayó mi diente!* [**Look mommy, my tooth fell!**]" A little girl shouts in Spanish from the video.

"*¡Nova que bueno! Ahora tienes que ponerlo debajo de tu almohada.* [**Nova that's great! Now you have to put it under your pillow.**]" The mother responded.

She said Nova's name, she must be her mother, but she is only recording a small Nova. I can't see what she looks like, until she moves closer to a mirror. My eyes widen, I have seen this woman before.

"You remember her, right? I mean how could you forget. I know I can't forget. The first time I saw Nova I was shocked she looked so much like her. I had to be sure, so I went to Nova's apartment and went through it to see if I could find a picture of her parents. "Sebastian monologues. "Unless you have been repressing it this whole-time little bro. Not something a child wants to see. I remember coming up behind you when we were kids and seeing her on the floor."

"Crespo, didn't kill her mother..." My fingers run through my hair with the revelation. It was like forgotten memories were flooding back.

"She doesn't need to know. She wants to kill Crespo, and we want him dead. She'll get justice for her mother."

"How is that justice?" I raise a brow at him.

He exhales, "We both know the person who killed her mother is dead. Giving her a new target benefits us as much as it benefits her."

He is right, now's not the time to get soft over tragedies. Crespo must be taken down and if we must use her to do it, then so be it.

Chapter 5

Nova

I woke up feeling horrible. I can't believe I've slept with two brothers. How sick am I? It still felt great though a part of me wanted to do it all over again, but the other side wanted to drown me in holy water. I can't let these triplets distract me from the path I had chosen. No matter how good their dicks felt inside me. My mind starts to wonder how they would feel together...ugh stop this horrible thinking.

A knock on my door wakes me. "Come in!" I yell out. Jameson walks in with his usual gorgeous smile.

"Gym today, time to go." He says softly, lying down next to me.

I grumble, "No, can't we just stay here and eat and be fat. That sounds like the better choice."

He laughs, "That would be nice. I could lay with you all day." His light green eyes investigate mine as the sweet words drip off his lips.

My heart skips a beat, but I have to remind myself why I'm here. "Don't do that." My voice lower than usual.

"Do what?" He asks.

"Flirt with me, I might think you actually like me." I say looking away from him and to the ceiling.

Jameson snickers, "God forbid."

"Don't act like you and your brothers are not going to let me rot in jail once I kill Crespo." It sounded like I was joking, but

I knew it was the truth.

Silence....

Of course, what else did I expect from mobsters. The niceties are just for show until our partnership is over. I meant nothing to them and that is what I should never let myself forget. The sex was just sex, the flirting was just flirting. I needed to focus. "We should get going." I say breaking the awkwardness.

Jameson drove me in his car today, it was an old classic Ferrari in navy blue. "Cool car." I commented looking at the inside of the car. I could tell it had been modified.

"Do you know what it is?" He asked tilting his head in my direction.

"Ferrari?"

He nods, "Yes, it's a 1961 California Spider."

"It's beautiful. I'm not really into cars, but they sure are nice to look at."

We stopped at a red light. "You want to drive it?"

I looked away embarrassed, "Um. Yeah, I can't drive. I'll crash this into...well anything."

"No one taught you?"

"Well, my friend's mom tried, she failed miserably. That summer I learned so many swear words in Mandarin. Good thing for subways."

He rubbed his temple, "Okay...we will need to work on that to."

We stopped at a gym called "Rope's." Jameson opened the door for me, and I walked into the see a normal more upgraded version of a normal boxing gym. "Nice gym."

"Thanks, we own this one and about seven more. "

"Really into boxing?" I raise a brow at him.

He shrugs, "Sure, let's say that."

Jameson and I walk over to a stand selling athletic wear. He does a handshake with the vendor and asks for some female gym wear. "Right now, Shot, I got these. But if she doesn't like them, we got more in the back, the new stuff that we are putting out tomorrow. The shipment just came in."

"Thanks Mar." Jameson then looks at me, "These, okay?"

I nod my head, "Yeah, there really nice. Thanks." I noticed that there wasn't anyone here today accept the workers. "Pretty dead in the mornings. Huh?"

"No, I wanted you to learn without distractions. I closed it down for us." He explained, as he threw his shirt on a nearby chair. It was weird, Jameson was leaner, but for some reason I think he is stronger out of the three.

He turned around, not looking at me. "Go ahead and change."

I took off my clothes and changed into the sportswear quickly. "Done."

He turned back around and went into the ring. I followed him and stood at the end of the ring. Jameson watched me closely, "I want you to land a hit on me."

I smirked, "Shit, I can do that. I'm not a bad fighter."

He rolled his eyes playfully, returning my smirk. He gestured me to get closer. I did when I was close enough, I swung, but he dodged it with ease. I was a brute fighter with no technique. His footwork was impressive. "You're swinging too wide. Keep your hands closer to your body, your dominate hand should always be in the back."

The next time I tried to punch him he grabbed me and slammed me on the floor. It hurt like a bitch. "Damn. And here I thought you would take it easy on me. You bully." I whined.

He broke out in laughter, "That was me going easy on

you."

I stepped back thinking about the notes he had given me, and the next time I threw a punch I almost had him, he flipped me again. I held my head from the pain. He got down beside me and checked to make sure I wasn't bleeding. "You trying to kill me?"

He continued to make sure I was all right, "It's either this or punching you directly and I doubt you want me to do that." He joked. "Well, no blood. Let's go again."

"I tap out!" I cried dramatically.

Jameson flicked me on the arm, "No tapping out."

Before I could whine again Jameson pinned me down. His hand pinned my wrist above my head and his other hand was on my neck. His knees on either side of my waist. "What are you doing?" I ask, genuinely confused.

"Figure out a way to get me off of you." He ordered. I wiggled in his grasp, which made his hand tighten around my neck. "Try again."

To be fair, I didn't really have much of a motivation to get him off me in the first place. His light eyes stare down at me as he tightens his grip again, "I don't know how." I confess.

He finally loosened his grip on my hands and neck. Then explained a few different ways I could get him off me, but he was still on top of me. How the hell was I supposed to focus?!

"Hey...are you going to get off?" I ask.

"No."

"Ok...that's cool." My voice was incredibly awkward.

"Try again."

We kept at it for a couple of hours before I was finally able to get him off me. Although, I'm sure though he let me that one time. When he finally called it quits, I did a childish move and jump on his back and put him in a head lock. He struggled a bit, but then flipped me onto the floor again. "Come on! Fuck!" I yelled. Laying on the floor looking at the ceiling.

He gives me his hand to stand up, "You'll get better." He reassures me.

"I hope." I sigh.

We grab our clothes use the gym showers. I knew that I was going to have to take another shower when I got home to comb out my hair. Getting out of a shower I put my clothes back on and met up with Jameson. "Hungry?"

"Yeah, I'm feeling pizza. There's a really great restaurant on the lower east side that has the best Sicilian pizza ever." I raved. He nodded and we got in the car and drove.

Once we got to the Pizzeria, Val smiled when he saw me, but his smile dropped quickly when he looked at Jameson.

"Welcome Nova and you as well Mr. Dominic. Nova, I didn't know you knew Mr. Dominic." His smile was nervous. Usually, Val is talkative and for some reason trying to get me to me marry his son. He's like a pushy uncle.

"We haven't known each other for long. We just recently met." I explained. He nodded, again nervously.

"You know I've been needing to talk to you Mr. Vito. But first, I have to get some food in her." Jameson's tone even made me nervous. He was able to switch so quickly from sensitive and sweet to a frightening enforcer. What did Val owe him? Was he going to hurt him?

"Can we get a couple of slices of Sicilian? Cheese for me."

I looked over at Jameson, "Yellow peppers and mushrooms." Jameson answers. I look at him disgustingly. He narrows his eyes in confusion. "What?' He asks.

"You're ruining a perfectly good pizza" I cringed.

"Veggies are good for you, *tesoro*." He called me treasure

47

again. Didn't I tell him to stop the flirting. I glare at him, but he just smiles sweetly, intertwining our fingers.

"Only thing that should go on pizza is meat." I say ripping them away playfully.

Val excused himself and took our menus. Victoria, Val's daughter, was waitressing today. She looked at her feet once she saw Jameson, but her face was red. I can't tell if she was scared or in love. Honestly, I don't blame her.

"Hey Nova, you on a date?" She asked shyly.

I looked to the side shyly, "No, were just friends."

"Ouch, I thought the date was going well." He teased.

We ate and Jameson told me to wait in the car while he had a word with Val. When he came back, he smiled and got in the driver's seat. "What did you do?" I asked nervously.

"Don't worry, we honestly just had a chat. I didn't even touch him. If that's what your worried about." He replied. "We got one more stop before we go home."

Jameson drove us to a mansion. As we walk through the doors there were women in next to nothing everywhere. They all stopped what they were doing and fawned over Jameson. Not gonna lie, all these beauties really made me feel less than. "Sunny!" Jameson shouted.

"Quit that hollerin' boy. Didn't your mama teach you any manners!" A woman with a thick southern accent screams back, making Jameson chuckle. When she finally came down the steps, she had on a beautiful red dress, hugging her curves exactly right. She had the clearest ebony skin, deep brown eyes, and a long ombré ponytail going down her back.

"Nova this is Eleanor "Sunny" Davis. Sunny this is Nova." Jameson introduced. "Sunny is a madam, she runs our- "

"Prostitutes?"

"Sex workers is more accurate baby. These girls get paid

very well for their services. I make sure to get them the best clientele." Sunny explained. "Jameson and I make sure no one dare to fuck with our girls. Our girls are very classy and should be treated as such. My lowest paid girl is going for about nine hundred dollars right now."

My eyes widen, "That's crazy." I stated.

"So, everything is under control I assume?" Jameson asked Sunny

She crosses her arms, "Yes, but I've been having a problem with a regular. He is here now if you wanna talk to him." She confesses.

"What's the issue?" Jameson asked.

"He slapped Vanessa. So, I bashed his head with a bat, but he came back today."

Jameson sighed, "Okay. Where is he?"

"Waiting for Vanessa. So, he thinks. I was going to shoot him, but since you're here. I don't see why I have to get my hands dirty. This manicure isn't cheap." She flipped her hair and walked back upstairs.

Jameson told me to follow him, and we went into what I'm assuming was Vanessa's room. There was a man sitting in a chair with his arms crossed looking at his phone. "Finally, you pay a girl more than she's worth and you-" The man didn't get the chance to finish Jameson had already flipped the chair, making the man hit his head against the floor.

Jameson runs his fingers through his hair, "Father Ward. How would god feel if he knew that you had struck one of his children?" Jameson mocks. "Now I have to make sure Vanessa gets checked out by a doctor, that is unnecessary spending for me. So now you're damaging my employees and costing me money."

"M-M-Mr. Dominic, I'm s-s-sorry I won't do it again I

swear." The man stutters. His blood was dripping down his face, from his head.

Jameson reaches from behind his back, and I realize he had a gun on him. "I know you won't Father Ward." With that he shot him in the head. I gasped and fell to the floor. Jameson turned around and leaned down to my level. He used his hand to lift my head, so I could stare into those light green eyes. "It gets easier."

I took a deep breath and Jameson helped me off the floor. Sunny walked into the room and said she would take care of the rest. I was in shock, but should I be? I knew what I signed up for with the triplets. They were killers and I needed to stop acting otherwise.

Jameson didn't let go of my hand the entire drive back to the house. When we got home, no one was there.

Jameson

I killed him on purpose. Needing to see how Nova would react if she truly had the killer instinct to *actually* kill. To a degree everyone is capable of killing under some type of circumstance, but I needed to know she could do it without the push. She can't and I see that now. Our car ride was quiet, her cheery mood was nowhere to be found. She didn't let go of my hand though, she held it tightly. I'm surprised, after killing someone in front of her, I didn't think she would want to touch me.

Bash and Ero were gone for the day, meetings for our legit businesses. I decided to help her out of her shock, I'd run her a bath. That's what my father would do for our mother when she would witness the aftermath of anything taking place at the time. I lead her to her bathroom; I turned around letting her get into the tub. I could hear her sliding into the tub.

"Thank you for doing this." She says quietly. I could hear her using the sponge to clean herself.

"Are you scared of me now?" I ask, genuinely wanting to

hear her answer.

She hesitates but answers, "No."

"You sure?" I laugh pitifully.

"Yeah, I'm just a little taken back. I've never seen anyone get killed right in front of me." She confessed.

In the back of my mind, I understand the reason for what I did, but this did harm her in a way, and it bothered me. I wanted her to forget about my test. I didn't want her to fear me, that wasn't my goal.

"Look at me Jameson, I'm not scared of you. I swear." She reassured.

It's as if she could read my mind. I turn around and sit next to the bath. Leaning against it, she flashes me a halfhearted smile. Without thinking my hand cups her cheek. She grabs it and kisses my hands, the same hand who shot that idiot priest in front of her. Those plump lips keep my mind racing.

I inhale at her warm touch. "I want to touch you." I confess.

She looks away embarrassed, "You really shouldn't." She laughs sadly.

I narrow my eyes at her, "Why?"

She lets go of my hand, "I slept with your brothers..." Her confession didn't shock me since I already knew that. I won't say it didn't bother me because it did but fuck it. I had never shared women with any of my brothers, but if I get to have even a fraction of her, I can let it go.

"That's your business. The moments I have you, are mine. What you do with them is between you and them, I don't need to know."

She looks at me confused not knowing what to do. I answer for her by pulling her into a kiss. As I went to pull away, she kissed me back forcefully, as if she had been waiting for this as much as I have. I wrapped my arms around her. Her body stood with me, wetting my clothes. "Your clothes are getting wet." Her doe eyes looking up at me.

I smile and kiss her, bringing her closer to me. My hands gripping her wet curls harshly. Her small hands going under my shirt. I take that as a sign to take my shirt off. I pull it over my head and throw it on the ground. Nova's tits press up against me, they are so big I can barely cover my whole hand with one. Everything about her screams sexy. Her beautiful curls, plump lips, curvy shape.

"*Realmente eres un tesoro. Te voy a disfrutar.* [**You truly are a treasure. I'm going to enjoy you.**]" I whisper into her ear in Spanish.

"Trying to charm me in my native language?" She giggled.

"Is it working?" I asked kissing her cheek, and down her neck.

She rolls her eyes playfully, "Maybe..." She moans in my ear.

Nova

Butterflies are in my stomach. I'm getting caught up in this intoxicatingly romantic mobster. I hate to admit it, but I like Jameson. He's sexy, strong, has a personality that clashes well with my own. Also, it does help that he makes my body feel like its melting. The wicked witch ain't got nothing on me right now. His kisses are so tender, but then his hands are incredibly rough. The greatest combination during sex. The suds of soap still dripping off my body as I sit on the edge of the tub. Jameson pulls away from me, his pants are still on which pushes me to get on my knees and pull them down. Jameson smirks and kicks the clothes to the side.

He softly strokes his thumb against my lips, as I stare up

at him naked on my knees. "Hopefully, my cock doesn't bruise those pretty lips." His words light a fire in me. My hands grip him firmly stroking him up and down. Soon after, half of his cock is in my mouth. "Only halfway?" He teases, but I can see he is enjoying fucking my mouth.

I lick his length and massage his balls in my hand. Moans and growls escape his mouth as he grabs a hold on my hair. I start to choke a bit on his cock, making my eyes water and making me cough once I removed myself. "Fuck," I cough.

The tears roll down my face, how fucking embarrassing is that? Yet, Jameson simply leans down and licks my tears. "No crying, *tesoro*. The only thing that should be running down your face is my cum." He whispers into my ear.

Jameson scoops me into his arms and places me on my bed. He parts my legs, leaving kisses along both sides of my thighs before sticking his fingers inside me. "Ah..fuck... Jameson..." My scattered moans escaping my mouth.

He picks up the pace, his fingers dancing in my pussy. "I could eat you for days. How does my tongue feel?"

Before I could answer, he slams another finger in deeper than before. My body is heating up, and at this point only his cum could quench my thirst.

"No answer?" His teasing is truly endless.

"It feels so fucking good." I blurt out throwing my head back. He smiles and continues sliding his tongue in and out of me until I reach my first orgasm. My breathing starts to slow.

Jameson lifts his face up to mine and kisses me deeply as he hovers over me. His hand creeps up to my neck, just like in the ring at the gym and squeezes. He thrusts himself in me. I had never been choked before but I couldn't say that I didn't like it. His strong hand taking my breath away as he fucked me harshly was surprisingly satisfying. "When I first had my hand around your neck, it took everything inside me not to fuck you in that ring." He growled. "Fuck...your pussy is going to suffocate me."

My internal laugh was shortened by my, not so quiet, moans. "You're going to make me cum again."

For a second, he slowed his thrusting, going in and out. It was like he was torturing me. "Do you like it, *tesoro*? When I choke that pretty neck of yours, then fuck that wet pussy. Should I cum in it? So that you can remember me through the day? My cum dripping into your panties all day."

My mind was so blinded by my horniness that I screamed, "Yes! Give me all of your cum..."

"Keep on and I'll cum." He warned, but I just took it as an invitation. He started to pick up the pace once again. I'm guessing he was getting tired of his own teasing. I could feel my cream dripping at my sides as he continued to thrust into me. His hand released my neck and he leaned down pressed his forehead against mine, his eyes focused on mine. It was so intimate; I've never had sex like this before. He slowly eased into me again. I could feel every sweet stoke banging against my walls. His light gaze not faltering, I felt entranced. but then again, I feel entranced by all these green-eyed mobsters. Their gazes hold a bit of power over me.

His lips softly crash into mine. Our tongues don't fight for dominance, it's just a sweet kiss. The overwhelming pleasure of his strokes and kiss send me over the edge once more into my second orgasm. "Wetting my dick again with your cum? I think I should return the favor." He grunts. With that I could feel his wetness coating my walls. No one has ever cum inside me before. My body tingled with the lasting feeling of Jameson's cock still buried into me.

"No one has cum inside me before..." I confess.

He smiles, "Glad to be the first." He kissed me soon after, making my lips widen with a smile.

Jameson slowly withdraws from me and lies on the side

of me. I don't know what to do and so I just lay down with my hands on my stomach.

I guess he can feel my awkwardness because he pulls me in close, my head resting on his chest. I place my hand on his shoulder and run my fingers along his neck. His eyes shut, but he's not asleep. His fingers trace my side. "Stop tickling me." He playfully groans.

"You started it." I laugh. He smiles at my response, his eyes still closed. "Sleepy?" I tease.

"No way, I could do this all day. I'm just envisioning." He lies.

"Fucking liar." I growl, which causes him to laugh. "Just say you're tired. Go to sleep if you want. I'll make sure the monsters under the bed don't hurt you." I joke.

I run my fingers through his hair, my subtle touches knocking him out. I cuddle in close to him, and in his sleep his grip tightens on me.

This scene gives me that magical feeling that I hadn't felt in a long time, but quickly I return to earth when I hear the next thing to come out of his mouth. "Lola...don't." He mumbles. I sigh, I feel stupid for even feeling weird about him saying another girl's name. *Come on Nova, you're not in some fairytale, stop getting attached!'* I yell at myself.

My phone rings with J. L's number. "Yo." I answer.

"Hey, get your ass to the hair salon! Did you forget we have appointment? Dani and Mya are finishing with their clients. We are next!" She yells through the phone.

"Fuck, I'm on my way." J.L always had the best timing. I remove Jameson's arms from around me, which makes him turn a bit and reach out for me.

I take a taxi to Babineaux Lux, the salon J.L and I have been going to since my mami was around. Mami learned English and French here when she first came from Cuba. Many of the hairdressers who were working, immigrated from Haiti and France. They tried to teach me, but kids don't want to learn shit, so my French is not the best.

Pulling up to the shop, I can already see Dani glaring at me through the window with a hot comb in her hand. There is a list of the worst things you could do and keeping your hairdresser waiting has to be in the top 100's. I walked in and see J.L sitting in Maya's chair. I walk over and sit in Dani's chair. "Please don't burn me." I beg, not looking her in the eye.

"*Je devrais vraiment te brûler.* **[I really should burn you]**." Dani growls in French.

J.L snorts out a laugh next to me. It felt like we were children trying not to get scolded by our aunties.

"Ok baby, how do you want your hair today?" She asks, a bit more lovingly.

"It's been kind of hot lately, I have so much hair that its tiring. So, two braids with silver rings."

Dani puts the hot comb away and Maya steps up to J.L. "What about you? Maya asks.

"Blowout for me." J.L answers.

The session starts and Dani and Maya are hard at work. "What have you girls been up to?" Dani asks.

"Medical school sucks, the usual." J.L answers.

I want to answer, but what do I say? I joined up with the rival mob to the guy that killed my mom and oh by the way I have been fucking triplets. Which is so wrong on so many levels, but here I fucking am. So, I simply answer, "Just enjoying this gap year. I think I might go to law school after this break." I lie.

"You better!" Maya shouts. A pain sits within me as I hear the joy in her voice.

By this year, the only thing I'll be in is a jail or a grave. I should remember that. I guess I'll have to have fun while I can. No regrets, right?

After the salon, J.L went to pick up Bo from her mom's. I stand in front of the salon checking a text I get from Jameson.

Where are you?

-Jameson

I get ready to type back, but before I know it, I'm rushed into a car. I go into full panic, trying to understand what is happening. I see a man with chestnut brown hair and bright brown eyes sitting across from me.

"Hi, it's so nice to finally meet you. I'm Santino Crespo. We have so much to talk about." He greeted with a smile.

Chapter 6

Jameson

A ten-year old version of myself is walking down the stairs of my childhood home. My little sister Lola is still a toddler, and she is trying to run to the kitchen. I run at her side, "Lola! Don't run!" I say in an angry whisper. Mama and Papa are not going to be happy about this. "Come back to bed." I whisper in a stern tone.

She ignores me and continues to run to the kitchen. In the end, I stay and get her a cookie so that she listens to me. " Thwank you Jamie." She says in her babyish words. Her wavy black hair bouncing as she waddles up the stairs with the box of cookies.

Bang!

The sound I can't forget. Lola screaming and crying and then-

I wake up in Nova's bed, but Nova is nowhere to be found. *"Why am I dreaming about that?"* I think to myself. Nova's sweet scent still lingers on the bed. I closed my eyes and replay myself inside of Nova. How good she felt, her loud moans engulfing my ear. A smile comes to my lips as I reminisce.

I get up and leave Nova's room and go into mine for a shower. I wonder where she went...

Three hours go by, and I still don't hear anything from Nova. I take out my phone and send her a text.

Where are you?

-Jameson

Another hour passes by and still nothing. I call the phone

directly, but it keeps going straight to voicemail. "Where the fuck is she?" I growl to myself. I send a message to Bash and Ero.

Nova is missing.

-Shot

What the fuck are you talking about?! You were supposed to watch her!

-Ero

Did the little minx finally realize it was too much for her and ran?

-Bash

I didn't fucking lose her! I woke up and she was gone!

-Shot

That little girl tire you out little brother? Clever girl.

-Bash

No... there is no way she would just leave. Was it a trick? Fuck, did she really fuck me over? I was right, she was not ready for all of this. Seeing me kill that barbaric preacher proved it. How stupid could I have been to think she could just brush it to the side. Fuck, my brothers are going to kill me.

But...

Something inside me doesn't want to believe it. She must be the best actor in the world, cause fuck her laugh is still replaying in my head. The sweet way she kissed my hand. The look in her eyes told me a whole different story. To even think she slept with me out of fear, makes me sick.

Sebastian

Turns out my obedient girl is not so obedient. How could she run from us? Does she know the truth maybe? No, she couldn't, even Shot doesn't know. I wonder what could make her run. Her phone is off I've called a numerous number of times. God, I'm acting like such a pussy. This girl doesn't even hold any true value to us. If she left, maybe we are better off.

Who was I fucking kidding? That girl doesn't just get to break our deal and run. This will be a fun chase my sweet girl. Her first mistake was thinking I was Shot and letting me fuck her. Either she brings Crespo to his knees, or she will spend the rest of her days living on hers.

I sent out multiple search parties to find her. I'm sure Shot and Ero have done this same. I know Ero has to be boiling, he has such a short temper, I can just imagine the fit he is throwing right now. He has to be swearing up a damn storm.

"Bash, what has you so distracted?" Gia asks angrily. She pushes her blonde hair back and glares at me with her icy blue eyes, looking back at me on her knees.

"I got to go." I say pulling up my pants.

"Excuse me?" She growls. "What the hell?"

I chuckle at her annoyed disposition. "Don't worry, next time I need good head. I'll make sure to call Isabella." I half joke.

She throws her heel at my head, but I dodge it and walk out of her room.

I hear a voice clear their throat, and suddenly I'm whacked with another heel. "Why do you come in here pissin' off my girls." Sunny growls.

"Gia needs to sharpen her skills, or you won't make a buck." I comment.

Sunny rolls her eyes, "I've been doing this longer than you sweet boy, I know how good my girls are. You've been through so much pussy; you can't feel anything anymore." She retorts grinning.

I roll my eyes at her snarky remark, "I'll see you later. I got a bad girl to hunt down."

Sunny scoffed and walked back down the hall.

Nova

I sit in a limo staring at the son of Crespo. Santino Crespo, according to what I knew about him is that he is the oldest son to Daniel Crespo and his wife, Sana Crespo, original surname being Gagliano.

"Why did you put me in this car?" I ask cautiously.

He smiles, "I'm not here to hurt you. I promise. I know it must look that way, being that I threw you in this car and all that."

"Could have fooled me. Last time I talked with your father he threatened me." I state.

"I'm sorry about that. He didn't mean it. He is just frustrated with the situation. Honestly, he would kill me if he knew I was here, but I can't stay away for much longer." He gleams.

What the hell is he talking about? He isn't making any sense. This just went from weird to creepy really quick. I look at my pocket and he notice.

He frowns, "I truly mean you no harm. I would never hurt you."

"Then can I leave?" My eyes narrow at him.

He sighs, "Of course you can, but I really wanted to talk to you more if I could. At least take my number. I just want to talk."

"Fine." I play along and he takes my phone, but its dead. So, he writes it down and gives it to me.

He allows me to leave, and I take a taxi and head home. The apartment is empty, and I start charging my phone in the kitchen. I hear the elevator coming, I see a man I don't know. He has dirty blonde hair and green eyes. His eyes are glued to his phone until he sees me, "You must be Nova" He chuckles.

"Who are you?" I ask curiously.

"I'm Donnie Dominic, I'm their cousin. They called me looking for you. You are in so much trouble. Have you checked your phone?" He laughed.

My eyes widen, "Fuck," I stare at my phone as it finally turns on. I see the many texted messages from Jameson and Romero. "My phone just turned on. "I groan. I didn't charge it because I ran to the damn salon without thinking.

I'm home. I'm sorry I went to the salon, and my phone died before I could text you back.

-Nova

Okay good. I'll be there soon.

-Jameson

Next was Romero.

I'm home cold one. My phone died after I went to the salon.

-Nova

He didn't reply. I tried Sebastian next.

If you care. I'm home. Phone died.

-Nova

My sweet girl, I hope you have no plans for the day. You're on timeout today.

-Sebastian

Fuck that.

-Nova

I roll my eyes at his comment. Donnie comes and sits next to me on the table. "So, you want to help us take down Crespo. Kinda ballsy of you." He raves.

Soon another man comes in with dark hair and even darker brown eyes. "You found her? Good fucking work." He gleams. He reaches a hand to me. "Hey, I'm Sam Riva."

I take his hand and shake it. "Nova." I greet. "So, you guys going to babysit me now?" I groan.

"Nope, we were just looking for you. We know your completely safe and clearly not going anywhere. So, we are going to head out. God those three are so damn intense." Donnie laughed. They complimented my newly done braids and headed out the door.

Like clockwork, Jameson walks in with his normal smile. I smile back, still having the butterflies from this morning. His fingers trace my new braids as my head lays across my arms. "Very cute." He compliments.

"Thanks." I say in a faint voice, still a bit embarrassed.

"You had us worried. We thought you ran away." He laughed.

"If I ever decide to run away, I'll send you a post card." I joke.

He tugs on my braid, lifting my head up, and kisses me. I kiss him back with the same passion. Even though I'm still a little annoyed about the whole 'Lola' thing. I know I have no right to even go there when I literally fucked his brothers. God I'm such a fucking hypocrite. Humans are such flawed creatures.

I pull back from the kiss, "I need to tell you guys something." I confess.

Romero

This girl lives to piss me off in the most irritating way possible. I sit in the car, heading home, and look at her text.

I quickly make it home and go up the elevator. Shot and Nova are in the kitchen sitting on the counter tops. "Hey, we gotta talk." Nova starts.

"You're fucking right we do. People have seen you with us. You no longer have the opportunity to go out and let your phone die!" I fumed.

"I think Crespo is on to us." She blurts out. "Today when I went to text Jameson back, I was pulled into a car by Santino Crespo."

"What the fuck?!" Shot snarls.

I am in shock. Why be so bold about it. There is no way they are that stupid to let us know they know. Crespo was never stupid, so this just doesn't make any sense. What could he possibly gain from letting us know? Unless he doesn't know and has some connection to Nova. She told us she wanted to kill him because she thinks he killed her mother, but she never told us exactly how that would even happen.

"How does Crespo know your mother?" I question.

"She grew up around his family until she was a teen because of her sister. Then left." She explained.

I think about the possibilities for the Crespo family's interest in Nova. Nova goes on to repeat what Santino said to her. Nothing about this interaction made sense to me. "This is useless..." I groan.

"I'm just telling you what happened." She growls back.

I run my fingers through my hair, "This is so fucking frustrating." When I run the scenarios in my head, the only thing I can produce is he is trying to scare us, or Nova and the Crespo's have some unfinished business she is not sharing with us. I don't have time for this.

"While you guys' debate what's going on, I'm going to crash." I realize that its already dark outside and I sigh.

"No. If we don't get to sleep neither do you." I scoff.

Nova glares at me and crosses her arms. "Why?" She wines, which causes Shot to laugh.

I don't find this amusing one bit, "You came to us, wanting to take down Crespo and now you're whining because you don't want to put in the work." I growl, which shuts down her playful mood. "I want Crespo's head on a spike!" I snap, before storming out of the room and into the upstairs office.

Nova

Romero was right. I'm getting too comfortable playing house here. I need to focus on my target and nothing else. I follow Romero up the stairs and into his office. He is on his laptop typing away. He looks up at me for a second then back to the screen. "Yes, Nova?" He asks in a 'leave me the fuck alone' tone.

I sit down in the chair in front of his desk. I take out my phone and dial and put it on speaker. Second later I hear an answer, "Santino." He answers. Romero looks at me with wide eyes.

"Hey, its Nova. I think I'm ready for that talk." I say cheerfully.

I can see the worried look on Romero's face as Santino replies, "Nova that's great. I'm actually throwing a gala in a couple of days. I would love for you to come. My dad will not be there, if it helps. Then we can have an honest talk."

"Sounds really fancy, but yeah that's fine." I agree.

"I'll text you all the info. I cannot wait. See you soon Nova." With that we hang up.

I look up and Romero who is drilling me with his eyes. "What the hell did you just do?" He growls.

"You told me to stop messing around, so I'm going to figure out what the Crespo's wants with me. I'm not going to sit around anymore. I'm doing this." I explain.

I get up to leave but he stops me, "No, it's not safe for you. You can barely defend yourself. If your alone with him, who knows what could happen?!" He protests.

I smile, "Worried about me?" I bat my lashes at him.

He quickly releases me. "No, but what's the point in losing an investment."

He really knows how to ruin things, "An investment...right." I scoff.

I go out to the terrace to get some fresh air. The view of the city from here really is breath taking. I don't think I've ever truly been able to admire the city. "There you are." A flirtatious voice says into my ear. I feel a large presents behind me.

"Can I help you, Sebastian?" My guard is completely up after his little text message.

He ignores me and wraps his arms around my waist. "You were a bad girl today, sweet. Making me worry like that." He purrs into my ear. I know it's all bullshit, he wasn't a bit worried about me.

"Liar." I growl.

He kisses the crook of my neck, "Oh, but I was...I couldn't imagine someone else touching you like this." His fingers making their way up my legs. The subtle touches make my breathing pick up a bit.

I try to break from his hold to not give him the satisfaction, but his arm is keeping me in place. "Let me go, Sebastian, I mean it." I snap.

"You sure?" He asked smugly. He removed his arms from me. "Fine, I'll play nice today, sweet." He says flicking my forehead.

I look over at him surprised. He takes a seat on one of the couches. "What?" I ask. Confused on why he was still here.

"What are you thinking about, sweet?"

I shrug

He chuckles, "I know you have a lot of thoughts in that big forehead of yours." He jokes. I took off my sneaker and threw it at him, but the fucker caught it.

"My foreheads not *that* big." I hissed back.

"It is." He snickers.

In turn it makes me laugh and decide to sit across from him on the other couch. "I'm doing something risky and I'm not going to lie. I'm scared."

"Scared to die?"

"Scared to fail. I don't care if I die, as long as he pays for what he did."

His hazel eyes stare off into the distance for a second before looking back at me. "So, what's the plan? He finally asks.

"I'm going to a gala hosted by Crespo's oldest son. He invited me."

"What the fuck for?" Sebastian's usual charm was gone. I guess his real personality is not as sweet.

"Romero will fill you in later, I'm sure." I take a deep breath, "Anyways, I'm doing it and I can't fuck up."

"Then don't." He simply says.

I rub my temples, "The pep talks around here really suck."

He stands and adjusts his suit jacket. "When is the gala?"

I look at my phone at Santino's text. "Four days from now."

That gives me time to teach you a few skills. I want to believe he's talking about defensive skills, but his smirk leads me to other ideas. I narrow my eyes, but he just flashes me his charming smile, "Can you shoot a gun?"

"No, but I've heard a lot of gunshots in my neighborhood, so I'm like a pro at figuring out the difference between fireworks and gunshots."

He snorts out a laugh, "Shooting lessons tomorrow." He takes out his phone. "I heard you met Cami, I'm sure she can help you pick a gown for the gala." I smile at the thought of seeing

Camila again. Sebastian noticed and glares, "Got a crush?" He growls.

I chuckle, "Maybe." I tease.

"Such a greedy girl." He says loosening his tie.

Chapter 7

Sebastian

T he gun range was cleared out today so Nova could focus. "Don't I have to put ear plugs on or something?" Nova asks holding the gun I gave her.

"No, our enemies don't give us time to put them on." I answered sarcastically.

She was a good shot, but too afraid of the sound up close. When I told Shot, I was taking her he seemed irritated. He got a taste and can't let go. I knew that fucker would get pussy whipped one day. Nova is a good lay, so I understand the need to want to be inside her every day. I don't even know how I managed to pull away the other day. All I wanted to do was fuck her on that terrace for the world to see. Sunny thinks I can't get it up anymore, but my body wants Nova.

This is not a 'she's special' type of bullshit. It's just physical chemistry, nothing more.

The following day Cami came over to help and accompany Nova to the gala.

Thump...

Thump...

Thump...

Nova came down the stairs in an emerald, green gown, with a slit to show off her short, but sexy legs. The gown showed off her shoulders. The green sat well along her beautiful brown skin. Her hair was still in two long braids going down her back with silver rings. Her lips painted in a dark bloody red. Ero and

Shot had the same mesmerized expression looking at her come down the stairs.

Cami cleared her throat, "Well how does she look guys?" Cami prodded.

"Stunning, sweet."

"Very pretty, *tesoro*."

"You look appropriate." Romero's comment caused me to snicker. This hard persona he has given himself is hilarious.

I stand next to Ero, "It's okay Ero, we all know you want her as much as we do. Shit maybe more. To see her tied up, on her knees choking on your cock. Tears running down her face from gagging." I whisper in his ear trying to provoke a reaction from my little brother. He glares at me in return.

My pants tighten at my own words. I need to have her soon, enough of the gentlemen crap. I want her begging me to keep fucking her. Claw marks on my back from her pulling me close inside her, her sweet moans in my ear crying my name. My sweet obedient girl.

Nova

Romero also known now as the "Ice King" and not in the funny *Adventure Time* way, really knew how to ruin a mood. He walks up to me and pushes the bottom of my dress aside and puts a holster on my leg with a small gun in it. His touch was soft as his fingers graced my thighs.

As he gets up and looks at me, his eyes looked almost like they were pleading. "Be smart, do not let your guard down." He orders. He then looks over at Cami, "Do not leave her side. I mean it."

Cami nods, "I won't Ero. I'll keep her safe I promise."

Romero looks at me once more for a second before turning away and walking back upstairs as he makes a call in Italian.

"Two hours max, sweet." Sebastian orders.

"Don't forget what we worked on." Jameson says before I start heading out.

Cami held my hand the entire car ride to the gala. "It's okay." She said rubbing my hand with her thumb. She really had that big sister personality.

Getting to the gala, we entered and there was an abundance of people. All in fancy suits and dresses. I felt weird and out of place but a little better with Cami by my side.

I looked through the crowds and finally saw Santino speaking with a couple of people. He turned his head finally spotting me. His smile was bright as he walked up. "You came!" He exclaims. His eyes twinkling in the light. His smile dims slightly when he looks at Cami.

"Hi, nice to see you." I greet.

"Do you mind if I talk to you alone." He asks politely.

I look at Cami and she nods, "I'll be around." She whispers. I nod and follow Santino to a beautiful cabana. There are fruits and snacks on the table.

I sit and he sits across from me. He inhales, "Shit, I'm nervous. I have been playing this out in my head for a long time and now, I am at a loss for words. It's been so long." He confesses. '*So long? What does he mean?*' I think to myself.

He takes out a pink book. "What's that?" I ask, now extremely curious.

"I think it's better if I just show you." He says handing me the book.

I open the book and the first thing I see is my mother carrying a baby. I continue to flip through pictures and see Crespo sitting on the side of her hospital bed. "What is this?" I ask, in a growl.

He looks at me a bit sadly, "That's your mother holding

you for the first time. When your mother gave birth to you." He chuckled.

I was in utter shock. This was not registering in my head. Crespo is my father? Yet he killed my mother? Why? How could he kill a woman he had a child with? To keep it from his wife? Because Santino just said my mother was mine and not his. "No...." Was all I could get out of my mouth.

"Excuse me?"

"So, he killed the mother of his child...why?"

He sighs, "He didn't kill your mother. Dad loved your mom. "

"He loved my mom, while being married to your mother?" I growl.

"I'm sure you understand that my parents' marriage was arranged. Dad could only marry an Italian woman from another mob family because his father forced him to boarder peace. Plus, your mother hated everything about the Made Man life. It ruined her sister's life and so to keep you from it, she forbade us from seeing you. I was so angry at first, but as I got older, I realized that dad just wanted to respect her wishes." He explained, the sadness on his face evident.

My mind went spiraling. He's lying, he has to be lying. Nothing makes sense. He loved my mother, but somehow, she ended up dead. "Then who killed my mother?"

"Dad won't tell me. He's the only one who knows. It must have been someone with a high-profile family background."

I don't know, what's real or fiction, but I can't just take his word for it. Us being siblings, if that's even true, doesn't make up for Crespo either killing my mother or letting me believe he did. My brain is completely fried. "I need time. I don't know if I believe you."

"I'll give you some of my DNA. You can test it with your

own. We are siblings I swear to you." He offers. "Spit, lock of hair, whatever you need. I am going against your mother and our fathers wishes, which I do not take lightly. I wanted to keep the secret, but one day we are all going to die, and I know deep down she never wanted us separated." He pleaded.

What do I do? What do I tell the Dominics? Romero said he wanted Crespo's head on a spike and so do I, but if I truly am Crespo's daughter, how will he react? How will they react? Will they kill me? Thinking I have been playing them from the start? They'll kill me. I have to keep this to myself. I don't know who to trust.

That night I didn't say anything on the ride home. I tried not to alarm Cami just in case. When I went up in the elevator, I walked in to see all three of them sitting on the couch of the living room, as if they had been waiting there since I left. "Hey guys. Missed me?" I tried to act as casual as possible. As I sit next to Jameson.

"What happened." Romero interrogates.

On the way back I had been thinking of a lie that they would believe, but honestly, I couldn't think of much, so I came up with this. "He wanted to ask me out." I lied.

"He pulled you into a car and asked you to go to a gala, so he could ask you on a date?" Sebastian questioned, incredibly suspicious. "Seems a bit much, don't you think?"

"Says the man who bought out my building. You mafia guys sure do it big." I continued, trying to make it believable as possible.

"What did you say?" Jameson cut in.

I smiled, "I told him, that I'm into women, which is not a lie. If I would have said boyfriend, whose to stop him from trying to find and kill the guy, right?" I explain.

"Thats what I would do." Sebastian chuckled.

Romero had his hands intertwined as he stared at me. The look in his eyes telling me he's running scenarios in his mind, trying to figure out if there could be any truth to my words. I'm nervous but I try with all my might to keep a natural playfulness to myself.

"Well, that was a waste of a good dress." I groan, continuing to play my part. Even if Romero doesn't believe me, he is going to try to make sense of it in some way before he decides to plot. That gives me some time to figure out what the hell is going on with my life right now.

'I know deep down she never wanted us separated.' Santino's words ringing in my head.

Is that what my mother wanted? What if he is telling the truth? What if Crespo loved my mother and didn't kill her? Would he tell me who did? All this shit is circumstantial at best. I barely know the Dominic's as well, and last time I checked; Romero basically called me an investment. He doesn't trust me and honestly, I don't trust them either. So, I don't owe them the truth of what Santino told me.

"And you accept this?" Romero finally spoke.

"What do you mean?" I ask.

"You, who wants the Crespo family to fall, is willing to take his words as is. Stubborn as you are. It seems a little out of character of you." His eyes continue to burn into me, causing Sebastian and Jameson to follow suit.

"I didn't say I believed him, it's just what happen. What was I supposed to do? Pull out my gun, that I barely know how to use and force him to tell me the truth?" I growl back, enough to not raise suspicions.

Romero sighs, "I guess not." He replies. I can tell by his voice, he still not buying my story. Romero is a strategist; he will continue running what I said in his head until he figures outs something that makes sense to him.

"Alright, I'm going to find a way out of this dress and sleep." I say getting up from the couch and down the hall.

I take off the jewelry and try to rip off my dress, but it's no use. I sit on the bed and rub my temples. A knock comes to my door. "Enter!" I call out.

Like the sneaky fox that he is, Sebastian slips through the door. "Need help?" He asks.

"Yes, this dress is trying to eat me." I laugh dryly. As I sit on the bed, Sebastian gets down on his knee and takes the gun from the holster and sets it down. Then takes the holster from my thigh. His fingers purposely touching my inner thigh to seek a reaction.

"Hurry it up, Fox." I mocked playfully.

He in turn smirks, "Is that what I am, sweet? What does that make you? A hen." He playfully retorts back. I can't stand the fact that I'm smiling right now when my mind is still freaking out. Sebastian and his stupid charm, he really has a way about him that is...I don't even know the word. I guess the word is alluring? "Turn around." He ordered.

I felt his hands undoing the laces that was keeping my dress together. The laces fall to the ground, making the dress way less restricting. "Ok, I think I got it now, Sebastian." I reassure.

His hands trace my bare shoulders, "You rejected me one too many times, sweet. How long can you keep a fox starving before he becomes rabid." He purrs, sliding off the gown until it hits the floor and I'm standing there in my panties. I wrap my arms around myself from the cold. My nipples perk up from the chilly air. "Cold? Why don't we take a hot shower?" He suggests.

I'm not oblivious to what will happened if he joins me in this shower, but my head hurts from tonight. I need to just forget for tonight and make it 'Future Me's' problem. "Fine you win, Fox. But I'm no hen." I flirt.

Sebastian

This little vixen is playing a dangerous game with the three of us but fuck it if I'm not willing to play. Having us wrapped around her pretty pussy. It may be my own fucked up thinking that allows me to look past her fucking my brothers, I mean we are identical, so it bothers me just a little bit less. I know, insane thinking, right?

Without making a move her lips devoured mine. My sweet girl really must want this. I pull away and turn her around, so that her back is facing me. I attack her neck with slow licks, "No need to hurry, sweet." I murmur into her neck. My hands snaking around the front of her body harshly grabbing her tits. A gasp escapes her mouth, and her ass backs into my cock. I was already so damn hard, I thought I would cum right then and there. I put my thumb against her anus. "Have my brothers fucked you here?" I ask, pushing the finger further in.

She almost jumps, "No. I've never done it before." She confesses breathlessly.

I smirk, "Why? You don't seem like a vanilla girl, sweet." My finger sliding in further. Her hands land on the shower wall to keep her balance.

"My ex tried it and it hurt like hell, so I didn't try it again."

I pull my finger out slowly and rub her hold with my thumb. "That's because you're so tight. My finger could barely get through. You need to relax." I move my finger to a slicker opening. "Don't worry I won't fuck you in the ass...yet. We will work on it until you're comfortable, so then next time when I bury my cock deep in that big round ass, all you will feel is pleasure. Do not let anyone fuck you here. I will be your first."

I grab her chin and force her to look up at me. "What?" She moans.

"Understand?" My tone darker than before.

She nods, "Yes, Sebastian." Fuck, my name on her lips drives me crazy.

"What a good girl you are. My sweet obedient girl." My fingers still plunging in and out of her sticky pussy. She tightens up on my fingers. "Look how well you squeeze my fingers." The hot water from the shower sits on my back as Nova faces away from me, but I want to see her. I want to see her face when I bury myself in her. Wanting to see her face twist in any pain or pleasure I provided her. I withdraw my fingers and tell her to turn around.

Her doe brown eyes look at me. Her hands suddenly reaching up and running her fingers through my hair as she gets closer to me. Her lips traveling from my neck, shoulders, and abdomen until she is on her knees. She looks up at me and licks her lips. Fuck, such a tease.

"I'm not the best at this...but I want to get better." She confesses licking the tip of my cock.

It takes everything inside me not to choke her with my cock. Therefore, I simply grab her two braids in my hands and hold tightly. "You look so good sucking my dick." I praise. She tries to take in my cock to the best of her abilities, and it's enough to make me cum. I cum into her mouth and she swallows it all. "You look so beautiful with my cum running down your mouth." I comment.

"So, you do taste different from him." She comments back.

It irritates me slightly and I pick her up and slam her into the shower wall. My cock teasing at her entrance. "Bad girls don't get to cum." I tease.

Her eyes widen with regret, "I'll be a good girl. I promise." She cries, wrapping her legs tighter around me.

"I know you will, sweet. Look how wet and sticky you are. All for me." I say into her ear. Even with all the teasing, I needed to fuck her long before she begged me.

I thrust deep into her within seconds. She was so warm, and I could feel her already start to tighten around me. I continued to thrust slowly inside of her. A punishment for her words. She continued to beg for me to speed up, but I just continued my slow rhythm until I felt content with my little petty revenge.

Our lips crashed, Nova's fingers gripping my hair harshly. "Oh...S-Sebastian...I'm going to cum...fuck!" She moans.

"Cum all over my cock, sweet." I can feel her reaching her breaking point and she finally cums with a shake. "There you go, you cum so well." I kiss her once more. "I can feel your juices all over my cock. You're so warm." I groan as I continue to fuck her roughly. She whimpers and shudders as I climax within her. I pull out of her and watch my cum slide down her cunt and onto the floor of the shower.

We both breathe heavily, trying to wind down from our completion. My hair is in my face as I look down panting, still holding her up the wall. I can't look up at her. I'm a bit scared if I look up, her doe eyes will keep me captive.

I set her down, but she still is having a challenging time keeping her balance. "It's okay sweet, if you slip, I'm sure your forehead will break your fall." I tease. She smacks my head in retribution, which makes me chuckle.

"Fuck...you." She pants. "You can...barely hold it together...yourself."

Her arms wrap around my neck for support, and in turn I wrap my arms around her. What is this? I want to feel her skin against mine. There is something comforting about this. Fuck, what is this little fox doing to me?

I cradle her in my arms and carry her to her bed. She wraps herself in her blanket. I dry off the small damp parts of her braids. "Sit up, you'll get sick if your hair is wet." I informed. She just groaned and flipped on her stomach. I grin at her bratty actions and dry her hair.

She soon fell asleep. I found myself tracing her chipmunk cheeks with my fingers. She really does have a cute face. As I grow closer to her, guilt sits in the back of my mind. We have made her a pawn in our game. If she ever finds out the truth, it's game over. The little fun we are having with this little fox will be over.

Romero

I sit in my office and stare at the ceiling. Nova just lied to me downstairs. Why is she lying to me? What did Crespo's son say to her? She was willing to tell us what happened the first time. Was that a lie to? No, everyone has a tell and she didn't appear to be lying. What does he know? Why didn't she tell us? Can she not trust us? That is it. She does know. I will deal with her later, but first this insignificant bug.

"*Donnie, ho un lavoro per te.* [**Donnie, I got a job for you.**]" I say in Italian through the phone. "*Il figlio di Crespo sta diventando un problema. Scopri cosa sa.* [**Crespo's son is becoming a problem. Find out what he knows.**] By any means necessary."

"Understood." He answers through the phone.

Memories flooding my head to an eight-year-old version of myself watching my father yell and scream at his soldiers. Bash reading his book beside me and Shot playing a video game. I just...watched. I watched everything my father did. How he conducted business, how he treated my mother, everything. I was a very observant child. My father realized this and decided that I would take over when he was gone.

He called me into his office that day. "Yes Papa?" I ask.

"You will come with me to the warehouse." He ordered. It was not a request.

He brought me to the warehouse and there was a woman tied up and blindfolded, then a small boy next to her also blindfolded.

"Why did you take from me Anthony? Do you need it for your family? I can understand that I have a wife and kids. I didn't realize I wasn't giving you enough." My father's voice ever so condescending. There was not an ounce of pity in his voice.

The man was terrified. That is how most people were around my father. The woman was crying, "Tony what did you do?!" She screamed.

Seconds after a bullet flew through her head. She fell on the floor, dead. I was taken back, but I was not scared. Even as an eight-year-old boy, I mostly brushed it off.

Anthony screamed, "No! God, no!" He cried. "You bastard!" He growled, tears pouring from his face. His son started to cry, going off his father's reaction. Crying for his now dead mother.

"Me a bastard? Now you only have one mouth to feed. I did you a favor. Kids don't eat that much when there this young. It will give you some time to build back the money you owe me."

"You're insane." The man cried looking at his wife.

"It's just business." He simply said.

I will never forget his words. That is how it worked. Nothing is personal, this is just a business. Just like any businessman, you don't want the company to fail. You have those that are bad for business. The company cannot fall. Santino Crespo has become bad for my business; it runs in the family.

Chapter 8

Nova

I wake up and wiggle my feet and realize I'm wearing socks. "Did Sebastian do this?" I murmur to myself. My body still a bit sore from Sebastian's intensity last night. I got to forget, and I thank him for that, but now future me is present me.

My life is a cluster fuck. So, what are my options here? Tell the Dominic's and risk them killing me, or trust Santino and the people who possibly killed my mother? They want to keep me quiet. No, they would have just killed me if that was the case. Ugh, fuck my entire life. I should have just gone to school...I just had to be some fucking vigilante.

I met up with J.L for lunch before her shift started. "I miss you girl. You quit the bar, and you've been M.I.A lately." J.L whines, while sipping on her espresso.

"Yeah, sorry just trying to focus on going back to school." I lie. I play with my braid and look up at the sky. "Hey, can I ask you a hypothetical question?"

She looks at me with narrow eyes, "Sure." She answers.

I inhale, then exhale, "If you found out that your dad was in the triad how would you react?"

She looks at me with raised brows, "Honestly, scared.... I mean you've seen the movies and documentaries. That's nothing to fuck with. They're borderline dangerous cults."

Well thanks J.L that makes me feel even better. If only you knew the shit, I'm in now. Would she even believe me though?

"Nova?" A voice says from behind me.

I turn around in my chair and see Cami. "Hey, Cami. What are you doing around here?" I ask getting up to hug her. J.L quickly clears her throat. "Oh, Cami this is J.L, my best friend, we grew up together." I then turn to J.L, "This is Camilla, she owns a boutique a couple block down from here." I introduce. They shake hands, but the handshake lingers for a second too long before I have to clear my throat. They instantly let go.

Cami laughs nervously, "I'm here because I was thinking of expanding the brand and building a way more affordable store. I went to see the empty space, but it is not the best. Yet, I still believe I can make it into something great." She explains.

"That's really great Cami. I'm happy for you."

She smiles brightly, "Thanks, so what are you gals up to today?"

"J.L strips at a really nice club, if your down to go watch her?"

Cami's face gleams, "I'd love to."

Romero told me to stop bartending because it took up too much time, but never said I couldn't visit the club. I see J.L being the baddest bitch on her pole. She really has a talent. I sit down and watch her put on a show. Cami and I cheer her on and dance along with her.

"You can't come to my work. Get the fuck out!" I hear Layla's voice. I turn to see her on the pole stopped, yelling at her ex. I forget his name but I'm sure she got a restraining order on him. I notice Cami walking up to the guy.

"I'm trying to watch a hot woman shake her ass in my face and you're disrupting that." Cami explains sweetly, which causes me to snort a laugh. She crosses her arms, "Leave or get thrown out." She warned.

"Stay out of it. Damn, you bitches never know when to

keep your fucking mouths closed." He growls back, he raises his hand like he's about to slap her and I move instantly. Before I could even help, Cami knees him and snaps his wrist. Then gives him the bitch slap of a lifetime, shit even I felt the embarrassment he must feel. Richard and Shakir, the bouncers, dragged him out. It was such a funny sight to see.

"Nice reflexes." J.L comments. "So, you like me shaking my ass in your face?" She flirts.

Cami drags a strand of hair back," I mean it's a beautiful ass." Cami flirts back. I am in utter shock watching them. Did they forget I was here?

"Hey guys, Ima head out." I whisper.

"Okay, get home safe. I'll keep J.L company." Cami says, her eyes looking J.L up and down.

J.L doing the same. "Yeah, Nova. We're good here." Damn these girls can't wait to get rid of me. I laugh internally at their obvious crushes.

When I got home, Romero was in the living room waiting on me. "Go change, I'm meeting with Matanza about pricing. He likes you, so you're coming." Romero orders.

I inhale and exhale, "So basically, you want me to be what? A shiny toy to keep him in a good mood." I growl. What else would I expect from Romero.

His cold stare remains, "If need be."

I smile sarcastically and bat my eyes, "Ok. I'll make sure to pretty myself up." My voice goes into a high girly tone.

We sat in the car in silence like always. I would look over at him from time to time. I wish I could read his mind. Romero seems like he's always lost in thought. Plotting his schemes of world domination, probably. I snicker aloud.

"What's funny?" Romero asks turning his attention to me.

"You." I answer.

He narrows his eyes at me, "Elaborate."

"You must be a very stressed-out person. All you do is over think. You're either at meetings or the office. I wonder what you do for fun. If you actually have a personality beside being cold and distant."

Romero looks off into the distance again and ignores me.

Sebastian

*"Figliolo, un giorno non sarò qui e tu sarai il capo di questa famiglia. Sei molto in grado di conoscere un amico del nemico.[**Son, one day I will not be here, and you will be the head of this family. You must be able to know friend from foe.**]" Papa says his voice stern.*

*"Capisco, papà. [**I understand, Papa**]" A ten-year-old Ero replies. Even though I was the oldest triplet, Papa did not believe that I was suited to take over after him. Ero was his heir and the rest of us his support.*

After Papa dismissed us from his office, I went to find Mama. She was lying in the guest bedroom again. She stared at the wall for a while. Her black curls a mess. Mama seemed like two people most of the time. Some days she would be cheerful and energized, then some days lay in bed for hours without speaking to us. Papa said that Mama is fine, but she does not seem that way. I read to her when she gets like this.

"Mama, Ms. Xavier and I went over literature. We read a book today by Shakespeare. It's called 'Othello.' Ms. Xavier explained it to me and it's a story about a man named Othello who falls in love with a girl named Desdemona. Then this guy Iago gets mad at Othello for not promoting him, so he decides to break up Othello and Desdemona, as revenge. So, in the end Othello believes that Desdemona cheats on him and so he kills her, and then himself." I explain. I can't tell if Mama is listening or not, but I hope she is. She's looking at me, but I'm not sure she is aware she is.

Shot comes in the room and lays next to Mama. He strokes her hair and snuggles up to her. Papa would be mad if he saw him doing that. He believed Shot was too soft. I don't think that's a terrible thing. It means he is a good person who cares for others.

I take a book out of the library in the living room. I remember my mother with books. I lie down on the couch and flip through pages of *Othello*.

I hear steps trickling down, "Hey, where is Nova?" Shot asks coming down the stairs.

"With Ero." *Flip*, "Why? Miss her already?" I tease.

"Fuck off. What if I do?"

"Don't be stupid. She's not staying for long. Don't start getting attached."

He scoffs, "Yeah, cause I'm the only one. Is that why you were cuddling up to her after you fucked her."

"I was tired." I lie. Fuck, he saw me. I thought I left with time. He must have come into her room when I passed out. She's fucking warm, I couldn't help it.

"Yeah, okay." He said rolling his eyes. I swear this triplet bond is going to be the death of me. "Why are you even home? You're usually at the club or bothering Sunny's girls."

"I'm sick. I got a fever or something." I groan.

"Or something" He joked.

"Yeah right, I'm clean. Unlike some people I get tested every two weeks."

"That's because you fuck a new girl every other day. I would to." He laughed.

Now that I think about it, I haven't fucked a single girl since the first night with Nova. I mean Gia tried sucking me off, but I couldn't get it up for shit. Hopefully, this sexual infatuation ends as soon as she is gone.

Nova

"I wish you would have told me earlier. I promised to do something with Jameson today." I huffed.

"You are not here to date my brother. You're here to become mutually useful to us."

"So, I'm not useful...yet?" I scoff, "But you need me to make deals with drug lords, ironic."

Romero shifts in his seat, he kind of reminds me of a quiet kid. The kid who is quiet and serious but gets pissed off about the smallest things. Yet, he never physically pushes me away. He doesn't pull back when I touch him. He likes me more than he's leading on.

The car stops and we are at a club, I know about. I used to sneak into this club as a teen all the time. I didn't realize it was owned by a drug lord. When we entered the club, we went to the back room. I saw unknown faces surrounding Matanza.

"*Niña*, you came back!" Matanza gleamed.

I offered him a smile, but I did not want to be here in the slightest. I wanted to hang out with Jameson. The only one of these bastards that will admit he likes having me around. Matanza and Romero were talking numbers about the drugs. I zoned out for most of it, until Matanza turned his attention on me. "*Niña*, you single?"

Romero

Nova looks at me, almost wanting me to answer his question for her. "Oh, my fault, I didn't realize she was yours Romero."

Nova's hand rested on my leg. "It's fine. I'm passed it." I rested my hand over hers. Why did I want to comfort her? In this moment, I didn't claim her for bravado, but because I could see she was uncomfortable, and it was bothering me. I hate this feeling. I shouldn't have brought her. What was I thinking? I expect her to act like one of us, but then parade her around like a sheep to a pack of wolves. I don't need her to close this deal. I lean over and whisper to Nova, "You can go home, I'm sorry."

She looks at me dumbfounded, "No, I want to stay. I'm fine."

I nod my head and we continue with the meeting. Before I could tell Nova was out of focus, but now she was listening to every word. Soaking in all the information and I hate to admit it, but I was slightly happy that she stayed. Seeing her talking to them as if she were one of us.

On the ride home, I looked out at my city. My phone rings with Shot's number. I answer, "What?"

"Bash is sick and acting like he's dying. This man will take a bullet but not a cold." Shot laughs, which causes me to chuckle. Bash always hated getting sick. He would always cry as a kid, which pissed off our father all the time.

Nova looked over at me confused, "Bash is sick and whining." I tell her.

She laughs, "Aw, little baby Bash. I can't wait to get home." She laughs sinisterly.

Once we got home, we could hear Bash's exaggerating whining from his room. "Bash, shut the fuck up already. You are fine." I growl. I hate whining.

"Nova come take care of me." Bash pleads.

She laughs and walks over to him. She puts her forehead against his. "You're really warm, fox. Ginger tea and *sopa de pollo* should fix any cold." She offers.

Sebastian

Nova thinks I'm warm she should feel her own skin. She's always so warm. She leaves my side to make the soup and I drift.

"It's okay, Sebastian. Mama is here. Don't listen to Papa, if you don't feel well, you tell me." Mama says stroking my hair as I lie

on her chest.

Papa walks into the room, "Sebastian, you cannot keep crying to Mama. You must learn to deal with pain. I say this to help you, not hurt you. The life we live is hard. It is not some movie; this life is real for our family. You four are my legacy. You cannot let the world eat you."

"I'm sorry, Papa." I whimper, still nuzzling up to Mama.

Mama continues to rake her fingers through my hair. "I think Papa does not realize that you are still young." Mama soothes.

"He won't be for long. He must learn now." His voice slightly raised. Papa never hurt Mama physically, but sometimes he would yell, and Mama would get angry.

"Sebastian..." A familiar voice calls out to me. I open my eyes and see Nova. "Hey, you knocked out. I just finished the soup." Nova puts down the bowl of soup on the nightstand.

"Feed me, sweet." I playfully beg. She narrows her eyes and pulls a strand of my hair; it makes me wince. "Be nice to me, I'm sick." I whine, forcing a cough. Nova smiles at me and runs her fingers through my hair.

"Sit up and eat." She orders.

The chicken soup is amazing. "I didn't know you could cook."

"That's cause you guys think I'm going to poison you." She jokes.

I mean she's not wrong. We usually don't let people cook for us. I mean take out is fine, but with all the enemies we have. We don't exactly go to people's houses and eat their food unless they are blood. "You could, can't be too careful." I comment. Yet, I didn't think twice about eating the food. Shit, I'm already almost done with it.

"I can make you more later." She laughs.

I put the bowl back on the nightstand and then drink the

ginger tea she made. "Disgusting." I growl as I sip the tea.

"It's good for you!"

"You sound like Shot. You decide to make me spicy water."

"Okay." She snatches the tea from me and starts to drink it.

I snatch it back, "I didn't say I was not going to drink it." *Sip*, "Now you're going to get my cold." I snickered.

"I don't want your cooties." She jokingly groans. I leaned and kissed her soft lips. She pulls back almost immediately, "You need to stop kissing me so casually." She comments, crossing her arms.

"Why?"

"We're not together. It's too intimate..."

I smirk, "Afraid you'll fall for me, sweet?"

"No. I won't fall for any of you. No matter how much you guys tease me. I know this is a game to you three, but lucky for me, I'm aware." Why did it hurt to hear her say that? "Plus, I wouldn't know if I was even in love. I've never been."

This caught my attention quickly, "Never?" My voice full of amusement.

"Never."

"What about your ex?"

"I mean I liked him. It was an infatuation that passed quickly. Like and love are two different things. When I read about love, it seems like when you are with someone you love...you're supposed to feel...warm inside...I guess. Fuck I don't know."

I chuckle, "Like Romeo and Juliet?" I mock.

"No. First off, Shakespeare didn't write about love. He wrote about infatuation. Romeo was so 'in love' with that other girl, but then here comes Juliet and boom, he's now in love with this Juliet girl. That's not love. Don't even get me started on Othello. This man swore he loved this girl and once he thought she cheated, he smothered her until she died. I don't know about you, but that's fucked up." She rants.

I burst out laughing, "I didn't know you were into literature."

"Yeah, my mom read to me a lot. It also helped her read and write in English. Those goosebumps books were our favorites though. Mami also liked Poe."

"So, she liked dark literature."

She smiled sadly, "Yeah, she did." Her brown eyes fading into distant memories.

Suddenly, my head get heavier, and I groan as I lie back down. Nova gets into the bed and pushes my head close to hers on the pillow and strokes my hair. My hazel eyes now getting lost in hers. It seemed too easy.

"You're fine. I'll stay with you until you fall asleep. Okay?" She cooed. Her fingers weaving through my hair as she closed her eyes. Making herself comfortable in my bed. Without thinking I wrapped my arms around her waist bringing her closer and nuzzling into her chest. It was like sleeping on a cloud, you know if the cloud had double D's. I hated to admit it, but I wanted her closer I wanted to feel her warmth. Guilt ran through me as I thought about the truth of her mother's death. The closer I got to Nova the harder I realize this was going to be.

"Mama, who's Lena?" I ask.

My mother stops washing the dishes instantly. "Who, sweet?"

"You have been saying her name when you lie down. I can hear you crying her name." I admit.

Mama dries off her hand and walks over to me. She gave me an apologetic look before sitting down by my side. "Sebastian, please do not say that name again. It would make Papa upset."

I didn't care much for my Papa. Mama and my brothers were all I cared for. "Ok, Mama" When Mama asked something from me, I didn't fight her on it. I did not want to make her sad in any way.

That night Mama and Papa took us to a family event. My cousin Donatello, or Donnie as we called him, was celebrating his birthday. Papa hated going to family events, Mama enjoyed being around so many people. It gave her a chance to talk to more than just us.

Donnie was playing with one of my father's soldier's child, Alexander. Donnie rushed over to me. "Bash! Play with us! Shot and Ero are already outside." Donnie offered.

I flipped through my book, "I'm okay. Go ahead without me." I answer. Donnie rolled his eyes and ran outside with Alex.

*"Perché non giochi fuori con gli altri bambini **[Why are you not outside playing with the other children]**?" Papa asks me.*

*"Voglio finire il mio libro. **[I want to finish my book.]**" I answered.*

*"Sebastian, devi essere socievole. È così che nascono le partnership. Devi essere sempre attento quando entri in una stanza. **[Sebastian, you must be social. That is how partnerships are made. You must always be alert when you walk into a room.]**" He explains, taking the book from my hand.*

Chapter 9

Nova

Waking up was odd. Sebastian was still in bed, maybe because of his sickness. The last two times we went to sleep together he was gone in the morning. He looked so.... innocent when he slept. I guess he can be sweet looking when his sly mouth isn't running rapid.

My fingers traced his sharp jawline. The closer I got to the Dominics, the more differences I could find in them. Sebastian has longer lashes than the others. Why do guys always have better lashes than girls? "Missing my touch already, sweet?" His sudden voice emerging. I thought he was asleep.

"Says the man who hasn't let go of me all night." I tease. He smiles, not smirks, smiles.

His finger plays with my frizzy morning curls as he closes his eyes once more.

"How are you feeling?" I ask trying to sit up, but his strong grip kept me in place.

His eyes slowly opened, gazing into mine. "Better."

"Well, since your better I'm going to head out."

"Damn, I'm just a piece of ass to you, sweet." Sebastian dramatically cried.

I raised a brow. "Duh." I stuck my tongue out.

He rolled his eyes and released me. I skipped to the door, but hit my forehead against the door, when I tripped. "I told you that big forehead is like a magnet." He laughed throwing a pillow at me.

"Fuck this stupid boujee door..." I growled walking out. I could still hear Sebastian's laughter down the hall.

DING

DING

I look down and see a text from Santino.

Let's meet in an hour. We need to talk.

-Santino

What do I do? Do I tell the Dominic's? I can't keep this from them. The more I go behind their backs, the worse I feel. I can't lie anymore I have to tell him.

Romero

I sit in my office, thinking about how to approach Nova about her lying to me the other day. What did Santino tell her? It is frustrating, if she were anyone else, I would have tortured the truth from her by now.

A sudden knock came to my door, making me raise my head. "Come in." I answer.

Nova walks right in and sits in the chair in front of me. "Romero, I have to tell you something." She confesses. Her fingers rubing with each other. "I lied to you the other day about what Santino said."

I suck in a breath, trying to stop myself at snapping at her. "Why?" I slightly growl.

Her cheeks puffed up with air, then deflated. "He told me that Crespo...is my father."

I closed my eyes, "So I was right."

"You knew?!" She growls standing up.

I narrow my eyes at her tone. "No, it was a hypothesis of

mine." I sigh, "If it's true, will you go back on your deal with us?"

"Of course not. I don't care if it is true. He's dead to me, for killing my mother." This time she was telling the truth. I believed every word.

"What does Santino want from you?"

"He wants us to be closer. He said that Crespo didn't know he contacted me."

"Do you believe him?"

"Maybe. I don't know. I only met him twice for like 5 minutes each time. He showed me pictures of me as a baby." She explained. Maybe Santino is telling a few truths. "He texted me this morning to meet up again in an hour."

She gives me her phone and I look at the message. "No more meeting with him alone. I don't know what he's up to. I'll go instead."

"Come with me?" she suggests. "What if he's telling the truth and he loses trust in me? I'll go and you can wait in the car."

"No." My reply blunt. "I won't risk it."

She smiles, "Are you worried about me?" Her doe eyes narrowing at me.

"No. I just don't need war to start over your big mouth. You still are in over your head. "I was not lying when I said that.

"Whatever. Keep keeping me in the dark and I'll never learn." She barks back. I was worried for her. She is still new to this world. She is too trusting, that will get her killed. I take a second and think this through.

Options:

1. ~~I let Nova speak to Santino. Consequence: He could kill her.~~
2. I go instead and trigger an early war.
3. I go with Nova and risk the element of sur-

prise that she is working with us.

4.   I take Santino hostage and use him as leverage? That is even if Crespo cares about his children.

I intertwine my fingers and rest my head on them. "I'll go in your stead. I can't risk something happening to you." I confess. I cannot even believe the words coming from my mouth.

Her infectious smile comes out and it is hard for me not to smile back, but I force my lips straight. "Okay, I'm glad we worked that out." She exhales getting up from the chair. The nerve of this girl, to think she could ever lie to me.

"Where do you think you're going?" I growl. Time for a punishment. Her eyes widen and she freezes. I get up from my chair. "Close the door and sit down." I order.

She narrowed her eyes refusing to back down. "Hey, I'm still sore. So, keep it in your pants." Her response made me roll my eyes. Bash and Shot are getting greedy.

"Do you remember what I said to you, I'll decide when you have had enough." I smirk. Walking closer to her. She bumps into the door, accidentally closing it. "Seeing you bent over my desk is going to be fun." I whisper into her ear.

Her breathing quickens as I leaned in for a kiss. Her eyes closed almost immediately. I smile as she opened one eye because I took too long. "Are you fucking with me? You are the biggest tease in tease history!" She whined.

I raise a brow at her. "Did you want me to bend you over my desk? Leave marks all along your body." I continue to tease. She closed her eyes once more. "Are you imagining it? My tongue and fingers between your thighs." I trace my fingers down her spine. "Or maybe I should fuck you against the window. Imagine so many eyes seeing the amount of pleasure I will give you. Seeing the erotic faces you make."

She lets out a sigh in irritation. "You think this is funny? You just watch, one day I'll make you beg. "She rants walking out

STEPHANIE PEREZ

of my office. She really was fun to tease. Nova is such a brat, but she makes me smile and at this point, I cannot deny it.

Now I have to meet with a Crespo. This should be...interesting. Santino had texted Nova a place. It was a restaurant nearby. When I pulled up to the restaurant and walked in, Daniel Crespo was sitting there instead of Santino. His smiles and gestures me to sit down. "I'm surprised to see you here Crespo." I start.

"Not a surprise to see you Romero, look at you...how does Papa's shoes feel?" He mocked.

"What do you want with Nova? I heard she is your daughter. Your son is a bit naïve, to be telling your secret like that." I retort.

He rubs his temples. "I'm not too surprised he did that. It was only a matter of time. He was so attached to her as a child. People and their patterns." He pauses for a second. "How do you know Nova?"

"Just met."

He raises a brow in amusement, "What are the odds?" He chuckled darkly. "Word has spread that she's your girl. Which surprises me, we don't marry outsiders."

"Who says I'm marrying her?" The words slip from my mouth but marrying a girl like Nova could be nice if I was not the boss of the *Casa Rosa*. From a business point of view, Nova was not an option. She cannot give me new territories to control or a treaty with any other rivals I have.

"Well, that's good. I wonder what she'd think if she knew who really is responsible for her mother's death?" His smile was gone. "You know I didn't even get to put her in the ground. I don't even know where her body is. Do you?" His voice, not so much angry, just curious.

I did not. I had no clue where she was buried. I remember her death, but what happen after is still a blank. I was never one to forget a kill, no matter how young I was, but for some reason my mind blocked it out for years, so much that I cannot remember what happen to her afterwards.

"I don't. Truly." I honestly confess. "I wish I did."

He sighs, "You know growing up, I hated my father. He was a week idiot. With no values. He could never do anything himself."

"Said the man who abandoned his child." I scoff.

His smile returns. "You know what I used to love about being a young kid like yourself?" He asks.

"Enlighten me." I dryly reply.

His smile widens, "You think you know it all. That no one can outsmart you. That you are untouchable. I witness firsthand that I could be hurt. This bravado you're strutting around with, can be destroyed with one phone call." He adjusts his tie. "I'm going to say this once. Tell my daughter that she's better off with her family."

Now it is my turn to laugh, "Family? You raised her for what? Ten minutes of her birth?"

"What's the matter? You obviously do not care for her. I'm trying to be civil, be smart." His voice may be soft, but I am no fool to know it is a threat.

"And if I don't?"

He gets up and puts on his suit jacket. "I'm not threatening you Romero. Your choices are your own. Whatever outcome comes from it will be your choice." With that he left in a car.

What was this deadbeat up to? I would not give her to them, ever.

Nova

I chose to put my trust in the Dominics, and to my surprise they were cool about it. They trust me now. I tip toe into Jameson's room, and he is in the process of cleaning his guns and knives. "Hi." I greet tilting my head into his room. He smiles and gestures me to come in. "Whatcha doing?" I ask plopping onto an accent chair.

"Cleaning day. What are you doing?" His light greens now focused on me.

I spin in the chair. "Reading law books in the living room for an hour. Now I have run out of things to do. Camilla and my best friend have been spending time together, they forgot I exist. So, I literally have nothing to do." I groan.

"Sounds like a pool day!" A somewhat familiar voice sings down the hall. Seconds later Donnie walks through the door. "So, let's grab some food and get the BBQ started. We can even invite the other cousins, so Nova will get to know some more Dominics. You know what? Let's invite Lola! I'm sure your tired of being surrounded by guys all day." *Lola*, that was the name of the girl Jameson said in his sleep. I wonder who she is to him...

Why did meeting more Dominics make me so fucking tense, "Um, yeah sounds great." I lie sheepishly.

Donnie grabs my hand, "Fuck, yeah! To the store we go!" He screamed. Jameson laughed. "Sam is waiting in the car. Nova is going to come to the store with us. We will be back soon." Donnie pulled me with him down the hall. I get the same energy from Donnie that I get from Jameson, easy to be around. I can just...relax.

When we reached the car garage, Sam was there waiting in a Lamborghini urus. I didn't know much about cars, but I remember seeing this car before and thinking it was amazing. I have never been able to sit in one before.

"Oh my god, this car is so beautiful. I'm not one for expensive cars, but if I had to have one it would be this one. Fuck this car, is like...I don't have the words." This must be what love feels like. Donnie laughed at my reaction to his car.

He opened the door and I hopped in the back. This car ride was not like riding with the triplets, Donnie, Sam, and I were talking up a storm and singing and rapping to songs. We went to the store and got hot dogs, burgers, *pastelitos*, *pan de bono* and of course some liquor.

We made it back and Sam hopped on the BBQ, while I changed into a swimsuit and put on sunblock. The sun did not agree with my skin. I was on bartender duty, obviously. I had made drinks for those of us that were here. Slowly but surely, the other Dominic's started to trickle in.

The first one to approach me was a guy with dirty blonde hair and brown eyes, "You must be Nova. I'm Leo, Donnie's brother. He was right, you are cute." With that he left and went to talk to Sam. Sweet talking is a Dominic trait. I then met Donnie's sister Michaela. Now that I think about it, they have ninja turtle names. If they have another sibling named Raphael or Rafaela, I'm going to be so excited.

Something hits me, I'm at a party with a bunch of mobsters. They are all part of *Casa Rossa*. I can't make the wrong move. Donnie swings his arm around me. "Calm down. We don't bite." He jokes, which loosens me up a bit. When Donnie gets up, I go behind him and push him into the pool. He comes up for air and I laugh, "Keep laughing, cause your next!" He yells and I hide behind Jameson, wrapping arms around his waist, since he's a whole foot taller than me.

Soon enough Romero comes into the scene looking annoyed per usual, still in the suit he left in. He looks dead at me, then at Donnie, then back at me. I release my arms from Jameson and jump into the pool. "Look who finally showed up!" Donnie hollered. He's so loud, I could hear him under the water. I came up for air and pushed my wet, now wavier, curls out of my face. Romero is gone by the time I came up but someone new was here. She was incredibly beautiful, she had short dark curly hair, mahogany brown eyes, and olive skin. "*Lola, vieni a conoscere Nova!* **[Lola, come meet Nova!]**" Donnie said getting out the pool.

I climbed out of the pool, "Hi, I'm Nova." I greet.

Lola looks me up and down with an unmistakable glare, "Lola." She barely greets before stepping passed me and into Jameson's arms. A sharp pain dug into my chest. Damn it, there I go again. Why do I even care? I take in the sight of them hugging, which didn't seem that serious, but it still bothered me.

Suddenly I was picked up by Donnie and he jumped in the pool with me. My arms still wrapped around him as I came up. "This makes us even." Donnie laughs. I unwrap my arms from his neck and slap his shoulder laughing. I get out the pool once more and gesture to Donnie that I'm watching him. I walk over to the bar and make myself a drink...then another...and another.

Jameson

Lola walked over to me after saying something to Nova I greeted her with a hug. "I missed you, Jamie." She greets hugging me tightly.

"Did you meet Nova?" I ask. She scowls and rolls her eyes. Lola never was a fan of other girls growing up. Mama and Papa tried many times to set up play dates, but she would never play with the other girls. "Be nice to Nova, Lola. I mean it." I ordered sternly.

She replied with another eye roll. I look over at Nova she is taking shots back-to-back. I get up and walk over to her. When I put a hand on her back she looks up with stunned eyes. "Hey J, what's up?" She asks, not really looking at me in the eye.

"Are you okay?" My eyes soften looking at Nova.

"I'm cool." She laughs dryly, "I'm just having a drink, are we not at a party?"

I can see that there is something wrong. I grab her hand

and bring her inside into my room. "What's going on?" I ask now more sternly.

She laughs once more, "Nothing, I'm fine I swear. So, you can go back to Lola now."

She shifted uncomfortably as if she didn't mean to say the last part. I start laughing and she glares. "Are you jealous of Lola?"

She plays with her fingers, "The first time we had sex you said her name in your sleep…" She pauses. "So, I guess she must have been…your girl or something."

I laughed even harder. "*Tesoro mio*, Lola is our younger sister. Trust me you have nothing to be jealous about." I pull her into my lap and lay a small kiss on her lips.

She looked so embarrassed, "Um…that was a plot twist."

I'm surprised Nova would feel jealousy towards any girl. Even if Lola was not our sister, I don't see anyone but Nova. I have never felt like this before about a girl. "Nova, you are all I see." I confess. "I want you all the time." I mumble into her neck. My lips leaving kisses down her neck and chest.

Little moans escape her mouth. Her fingers intertwined into my hair as my tongue licks one of her nipples. She already had tan lines from today, which made her look even sexier. Suddenly Nova pulls away from me.

"Someone will be looking for us soon we should get going." Her voice a bit breathless. I nod and walk back outside with her. Before she can do anything, I grab a towel and sit her on my lap. I push her bikini bottom and point my dick into her opening. She looks back at me lustful but nervous. I entered her slowly to not have her moan too loud and draw attention. I had no trouble getting my dick into her, she was incredibly wet already.

"Fuck…" I groan. Her walls starting to clamp onto me. I needed her so bad I am willing to fuck her while my family was around. Damn, what will I do when she's gone.

"Your family will catch us." She whispers. Another quiet moan escapes.

"Ignore them." I turn her head slightly to look at me. "Just focus on me. Let me make you feel good, *tesero*." My voice a bit breathless as I push deeper into her. She digs her nails into my thighs. Her chest heaving slowly as I enter her and pull out. Since everyone was at proximity I couldn't move as fast as I wanted. I may have not thought this through. I am definitely thinking with my dick. I couldn't wait another minute to be inside her.

She leans back on me. The back of her head resting on my shoulder. "Jameson..." She moans. I kiss her warm cheeks. My fingers rub her clit as I ease in and out of her.

Nova

Pleasure flowed through me, despite the fear I felt if any of the Dominic's figured out Jameson was fucking me under this towel. I knew what we were doing was so wrong but why did it turn me on even more. Am I an exhibitionist? I was never like this before; I mean I wasn't a prude but fuck these Dominic triplets bring out something in me that I've never felt before. Jameson was working magic with his fingers. I felt my climax coming soon. All I could do was moan his name over and over as quietly as possible.

"You can cum if you want to." He whispered into my ear.

My eyes closed shut. "What about you?"

"We are not done for the day. You'll make it up to me later. When I cum, I want to see it dripping down your legs." He whispered, kissing the back of my neck. "In your mouth and on your breasts."

Fuck...yes that did it. Jameson's dirty words bring me to complete completion. I shudder as I cum and Jameson wraps his arms around me. "I came." I breathed.

"I know, *tesero*." He says sliding out of me.

His fingers then sliding in filling me up again. "Jameson, I'm sore." I whimper.

He slides his finger out of me and licks them. "So sweet, *tesero*." He pauses, "Taste how sweet you are." He pushes his finger to my mouth, and I lick my sweet cum off his finger.

I turn around completely and kiss him. Then nuzzled my head into the crook of his neck. I feel him smiling, which in turn makes me smile wider. Jameson really is someone I could fall in love with. I know I shouldn't think like that, but it's hard to not fall for him.

Chapter 10

Nova

Meeting the Dominic's was surreal. They were all really sweet, well…mostly. Lola definitely does not like me. Donnie and Sam stayed over. They were passed out in my room, I slept in Jameson's bed. I have no clue where Romero went. I hadn't seen him since he got home yesterday. Now that I think about it, I haven't seen Sebastian either. I wonder where they went.

Jameson shifted in his sleep. "You're staring, *tesoro*." He mumbles.

"Well, I'm up and you're not. What else should I do?" I whine. He smiles, but his eyes remain closed.

"Go back to sleep. You're always up early." He yawns, throwing the blanket over our heads.

I laugh and get up from the bed. "Fine, I'll go make breakfast." I sing skipping down the hall. I get in the kitchen and work *my* magic. I make some pancakes, bacon, eggs, *tostada, café con leche*, and cut up some fruit for freshness. Also, on the side hangover soup. I set the dining table all nice for the breakfast and went to wake Donnie and Sam. I knock first but I don't get an answer, so I start opening the door.

Before I can open the door all the way, Donnie blocks the door. "Morning!" He says brightly with a big smile plastered all over his face. "Something smells good." He sang.

Kinda weird that he blocked the door, but I didn't think too hard about it and said, "Yeah foods ready. Get it before it's gone." I stick out my tongue at him as I walk back to Jameson's room.

Romero

I sit on our jet as Bash sits across from me. The jet is headed to Italy. It has been years since I visited this place. As a kid it was a second home to me, but now it is just a place of forgotten memories.

"Lastra is stealing huh?" Bash gripes.

"Sartori called me yesterday. He says the product being sold does not match the numbers. When Lastra ran the numbers, he said it was lining up, but Sartori ran them to be sure, and they have been low for three weeks." I explain. "Since when has Lastra ever ran numbers and got them wrong. That's too many coincidences for me."

"How short?"

"$100k." I chuckled darkly. "Not much, but still."

Bash returned my laugh. "Chump change, but it's *our* change." He pauses, "Why not send Shot?"

"We can break some limbs just fine, plus I need the best fighter to watch Nova. Donnie and Sam are also going to stay until we get back."

"Any other reason why we're here? One of us would have been fine." He groans.

I closed my eyes and sigh, "I'm visiting our parents graves."

Bash's face went dark. "Why?" He asks, narrowing his eyes at me.

"Crespo wants Nova. I don't know why, but I thought if I went to Mama and Papa's graves, I could put together an answer." I laugh sadly. "Childish, I know."

"We can't give her to him." Bash growls. He tilts his head back and pinches his nose, "What is this little fox turning us into. The plan was to use her and toss her aside, now we are testing fate to keep her." Bash whines. I snicker at him. He has become more like Nova. He was always a brat, but now so more than ever.

Nova

"Where's Romero and Sebastian?" I ask with a mouth full of bread.

Donnie and Sam look at Jameson. Even though Romero is the boss of *Casa Rosa*, I guess to everyone else all three have seniority. "Italy." Jameson responded.

"What?" I whine. "All the boring shit you guys have me do, but I couldn't go to Italy with them?"

Jameson flicks my forehead. "I'll take you. If you want to go that bad."

My eyes shine, "Wait, really?"

"Where else would you want to go?" Donnie asked.

"Cuba. My grandmother is over there and she's getting old. My mother escaped Cuba, so she's not allowed back. I talk to my grandmother from time to time, but I really would like to meet her in person before she dies. She will be 89 this year." I smile sadly. My grandmother has dementia and every time I talk to her, I have to remind her that I'm an adult now. She only remembers me as a kid.

We bounced around topics for a while. "I hear your mother is trying to have you married to that blonde debutant. What was her name? Alba...Ana?" Jameson pondered.

"Chiara." Donnie answered flatly.

"You seem excited." I said sarcastically.

"I don't want to get married. Being tied down like that makes no sense. I'm young, all I want to do is party and live life.

"True. Is that normal for you guys to marry so young? I mean we are all still in our twenties." I laugh.

"Yeah, fucking sucks." Donnie groans, shoving another pancake in his mouth. "Anything that better strengthens *Casa Rossa*." Donnie's words send nerves around me. If I were raised by Crespo, would I have been in some political marriage like the rest of them. They really die by their mob. I can't imagine having such limited choices.

"So...do you guys really only marry Italian girls?" I was curious about this. I remember Santino saying it once.

"Usually yes, but it could be any girl that brings value to the family. Like a girl with a rich family or has family in government." Jameson answered. "Anyone not directly in a mob family is considered an outsider. It's just easier, people who are not raised in this life, usually do not survive." Jameson explained.

"So, I'm considered an outsider." I smile sheepishly. That day I really learned how the Dominics viewed me and where I stood in their lives. An outsider, I wasn't one of them.

Jameson opened his mouth to speak, but the alarm went off and everyone stood up. Everyone drew their guns and Jameson and Donnie started calling people in Italian. Everything was happening so fast.

"Go to the panic room. Now." Jameson calmly said to me.

I nodded and ran, but before I could get far, I felt something burning on my side. I touch my side and my hands are covered in blood. "J-J-Jameson...!" I cried.

He looked at me in horror and ran to my side. "Call an ambulance!" He yelled. My vision got hazy and soon everything went black.

Romero

I left Bash to deal with these idiots, while I went to my parents' graves to figure out what I should do. I sit on the ground in front of my parent's graves. I took a deep breath, then spoke, *"Ciao, ma, che piacere vederti. Vorrei che potessimo parlare. Chissà ' se te lo aspettavi. Papà, sei stato l'uomo più ' brutale che conosca. Se tu fossi qui mi daresti una lezione su come nulla viene prima della famiglia, ma non posso lasciare andare questa ragazza. E 'così' che ti sentivi con la ma quando volevi proteggerla?* **[Hello ma, good to see you. I wish we could talk. I wonder if you saw this coming. Papa, you were the most brutal man I know. If you were here, you would give me a lecture about how nothing comes before the family, but I cannot let this girl go. Is this how you felt with ma when you wanted to protect her?]**" The thoughts running through my head. "I just need like a sign or something. Fuck, I don't know—excuse my language Ma." I laugh. I look like Mama when she would talk to Papa's dead sister.

I get a phone call from Sebastian. "We definitely have to go to church this Sunday." Bash laughed. "Also, will definitely have to get a new suit. God, blood really sinks into your clothing."

"I guess the meeting went well?"

"Sartori will make sure there are no longer any problems. Also, I may have killed three soldiers including that rat Lastra. Satori's sons are of age now. They will be joining him. Maybe try to not tell Cami. She's not going to like her little brothers being away." Bash joked. He pauses, "Donnie's calling me I'll call you back."

I hang up and then my phone starts to go off as well. When I look at the text, I drop my phone. Something inside me takes over my body. A feeling I hadn't felt in a long time...fear?"

Nova has been shot.

-Shot

Jameson

Nova is being rushed into the emergency room and these

idiots won't let me go with her. I have all the exits covered with *Casa Rossa* soldiers. That shit did not come from someone in the house. That was an outside sniper. Why shoot Nova though? I can't make sense of anything right now my mind is too scrambled. I need to calm down, I can't think like this. My phone rings and it's Ero. I answer but don't say anything.

"What the fuck is going on? Where is she? How is she?" Romero seemed calmer than I thought he would be.

"She's in the emergency room. I have soldiers on every floor in the hospital. Ero this wasn't random. This was a hit. A sniper shot a bullet through the terrace window. I don't know who it is. I can't even make sense of anything right now." I ramble.

"Calm down. She needs you." He growls. For a second a storm of 'fucks' are thrown out before he's back on the phone. "Get updates on her every thirty minutes. I'll be there as soon as possible." With that he hangs up and I'm left with my fear of what is happening with her.

Hours later

I sat in the waiting room with Donnie. "Mr. Dominic?" Dr. Moretti walked over with her clipboard in hand. She was our family doctor for problems like this. Bullet wounds we couldn't explain and anything else.

"How is she?" I ask, trying my best to sound unshaken.

"She's sleeping and stable. You can see her now. The bullet wasn't found in her body. She's lucky, the bullet just scraped her. It will scar but she's fine." She explained.

My chest still felt tight, even with this added information. I followed Dr. Moretti into Nova's room. Entering, I see Nova's sleeping face. Her long dark curls scattered along the bed. I walk up to her and intertwined my fingers with her. Her normal warmness was still present, which calmed me.

I update Bash and Ero on her status. I get into the bed with her and rub her head with my thumb. "I'm sorry, *tesoro*." I whisper to her. Her usually brown skin always had a bright golden undertone that made her seemed like she was always glowing, was gone. The doctor said she'd be fine, but fuck--I can't shake this feeling. I feel.... helpless. I want to burn this city to find who did this. Sitting here waiting for my brothers is torture. I want blood to flow. That is the only thing that will bring me solace.

Soon after Cami comes through the door with J.L, Nova's best friend. I get off the bed and collect myself. J.L to Nova's side. "What happened to her?" Her voice on the brink of tears.

"Biker ran into her cutting her side slightly. She's fine. She's just sleeping." I lie. I glare at Cami for even bring J.L in the first place.

J.L narrows her eyes at me, "Why are you here with her?"

"Nova and I have been getting to know each other." I explain. She nods but I don't think she believes anything I'm saying.

"Weird, I'm surprised she didn't mention you." her stare narrowing even more. I don't blame her suspicion. She knows nothing about me and I'm in a hospital bed with her best friend.

"It's still new." I simply state.

J.L strokes Nova's cheek. Cami grabs J. L's hand. "He's my childhood friend. He's trustworthy, I promise. It's late, lets come back in the morning. She'll be happier to see us with food." Cami insists. J.L nods in agreement and kisses Nova's forehead before leaving with Cami.

It's now three in the morning and I still can't sleep. I bang my head against the wall as I still in the chair across from her hospital bed. My bloodlust is in full drive, and I have to sit here on my ass. Dr. Moretti said she was sleeping, but fuck she's been sleeping for hours.

"Is she okay?!" Bash's loud voice comes through the door.

I glare, "Shut the fuck up!" I angrily whisper. "She's still sleeping."

Bash walks over to her and runs his thumb over her lips. "Anyone have an idea who did this?" Bash growls.

"If I did, they would be dead by now don't you think?" I growl back. Romero is unusually quiet. "Ero?" I raise a brow to him.

"This is going to sound crazy. I may just be in shock, but...I asked our parents for a sign on what to do about Crespo."

"And?' Bash and I ask in unison.

"And then Nova gets grazed with a bullet, through our bullet proof windows." Ero explains. He is in shock. Bash and I look at each other in confusion. Ero is too fucking smart to believe the words that just came out of this mouth. He is in clear shock. I don't think he has ever been in shock before.

"Ero, even if that were true-"

"Which it's not." Bash adds.

"What would that even mean?"

Ero crosses his arms and leans against the wall. "I don't fucking know. Mom wasn't exactly all the way there." He groans. "Maybe, they don't think she's worth the battle with Crespo?"

"I'm not going to say it *again*. "Bash fumed. "She's not going *anywhere*."

"What's our end game here? Because at some point, she will be gone." I ask.

"In the beginning, she was just a sacrificial lamb, but now.... I don't know." Bash sighs, taking a seat next to her, stroking her curls. Ero looks over at Bash, then Nova. "We have to tell her the truth and hope she forgives us."

"What truth?" I ask. "The hell are you talking about?"

I was seriously confused. Nova already knows every-thing, what have we hid from her?

Bash clears his voice, "Let's talk outside, Shot."

Sebastian

A ten-year-old version of myself wakes up noticing that Ero and Shot are gone from their beds. I got to Lola's room and she's not their either. I run to the study and see if Mama and Papa were in there. Just like I thought, I could hear Mama rambling.

"Let's talk through this. Don't do this. Your children need you." Another woman's voice said, she seems scared. She had dark skin, and noticeably short curly hair. I had never seen her before.

"I have to." Mama cried. "I will only hurt them." I peak in and see Mama holding a gun in her hands. I can see Ero hiding behind a chair. I try to walk into the room by going behind a bookcase to get to Ero.

Papa walks in and his eyes widen. "What are you doing? Give me that gun now!" He shouts. He walks closer to her, but she only aims it at them. "Ramira, leave now." He orders the woman.

The woman carefully takes a step. "No!" Mama yells and shoots her. Papa charges to take the gun from Mama's hands, but she pulls the trigger killing herself.

Shot looks at me stunned. "She killed her mother?" This didn't make sense. "Why was she even there to be begin with?"

"I don't know, I'm sure Crespo knows and that's why he killed so many Dominic's, taking two of our territories in the process."

"Why tell me now?"

"I didn't think it was important. Nova's mother doesn't matter to us. She was just another person caught it the *Casa Rossa* fire. You were the first one of us to start to care for Nova. We could all see it and I thought it would be easier if you didn't have to lie to her."

"So that was the plan, let her die trying to kill Crespo. Knowing full well our mother killed her, not Crespo." Shot took a breath and I could see the disgust in his face. "That's fucked even for us."

"It's just business. You know that. Your hands carry the same stains of blood." He sighs. His fingers running through his hair. "If we plan to let her be one of us. We have to tell her and let her decide."

"What if she goes to Crespo? He is her father. She put her trust in us...and we used it to our advantage." He laughs darkly. "We need to find out who did this, quickly. I'm itching to kill something."

"Me too little brother. Don't worry we will paint the walls with their blood..." I swear. Not just for almost killing Nova but thinking they could try and attack *Cassa Rossa*.

Nova

My vision is red... wait no... I haven't opened my eyes yet. The sun must be shining. I peak with one eye and see different shades of greens watching me attentively. "Damn Nova! You got shot, how's it feel?" Donnie jokes jumping on my bed.

I snort a laugh. "Stop jumping, on the bed. "I scolded in a whiney voice. He jumps off, but his bright smile is still there.

Romero slaps the back of his head, "Go wait outside." He growls.

"Feel better!" He waves leaving the room.

The big three gather around me. Bash pinches my cheek, "How do you feel, sweet?" His voice was soft and sounded genuinely worried.

"I'm fine. I can't believe I got shot. It's still hurts, but in a way, it's like a cool memory." I gleam, my voice still a bit dry.

Romero raises a brow at me. "Yeah, let's not make it a habit, besides, it only grazed you. Don't start patting yourself on the back." He scoffs.

"Were you born a hater? Did no one pick you in team activities as a kid or some shit?" I growl. "How many times have you been shot? Huh?" I ask mockingly.

He thinks about it for a second, before he speaks. "Successfully? Three times."

"Same here." Sebastian cuts in.

"I've been shot five times." Jameson confesses proudly. "Which means I'm pretty much immortal." He jokes.

"Or an easy target." Romero jokes.

I narrow my eyes at them, "Bullshit, I've never seen any scars on your bodies."

"Why do you think we have all these tattoos." Jameson chuckled. "They're healed now of course but the scar is still there. You just can't see it with the tattoos. You would have to really be paying attention." He explained. He grabs my hand and drags it to his shoulder. I rub the spot with my fingers and feel the scar. It really is hard to notice I can barely see it.

I lie back down and sigh, "So who's trying to kill you guys?" I ask. "Think it's Crespo?"

"Could be, but I don't think he'd risk killing you." Romero noted.

I roll my eyes, "He killed my mother, you think it's far-fetched that he'd let me die if it meant killing you guys." I scoff. "Why kill one bird if you can kill more with one stone, right?"

Silence...

"Guys?" I wait for suggestions.

"Maybe, but highly unlikely. It's too messy to be a Crespo move. This person seems sloppy." Sebastian stated.

"This person definitely knows us. There's a rat. It has to be." Jameson states. We all look at him observantly.

"Possibly." Romero sighs.

"But why shoot Nova and leave?" Sebastian growls.

Jameson rubs his temple. "They were fast, the bullets seemed random, more like a diversion." He speculates. "Nova's shot was an accident. How do you shoot bullets into a room and miss? You'd have to be the worst shot-"

"Or a good shot." Romero adds. "Call Sean."

"Who's Sean?" I ask.

"Sunny's brother. He's been our cop on the inside. Just to make sure we don't have any cops sniffing around us or if they are, we can get the heads up." Jameson explains. "Always be 100 steps ahead."

Oh, speaking of, I need to pay Sunny a visit. "Hey, not to change the subject but is there any chance I can see Sunny sometime this week?"

"Why?" Romero narrows.

"She's a woman who has been part of the criminal underworld. I'm sure she can teach me more than any of you *men* can. No offense." I smile brightly.

They all roll their eyes at me, but I simply keep the smile on my face. "You seem oddly chipper for someone who got shot." Sebastian observes.

"Grazed." Romero corrects. I glare at him in response.

I tilt my head, then sigh. "I mean it was scary, but I'm a nobody. I'm sure someone is after you guys not me."

"Yes, but you realize that you are now attached to us, which means you're just as much in danger as we are. Especially since Ero decided to claim you in front of Matanza." Jameson growls. "Word travels fast. We don't claim women we aren't tied down to by marriage. Even though Ero claimed you to keep Matanza at a distance, it now puts a target on your back."

I look down at my hands and I start to realize the gravity of the situation. It really isn't something to take lightly. Jameson's right, if people think I'm Romero's girl, they will try to hurt me to get to him. Fuck…anything could happen to me. I need to be more careful. Next time, I won't be so lucky.

Chapter 11

Nova

These few weeks of recovery have sucked. Having to come up with a bullshit reason for why I'm not living at my place to J.L. Thankfully, Cami is good at keeping J.L occupied. I hate lying to her, but again I don't think I could ever tell her the truth. I would only put her at risk if she knew a fraction of what's going on in my life right now.

Jameson has been trying to shove vegetables and greens down my throat, which is the fucking worst. That man must have the cleanest body ever. All he eats is healthy food. How the fuck does he do it? Every time he tries to make me healthy food, I ask for the unhealthiest shit ever. The crazy part is he *actually* enjoys eating healthy. I know he means well, but fuck I just want pancakes and pizza.

"No pizza." Jameson scolds.

I open my eyes and look at him in shock. "How did you know?"

He smiles slightly. "You do a little dance when you think about food you're going to eat."

Damn it, he really is fucking observant.

Since the shoot out everything has gone back to being quiet. Romero and Sebastian have been a little distant. Jameson seems the most normal, but he's been off too. Did I do something? Should I ask? I'll just leave it alone. I'm sure things will return to normal in a week or so. They must be stressed about not having any leads on the shooting fiasco. Romero especially,

I'm sure the attack is pissing him off tremendously. He's been either locked up in his office or gone from here.

Jameson looks at his phone and gets up from the couch. "I'll be back later. I got to go handle something."

I yawn and get more comfortable on the couch. "Where are you going?"

"Just some errands." His vague response doesn't sit well with me. That's what I'm talking about. They all seem to be keeping something from me.

I nod and soon after he is gone, and I'm left home with Romero. Romero is of course locked up in his office, planning revenge like a supervillain. Once he has a target, I'm sure things will only get worse.

Today I'll be visiting Sunny. Last time I saw Sunny, she seemed like she just ran shit, she didn't even take shit from the Dominics. One of the Dominic's drivers took me to see Sunny. I took advice Romero once gave me and dressed in the new clothes he bought me and made myself look presentable. I wanted Sunny to take me seriously.

Arriving at the mansion. A girl with blonde hair reaching her shoulders, crystal blue eyes, and skin the color of milk. She reminded me of Cinderella.

"Hey, I'm Nova. I'm looking for Sunny." I greet.

Her eyes widen a bit and nods opening the door and letting me in. "Yes, she said you were coming today. I'm Gia, I work for Sunny."

"Really? How is that? What kind of boss is she?"

Gia smiles, "She's amazing. She really looks out for us. We're lucky, few sex workers are treated with respect. She's more like a mom than a boss though. Tough when she needs to be, but fair. Plus, she makes sure idiots don't bother us." She giggles.

"Don't be givin' away all my secrets, Gia." Sunny scolds

from the top of the stairs. "Now go on. Your supper awaits. Chef Abandi is not going to be happy if your food gets cold."

Gia nodded, "Nice meeting you." Gia says before walking down the hall.

"I was informed that you wanted to speak with me?" She inquires, finally down the steps.

"Yes. I would like to learn about you."

"Me? Why?"

"You're a madam. A boss in your own right. I want to learn from you."

She smiles at me, "Well now, I can't say no to such a request." She gestures me to follow into a living room area. "Where should I start? I was born in New Orlene's, Louisiana. I grew up in a city called St. Claude. My life consisted of a baby sister, older brother and a mama and daddy who were very in love, but times were hard. Mama started working night shifts, that's what she called it."

"How did your dad react?"

"Daddy died before she could confess. Mama brought in a lot of money, but she could never tell daddy the actual amount. She would lie and say she made $300 this week when she really made $800 or more. Mama was a very pretty girl, and she had a ton of wealthy clients. She never stepped out on daddy, she loved him with her whole heart. It was just a job. People back then and now still don't understand that this is just a job." She pauses and pours the whisky sitting at a nearby table, then brings it back to us. "After daddy died, Mama moved us to New York and started running *Les courtisans de la reine*." It was French for The Queens Courters.

"So, this place has a name." I say looking around.

"It wasn't always this nice. It was going to be demolished, due to the conditions, but mama used the money she made to

119

buy it out. She remodeled the whole place, but then I remodeled it because it wasn't my taste." She snickered.

"And how'd she take that?" I chuckle.

"Oh, she whined a heck of a storm. You know them old southern women are so damn head strong! She was critiquin' every damn thing in this place when I changed it." Sunny huffed.

"So, she was the former madam?"

"Yes, once she fixed this place up, she made it into an amazing brothel. Mama made sure the girls were taken care of. Lots of people in this world, see women as disposable. Prostitution is a universal job, some do it because they want to, and others are forced into it. It's easy for people to pray on those with nothing. I have plenty of people that come to me looking for work because they have no place to go. Most people would take them in and work them to make a buck, knowing they have no willingness to work in this industry."

"So, what do you do with them?"

"I have a shelter that my little sister runs." She takes a sip of whiskey. "No one should be forced into sex work. It should always be a choice. There are people all over the world who are being forced into sex work because of lack of resources or just plain trafficking. Mama always said, 'Women get really fucked in this world, why not make a profit?' I was thirteen when she told me that." She laughed.

Her mom was not here for the bullshit. "Your mom sounds like a bad ass."

"She is, but she's really old now and all she cares to talk about is her days as New York's finest madam. I've surpassed her in sales already in my first few years, but she won't accept it for shit." She whined. It made me cover my mouth to hide my laughter.

"So how did you start working with the Dominic's?"

She pushes a piece of her hair out of her face. "I dated their daddy before he was married."

My eyes widen, "Wait, what? You dated their dad?" I questioned. I was completely shocked; I mean she looks only a few years older than me. "How old are you if you don't mind me asking?"

"A lady never tells, but I'll say it this once. I am forty-six years old. I met Servino when he first came to America from Italy. He was about fourteen and I had just moved with my mother and siblings to New York at thirteen. My mother had sent me with my brother to get some groceries. I really wanted the candy on the top shelve and so I tried to reach for it, and it came crashing down and spilled everywhere. The grocery worker was pissed and told me I had to pay for the damages."

"What a dick."

"No manners whatsoever. Servino and his mama were shopping, and she saw the way that man was treating me so she paid for the candy and told my brother and I to pick anything we wanted from the store, and she would pay for it. Extremely sweet woman, she carried herself with the most grace I tell you. She reminded me of my mama. Except mine was more of a spitfire. Besides the point, Servino and I kept seeing each other around and one day he just decided to talk to me, and we became fast friends. Servino's father was not happy about it one bit. Quite the bigot he was."

"So did you guys sneak around?"

"I mean.... we didn't have to sneak much. We would just sleep together from time to time. When his father figured it out, he found Servino an Italian woman to marry. He married her that same year."

"So, he broke if off with you?"

She slams the whisky glass on the table. "Hell no! I broke it off with him first! I deserved better, and I wasn't going to settle for some *boy* who couldn't stand up to his low-down daddy. I needed a man and so I got one, who treated me like the queen *I* am."

"Does he know, about what you do?"

"Yes, once I knew I could trust him."

"Wait, but if you broke it off with Servino then why..." Why are the Dominic's still working with her?

She picks up the glass again. "A year into his marriage, he killed his father as an apology to me. I mean he always wanted the bastard dead, so it works out. We stayed friends after that. He helped my business by donating some money and helped open up the shelter."

I smile into my glass of whiskey. I wonder what would happen if they had stayed together.

"Enough of that low down mama's boy, back to me. Basically, my girls get protection from the Dominics, and I send some of my girls to work in their clubs."

"Ah..." I nod. "Do they live here?"

"Not all, but some. Some of my workers grew up without people around and so they feel better staying here than alone in some apartment in the city."

"You live here to?"

"Of course, a mother bird is not leaving her nest. I must always be here to make sure there are no issues at all times."

"Do you have any children?"

"Oh god no. Make no mistake, children are god sent, but I already have my hands full with these brats, who I love dearly, walking these very halls. Every person that works for me gets a psych evaluation first. So that I can figure out how to help them or hire them. In a sense, I have children, there just not biologically mine."

"Did you ever want a child with Servino?" I ask, testing the waters.

She was quiet at first, she seemed to be thinking about the answer. "If he wasn't part of the *Casa Rossa*, yes, but otherwise no. I would not subject my child to that life. Boys are made into Made Men at an early age. To take a child's innocence, is something I could never forgive. The daughters have it a bit easier depending on the parent. Either you're a breeder to be sold off to a *capo* if you're lucky or a soldier, or you bring something to help the family like a good business."

"That's horrible...I can't imagine."

She crossed her arms. "I think my chapter has closed. Now I want to know a bit about you missy. Why are you working with the Dominics?"

I look down, "My mother was killed by Daniel Crespo when I was young. I gave the law a chance to do right by her and they failed. So, now I want to do right by her and end him."

She sighs looking up and down at me. "You kill him and then what?"

Then what...?

"Honey, tell me about your mama."

"She came here from Cuba, gave birth to me at when she was a teenager. Life was always fun. Mami would speak to me in Spanish, and I would speak to her in English. It was really funny and confusing. My mom really liked engineering; she could fix anything. She liked to eat a lot. Loved learning about the world."

"Sounds like a woman who always found a way through." She smiled.

"Yeah, she did."

"Do you think she would be happy with your choice? Do you genuinely believe in your heart that you are doing what your mama wanted for you? To kill Crespo or die trying? Killing Crespo won't bring your mama peace, but seeing you be the woman she raised you to be is. You only get one life. Take it from someone who's lived it. You know her better than I. What would she want you to do?"

It ruined her sister's life and so to keep you from it she forbade us from seeing you.

Santino's words ringing strong in my mind. My mother tried to keep me from this her whole life. She even told me herself about her sister's story and I spat in the face of that. What am I doing? Being a lawyer like my mother dreamed is what I should be doing. It's too late now, the Dominic's aren't going to let me renege on our deal.

Leaving Sunny's left me thinking about my choices. About how I truly am leaving a mark on my mother's legacy. She came here to get a better life and I'm just wasting mine on revenge, that at this point could not even be the real story. I never got actual proof that he killed her, I just assumed.

A call comes in from Santino, I pick it up. "Hey Nova, it's me, Santino. I'm so sorry dad took my phone and sent you that message. I know it must sound like a lie, but it's the truth. I want to see you again. Last time, I told you too much, too fast and that's on me. I should have given it to you in pieces. The Crespo's are doing a family event in four weeks. Please come. We all need to talk this through, for the last time. "

"I'll come."

"Really?"

"Yeah, I want the truth and I want to hear it from his mouth." I'm done playing games. I want to hear the full story. I can't keep thinking about what happened., I need to know what *actually* happen. Then I'll figure out what I need to do. I can't tell the Dominic's I'm going. Romero will never let me leave the house. I have to do this alone and then I'll tell them. I can already hear Romero nagging.

"We can all finally talk, and this bullshit can end."

"I hope so."

We hang up and I look up at the ceiling as I lay in my bed. Usually, if I were in my room one of the Dominic's would come in, but like I said before, they've been weirdly distant.

Having everything ready for the upcoming weeks, I head over to J.L and use my key to get inside. "Yo! Anyone home?" I shout.

"Auntie Nova! I missed you. Do you feel better now?" Bo ran into my arms, and I lift him squeezing him tighter.

"I missed you to! And yes, I feel way better now." I smother him with kisses.

"I'm in the kitchen!" J.L yells.

I set Bo down and walk into the kitchen slapping J.L ass. "Damn ma, all that ass for me?" I joke. She laughs and slaps my arm.

I pretend to wince, "Did you just hit me? I am in re-co-ver-y." I fake cry.

"Fuck your recovery." She snarled, then pulling me into a hug. "I'm glad you're better, though."

"Me to." I smile.

"So, what brings you over?"

"I missed you like crazy. I hadn't seen you in a week." I say wrapping my arms around her neck and kissing her cheek.

"You're so clingy..." She gripes, but deep down she loves me.

I let go of her and sit in on one of her bar stools. "So... how are things going between you and Cami. You guys grew close pretty fast."

She puts down the heat on the stove and jumps up to sit on the counter. "I mean, I don't think I've met someone like her before. You should see her sketches for her clothing, absolutely amazing. She just so fucking talented, and I don't know...she makes me feel..."

"Warm?"

"Yeah. She's fun to talk to and she's gorgeous. Also, she doesn't take any shit and she's not annoying about it, but just cool. You know when you meet someone, and something just clicks."

My mind goes directly to the triplets. In a way, I had an instant connect with all of them, well maybe not Romero at first. Yet lately I've felt like I've been further and further away from them, these past couple of weeks.

Sebastian

Shot and I have been paying a visit to a few old enemies. *Casa Rossa* has an abundance of those. My papa was a ruthless man and didn't do things lightly. Everything always served a purpose. He was loyal to those loyal to him and turns out he had more rats than friends.

"What has Yuri Sidorov been up to these days?" I ask Gregory. He used to spy on the Russians for Papa.

"He's retired. Given his son, Stephan, the reins now, but you won't have to worry about them. He relocated to Miami for a while."

"Oh right, I forgot he had a bunch of bastards. I guess he has a favorite then."

"Yes."

"Is that everything?" I bait. There's something he's leaving out. Withholding information from me will never end well.

"Yes"

I chuckle, "Funny, because I heard a different story. Andrei is taking his place, not Stephan." I take my gun out of the holster. "Why are you lying to me Gregory?"

His eyes widen, "I'm not lying. I heard it out of his daughters' mouth."

"I'd hate to think you're lying to me, Gregory. Listen, I'm going to believe it was an honest mistake, bring me something good and all is well."

He nods his head quickly, "Of course Mr. Dominic."

I give him a sarcastic smile before I put the gun back into my holster and leave the apartment.

Jameson

"It's been a while. I missed you." Valeria flirts. "*¿Cuánto tiempo ha pasado? ¿Dos años?* [**How much time has passed? Two years?**]"

"What have you been up to lately?" I Interrogate.

"You know, killing people. Nothing new." Her Columbian accent coming through as she speaks.

Valeria was a gun for hire, a real fucking assassin. She worked for us a couple times. We didn't end our business or personal relationship badly, but she never let anything come before the money. I wouldn't put it passed her that someone hired her to fuck with us.

Suddenly she bursts out laughing. "If you want to accuse me of something, just ask. I can see that look on your face. You look like a hungry *gato* trying to catch a rat."

"Did you shoot up my place?" I ask, raising a brow to her.

"Yes." She confessed. Valeria was always known for her honestly.

I rub my temples, "Why?"

"It's just business Shot; you know that. I can't sell out my buyer. Bad for business, you understand."

I sigh sitting down opposite of her. "What can you tell me?" I ask.

"This person is a nobody. I don't know or care. As long as I get paid."

I grew increasingly frustrated talking to Valeria. I try not to kill women if I don't have to, but fuck Valeria is testing her luck. "How about a trade? A favor for a favor."

Her ears seem to perk up as she sits upright. "I'm listening..."

"Give me a name. And I will owe you a favor, one favor."

We shake on it. I will always keep my word and she knew it. "I got a name, but honestly sounds made up to me. I don't know what good it would do. I never got to meet the person either, I was always communicating with their 'representation' or whatever."

"Give it to me." I insist.

She shrugs her shoulders. "Fine. Madrid, Jules." She laughs slightly. She was right that name sounded completely made up. Fuck me, this isn't helping at all. She gets up and grabs an envelope and gives it to me. "This is what they sent me the first time. Maybe this can help."

"Thanks." I get up and walk towards the door.

"Shot, you don't have to leave so soon."

"I do." With that I walk out and slam the door behind me.

Nova

J.L and I had been up with Bo doing a Disney marathon. "Is it weird that growing up I was in love with Tramp." I confess.

"They shouldn't have made a cartoon dog sound and act so attractive. Don't even get me started on Kovu from *The Lion*

King." She squeals.

"Yes! He's in my top ten Disney crushes."

"Who's in the top ten?" She narrows.

"1. General Li Shang, 2. Pocahontas, 3. Prince Naveen, 4.Mulan, 5. Tramp, 6. Kovu, 7. Merida, 8. Tinkerbell, 9. Simba, and 10. Mulan in the second movie."

"Pretty valid list."

I snort out a laugh, "What about you Bo?"

"Princess Jasmine." He answered.

J.L and I nodded in unison. "Good choice."

I look at my phone and noticed how late it was. "Hey I'm gonna head out." I say, kissing Bo and J.L on the cheek.

I get home at around 2am. First thing I go into is the kitchen. I've been craving everything. I don't even know where to start. Popcorn? Pancakes? Soup?

"Coming in a bit late, sweet." Sebastian voice says closing the terrace door behind him.

"Lost track of time." I say, with a spoon of *Mantecado* ice cream in my mouth.

He snickers, "Don't let Shot see you eat that."

I return the laugh and put the cup of ice cream down. Sebastian comes close to the island I'm currently sitting on and parts my legs slightly to get closer to me. "Where were you tonight?" He asks. His fingers tracing my legs softly. "Have you forgot there are idiots trying to kill us?"

"Can't a girl have a night out? It's not like you guys are keeping me entertained. You guys leave me here alone every day. Especially you and Romero have barely talked to me in five weeks."

His hazel eyes get even closer. "Have you been feeling neglected, sweet?"

"Yeah, a little. You guys aren't telling me anything, and it makes me feel more like an outsider. Like you guys can't rely on me or something."

He smiles apologetically, "Sweet, you were shot. We just wanted you to rest. You realize we have been just the three of us for a long time. It's what we are used to. It's easier for us to get things done this way. Next time just say something."

He's right...I should have just said something. Wait? Am I agreeing with Sebastian? "Since when are you so nice?" I narrow.

He smiles sinfully, "I'm always nice to you. I only call your forehead big once a week when it is clearly big every day."

I closed my eyes and bite my lip, trying to hold back all things I could mess with him for. "Like I told Romero. One day you'll both beg for me."

"One day? I'm begging for you *now*. You feel all the way better, correct?" His lips gracing my neck.

I couldn't help but tense up. It would be a lie if the Dominics didn't throw me off my game. Why do I crave their attention? I've never been the girl who needed someone's' attention, which is why I was single for so long. Yet, I'm not going to sit here like I don't want them because I do. Selfishly, I want to keep them all. Am I really surprised? I have been selfish since I got here. Revenge for my mother wasn't for her, it was for me.

A tear falls from my face. Sebastian wipes the tear away. He looks at me with panic in his eyes, "What's wrong, sweet?" His voice just as panicked as the expression on his face.

I force a laugh through my tears. "I'm a selfish person. I made my mother's death about myself. The fact that it took me this long to notice, just proves that." I sob. My breathing becoming more inconsistent.

Sebastian wraps his arms around me and rubs my back. "It's okay, sweet. Your mother knows that you're a good person." He pulls apart from me so that I can see his face once again. "And it's okay to go against your parents' wishes sometimes. They lived their lives and now we much live ours and make our own choices, whether they are good or bad. We have to grow on our own. Make our own fuck ups."

Suddenly Sebastian picked me up. My legs instantly wrap around him, while my head is still on his chest. I see that we are heading towards his room. "Are you really trying to have sex right now?" I say, as he sets me down on his bed.

He flicks me on the forehead. "Just thought you wouldn't want to sleep alone tonight."

I rub my head from the sting of his finger. "Thanks."

Chapter 12

Nova

This feeling, it's the same feeling I get when I'm around Jameson. Not just sexual arousal, but real butterflies. Sebastian takes a moment to take off his shirt and throw it on the floor and I do the same with the pants I came in with. I was one to just sleep in panties and a sweatshirt or naked. I didn't really like clothes to begin with. Sebastian's eyes looked a lot darker after he shut off the light. I didn't feel too sleepy, so I just watched him relax and fall asleep. I really do have a weird habit of watching them sleep. They just look so angelic when they sleep.

Without warning, his hand slid to the small of my back. I could feel a blazing sensation trying to rise through my panties. I just scolded him and I'm the horny one. Not having them touch me for five weeks left me yearning.

"You seem jumpy, sweet." He yawns. His fingers still lingering and sliding up my back and down again.

"Cause your touching me." I growl.

"Am I?"

"Yes"

His smiles get smugger as he opens one eye. "Am I?"

I flick him on the forehead and turn around. He chuckles at my actions and pulls me closer to him. His obvious erection pointed at my back as his grip gets tighter. Before Sebastian can try anything else a knock comes to the door.

"What?!" Sebastian growled loudly.

The door opened and the light was flickered on to reveal Jameson. His eyes go to me quickly. "There you are." He says, I guess he was looking for me to. He then turns to Sebastian. "Come on, Romero wants us in the office."

Sebastian nudges me slightly. "Come on, sweet."

"Let her sleep, it's late." Jameson hushes.

I get right up. "I'm coming." I grunt. I walk past Jameson and make my way to Romero's office.

Not a surprised Romero's eyes were fixated on his laptop. Jameson and Sebastian walked through moments later.

"Valeria was the shooter, which makes sense that no one was hurt badly. She was hired by someone, but they used a fake name." Jameson started.

"Is she an assassin?" I ask.

"Sometimes. She used to work for us." Sebastian explains.

Romero closed his computer and looks up at us. "Where is she now?" Romero asked.

"On to the next job I guess." Jameson answered.

"I want her found and killed." Romero's blunt words don't surprise me but are still hard to hear all the same. Jameson seemed bothered from Romero's orders. Romero narrows his eyes at Jameson. "Is that going to be a problem?"

"Of course not." Jameson reassures.

I look over at Sebastian and he leans down to my ear. "Ex-girlfriend." He whispered.

My eyes widen in shock. Jameson can kill someone who he had a relationship with just because Romero told him to. Also, how could Romero ask him to kill his ex? Like you have to have no heart at all to ask someone to do something like that. I know she did shoot at us first, but still.

"Why are your eyes red?" Romero abruptly asked.

Fuck, I forgot that I had been crying not long ago. "I'm fine." I answer.

"Anyone else have an actual answer?" Romero asks the room.

Sebastian smugly smiles, "Well, Nova believes that we have neglected her these past weeks. Don't you, sweet? Our lack of attention, drove her to tears." He lied. I smiled knowing he was keeping the real reason for my break down a secret.

"Is that true?" Romero's attention focused once again.

"No. I got something in my eye on the way home." I lie.

"Where were you?" He interrogates.

"Out with a friend."

Romero straightens in his chair. "What friend?"

"None of your business I don't have to tell you who I'm with, Daddy." I mock, which brings about a devilish smirk on his face.

Sebastian chuckles, "That mouth of yours is going to earn you a punishment." Romero response.

"Maybe a punishment is just what she needs for being out late." Sebastian's voice dripping with need from minutes ago. He leans down into my ear once more. "How about it, sweet?"

I look at them panicked. What the hell could be going through their minds. I look over Jameson, the most sensible one. He looks like he's in deep thought. I try to make a b-line to the door, but I'm caught by the sneaky fox. He sits me down on Romero's desk. The desk felt cold on my legs, but it wasn't what was causing my goosebumps.

Sebastians finger slid past my panties and inside me, causing me to gasp. "Relax, sweet. You look so pretty when you're in heat." Sebastian taunts.

I inhale and push my lips together. "I'm not in heat, you

are, sneaky fox." Damn it, I'm already breathless.

"Quiet, I don't remember giving you permission to speak." Romero growls, his hands making their way to my breasts and giving my nipples a harsh tug. Although, Romero's and Sebastian's teasing felt amazing, my eyes fell to Jameson, who watched them bring all sort of noises out of my mouth. I remember Jameson saying he didn't want to share with his brothers.

Jameson walked over and pulled my sweatshirt off me, than pushed my naked skin on the cold desk. "Leaving me out, Nova?" He says licking one of my nipples, while Romero played with the other.

"No- "Before I could finish, Romero's lips devoured mine.

Romero's kiss was harsh and possessive. "Didn't I tell you before, no speaking. Time for a punishment."

"You know Nova has never taken it up the ass." Sebastian points out.

"Really?" Jameson asks curiously.

"You don't say." Romero interjects.

Sebastian unzips his pants and parts my legs further. "I'll be the first inside." He revels.

Jameson and Romero glare. "Why do you get to have her ass first?" Jameson growls.

"Sweet gave me her blessing." Sebastian smirked. I looked away in embarrassment because it was true.

Jameson and Romero move to the side, which allows Sebastian to bend me over on the desk. While my head is resting on Jameson's lap. His fingers comb my hair, trying to get me to relax my body a bit more before Sebastian enters. I can feel Jameson's bulge on my cheek. I unzip his pants and take his cock into my hands.

"Nova…" Jameson moans as I start licking the bits of precum from his tip. I wanted to please him, all of them.

"What a giving girl." Sebastian says, his fingers still inside me, rubbing ever so sweetly. I squeal with Jameson's cock down my throat. I can feel Sebastian lining himself up with my ass. I don't believe there's even a chance it will go in. I'm too tight and he's too big, just the facts here.

Romero is just watching me as I suck Jameson off and it's making me nervous. It's like he's studying me. Little did he know, having him watch me was just so...erotic. He didn't need to be touching me like the others to keep my heat puddling. I could feel Sebastian rubbing something liquid and warm in my ass.

"Ow!" I hiss as Sebastian enters my ass. "It hurts..." I growl at him.

He laughs slightly, "I barely have the tip in, sweet. Relax..." His fingers trace my back slowly. The soft touches help me relax a little more. After about eight minutes of trying to enter me completely, he stills inside me. Letting me get used to his size. I stopped sucking Jameson to get used to Sebastians length in my ass. Jameson caresses my cheek with his thumb as I shake slightly from the pain.

Then suddenly the pain subsides, and I feel something mixed in with the pain. "You can move now." I say, tapping Sebastian's hand, that's placed on my hip, with my own. His arms wrap around my stomach as he slightly withdrawals before he slams back in. I didn't expect him to be so harsh. I whimpered from the fierce pressure.

"Fuck, Nova you're so tight. Damn I can barely even get through again." Sebastian groans.

"Don't light up. Fuck her harder." Romero orders. I glare at him. He's punishing me, that's why he let Sebastian fuck me in the ass. He wanted to see me in pain for disobeying his made-up rules.

"Don't have to tell me twice." Sebastian chuckles. Pushing into me with greater force, but it didn't hurt like I thought it would. I could feel the juices from my pussy run down my legs. Sebastian hovers over my back and kisses it. "You like me fucking you in your virgin ass, sweet? I knew you would."

"Harder!" I cried. He slapped my ass and proceeded to fuck me ruthlessly. I look over at Romero and again he's watching me.

Romero finally walks up to us and pulls my hair back, removing my mouth from Jameson's cock and forcing me to stare into those menacing eyes. "Couch." Was all he said. I look over at the couch in his office and fumble there when Sebastian slides out of me. Romero takes off his clothes, lies on the couch, and pulls me on top of him.

"Ride my dick till you're sore and then keep going." He orders. I lower myself onto his cock and moan loudly. "Whose cock do you want the most?" He asks, but I don't know if he's actually asking.

"Depends on who can make me cum the fastest." I retort.

"What did I say about talking? Bash, I think her bratty mouth needs to be filled, don't you?"

Sebastian walks over and pushes my hair back and lifts my chin. "Don't be afraid to let those tears flow when you choke on my cock." Sebastian whispers into my ear before shoving his cock into my mouth, I choke immediately. "Shot, her ass is all yours."

Jameson jumps off the desk smiling. He rubs my ass cheeks before he spreads them wide and inserts his hot cock in my ass. "He wasn't kidding, *tesero*. You're so fucking tight." Jameson groans. "If I'm not careful, I'll come in you too quickly."

Sebastian let me take a breath and I take it. "Please do. I want you to cum in my ass." I admit. Jameson picks up his pace as does Romero. Feeling both fucking me at the same time felt amazing. I could feel them rubbing inside me. Filling me up with their liquid heat. Even with both of my holes filled with their cum, they haven't stopped fucking me.

Jameson and Romero suddenly switch positions. "Do you like having all of us inside you?" Romero asks. "You can answer"

Moans escape me quickly. "Your dicks feel amazing inside me. They rub my ass and pussy so well together. I'm going to-"I huff, barely able to stop shaking from the amount of pleasure rushing through me. "Oh, fuck!" I choke out before I cum. My body shakes and I lay on Jameson's chest, breathing deeply.

"Are you sore?" Romero asks from behind me. His cock still deep inside. I turn to look at him, over my shoulder, and nod. "What did I tell you to do if you were."

"Keep riding." I answer.

Romero slams into me. "Good girl."

Jameson joins him in keeping a solid rhythm. It feels good but I'm so sore I feel like I'm going to pass out. Sebastian is jacking himself off as he watches his brothers fuck me. It fuels the fire within me, helping me keep up with the Dominics.

Jameson continues to pound into me harder and harder, chasing is climax once again. He digs his fingers into my sides holding me in place. "God, your pussy is so slick. Fuck, Nova!" Jameson pants.

"Still so tight, even after having all three of us in your ass. What a dirty girl, having all of us fill you with our cum." Romero teases. Seconds later Romero and Jameson cum inside me once again.

My body finally falls limp. Romero slides out of me and gets off the couch. Jameson also slides out of me, his cock still submerged in my folds. Sebastian comes over and picks me up setting me on the desk. "Sweet, did you think you were done? I haven't cum yet." Sebastian says plunging his dick into my cum filled cunt. "Don't worry I'll make you cum again, sweet."

His movements are powerful with every stroke, I can barely quit my shaking. My hips were almost trying to push against him, with the little strength I still had. "Fuck Sebastian! I'm so fucking sore." I cried.

He kissed my neck and slowed his pace down. "You can take it." His sweet tone was almost overshadowed by his groans. "I'm trying to go slower—fuck it's hard."

I dig my nails into his back. "It's okay, fuck me as hard as you want." I whimper.

His speeds up his pace, but I can tell he's still not going as a hard as he wants to. His pacing was honestly perfect, and I could feel myself, although sore, rising to another climax soon.

Sebastian moves to kiss and lick the other side of my neck and I make a small yelp sound. "You like our cum inside you? Can you feel it now? Me pushing it deeper and deeper into you?" He growled.

"Yes!" I wrap my arms around him to close the back. "Cum inside me Sebastian. I need to feel your hot cum dripping out of me."

That's all it took for Sebastian to cover my walls. He gently pulled out of me and behind his cock was cum seeping through my cunt. "The girls before me probably were way better at handling you all at once." I laughed, still out of breath.

Jameson kissed my temple. "You're the first one."

I look around at Sebastian and Romero. "We have never shared before, sweet." Sebastian admits.

"Oh." I don't know if that's a good thing or a bad thing.

"Sorry again for neglecting you." Jameson sweet smile looks down at me.

I can barely move before Romero picks me up in his arms. "Meetings over." He states. Leaving the office with me swaying in his arms as he walks down the hall into his bathroom.

Romero

Nova's warm body pressed against my chest as I picked her up and took her to my bathroom. Her breathing that was once racing had slowed into a slumber. Seeing what we just did, was a shock to me as much as Nova. I had never even thought of sharing anyone with my brothers, regardless of if I cared about them or not, but in this moment we were beyond ravenous. We wanted her, even if that meant sharing the experience. Seeing her bruised lips, her messy curls, the way she looked exhausted but still push through to satisfy us; it was beyond the best experience to watch. Her body completely submitting to us all at once. What a beautiful display.

I run her a bath to clean her. I cleaned off any of the cum we had so happily left inside her. She jerked around when I cleaned off her cunt. It was still sore. Her eyes were closed as I cleaned her. "Are you asleep?" I ask.

"Getting there." She answers a bit drowsy. "Thank you."

His brows raise slightly. "For what?"

"Taking care of me. Even though it's not exactly your first nature."

I glare at her. "That's not a compliment."

She smirks, eyes still tightly closed. "Yeah, that's what I think every time you 'compliment' me…"

I roll my eyes and set her in the bath. I take her hair out of her scrunchy, her curls are bunched up and knotted. I get up and walk down the stairs to Nova's bathroom and got her hair products and brought them back to my bathroom. I started with her shampoo, it smelled like coconut and some citrus smell I could not pinpoint. I massaged the shampoo into her hair which causes her body to hum.

"That feels so good." She coos with a smile plastered on

her face. "Do you want me to tell you what to do next?"

I narrow my eyes; I have never washed anyone's hair before besides my own. It should not be any different from mines, but our different hair textures might make the process a bit different. Is that what she is referring to? I continue to massage the shampoo in for about eight minutes and then rinse out the shampoo. Conditioner is up next, and I massage that into her hair. It makes her hair a bit less untangled, but I might have to run a brush through her hair to completely untangle it.

"Need help?" She teases, pointing to the brush with spikes with little balls on the end. Her teasing does not sit well with me and so I childishly pull on a strand of her hair. "Are you five?!" She hisses.

I ignore her and focus back on her hair. Nova has such long hair, how the fuck does she brush her hair every day? I see why she braided her hair the other time. I divide her hair and begin working.

"You don't have to. I know my hair is long. It takes a while to brush it all through."

I shake my head and continue brushing. "It's fine, I want to learn. You'll be with us for a while and I'm sure it's irritating to brush such long hair every day, so I'll help you if I can." I responded.

Nova

Romero can be a cold king sitting at the top of his arrogant tower, but then he has these really fucking sweet moments that makes me feel all warm inside and it's fucking confusing. "Stop being nice to me. You're confusing me. You all are." I say quietly.

"You want us to treat you badly? Don't tempt me." He chuckles as he takes another piece of hair to brush. "Because I'd like nothing more than to give you a good spanking for all that behavior."

"Promise?" My voice filled with laughter. The look on his face always told me how far I could play with him before he made good on his promises.

He tugged on my hair. "You can barely sit in this tub after our session. Do you want add to your punishment?" I roll my eyes, but he was right. It was hard sitting in the tub. My entire body was sore, but especially my ass. All three Dominic's entering me there, on my first time is something I will not soon forget.

Romero's hand let go of my hair and caressed my face. He leaned in close to my lips. "Romero, I can't I'm sore." I beg.

"I know, but your lips are fine." He retorts.

He leans in further, landing a soft kiss on my lips. This kiss was different, not just out of sexual need. I could feel the passion in his kiss, the affection. He was careful not to hurt me since my lips were slightly bruised.

I pull away. "What are you trying to do? Make me fall for you?"

He kisses me once more, putting even more passion into the kiss, if that is even possible. "Would you?" He asks.

"Huh?" I knew what he was asking but I played dumb, not wanting to even entertain the idea. None of them would ever seriously have a relationship with me. No matter how many kisses they steal, no matter how many times they make me cum.

Romero could tell I was deflecting so he moved on and went back to brushing my hair.

Chapter 13

Nova

I look up at the ceiling thinking about Romero's words the other day. Would I fall for him? I don't know. Could I see myself with Romero? I have no fucking idea. Jameson? Yes. Sebastian? Maybe. With Romero I never know where I stand, he's so damn hot and cold it makes him unreadable. Does he care about me or is he just bored? Not that Sebastian has given me any confessions, but he's not actively trying to torture me. Then there's Jameson, he told me that all he sees is me, but I don't know if I can just believe his words because it comes out of his sweet mouth. These thoughts had my stomach in knots.

"What are you wearing to the party? Should we match?" Cami's voice brings me back.

"I think, I'm going to just wear the red dress. What do you think?"

Cami face brightens, "I was thinking the same thing! But let's try it with these heels."

I frown. "I suck at walking in them." I whined.

She narrows her eyes and crosses her arms. "Don't be that way. You'll be fine." She picked up the heels and put them on the counter.

The Dominic's aunt, Donnie's mom, was throwing a party for Donnie's birthday. Donnie says it's all a ploy to get him to meet up with that girl she wants him to marry. He said her name was Chiara.

"Cami, can't I just wear sneakers and a sweatshirt, why is everything so dressy with the Dominics. You know all us Hispanics need is music, food, and liquor to throw a party. No one gives a fuck what you wear. As long as that ass is in motion."

She snorted a laugh. "*Casa Rossa* is an old fashion family- "

"By old fashioned, do you mean stuck up?" I cut in.

She snickers, "Well…yeah, but they mean well." She goes back into the closet. "But c'mon that party starts in three hours, and we haven't decided on anything." She whines.

After a grueling hour of clothe choices, we settled on the red dresses I picked from the beginning. The party was filled with members of *Casa Rossa.*

"Camilla!" I man calls out.

Cami turns around and runs straight into the man's arms. "*Papà, non sapevo fossi tornato dall'Italia!* [**Dad, I didn't know you were back from Italy!**]" She squealed.

She then runs over and pulls me towards him. "*Papà*, this is Nova. She's my new friend." She says with her arm linked in mine. She turns to me. "Nova this is my dad, Dario Sartori."

We exchange cheek kisses, "Nice to meet you Mr. Sartori. Your daughter has been an amazing friend to me."

"I'm glad to hear that. I can see from the smile on my daughter's face that you have been a great one as well. " His strong Italian accent ran through, but he was still incredibly well spoken.

We carried on a conversation for a while before I was pulled away by Jameson. He looked incredible, usually his loose curls are everywhere, but tonight is hair was perfectly placed. His suit looked expensive, *he* looked expensive. He really looked like those hot mobsters you read about in books. All he was missing was a lit cigarette to really pull off the mobster look.

"You look beautiful." He compliments.

"You look...so edible." I let slip out.

His sweet smile ruined his whole bad boy vibe, but I didn't care because he was still a bad boy, just a sweet one. "Do I?" He asks leaving a small kiss on my lips.

"Fuck yes." I groan quietly.

"The party just started. We can't get all hot and bothered already." The look in his eyes gave me the impression he meant the opposite of what he was saying.

I smiled and he escorted me away from the crowd. We sat outside on a couch. "Have you seen the birthday boy?" I ask.

"Nope. Which is weird he loves being the center of attention. I have a small meeting to get to. You can go look for him. His old room is upstairs, the last door on the hall." Jameson suggests.

I nod and head my way up the stairs in search of the loud birthday boy. I walk up to the last door and knock. I don't get a response, so I try to open the door and to my shock it's not locked. I go into the room and its dark, so I turn on the light no one is in the room, but there is a light coming from the bathroom.

"Fuck!" I hear someone moan.

"Is it Donnie?" I wonder.

"Stay fucking still. I love fucking you." Donnie 's voice said once more. My cheeks start to feel hot and honestly, I'm extremely turned on right now.

"What should I do? I should leave. That's what I should do." I whisper to myself. I feel like a deer in the headlights. I snap out of it, turn off the light and leave the room as quietly as possible. I lean against the wall in the hall. "Birthday boy wanted some birthday sex." I whispered aloud. Good for Donnie, but now I wanted some birthday sex too.

I walk back down the stairs and mingle with the wives of *Casa Rossa, since* the boys had some damn mafia meeting and of course excludes women. Cami was back at my side, and we dance together to pass the time.

"I'm here!" Donnie's loud ass yells coming down the stairs with Sam at his side. Wait...no... wait.

"About time! Where were you?" I pry.

"Sam and I forgot our guns. Gotta stay strapped even at my own birthday party." *He lied.* Donnie gave me a kiss on the cheek. "Glad you're better." He smiled.

"Me to." I smiled. I pulled him into a big hug. "Happy Birthday! How are we going to turn the fuck up in this party?"

He smiled evilly. "Oh, don't worry. This party is just for the old people, but after, it's our time to shine."

"Strip club?" I narrow.

"Strip club." He repeats. We do a little lowkey handshake and smile at each other.

"What are you plotting?" Romero comes from behind Donnie.

He hugs Donnie and wishes him a Happy Birthday. Sebastian follows suit behind him, then Jameson.

"Donatello! There you are!" A woman's voice gets our attention.

"Mother, please stop embarrassing me. It's my birthday, I'm not dealing with you today." Donnie groans.

"Chiara is here to speak with you." She insists. He rolls his eyes and runs his fingers through his hair.

Does he not want to marry Chiara because he's gay...or bi? Should I do something? It's not my place, but he seems almost angry, and Donnie is always so cheerful, it's making me uncomfortable that he's not his usual self.

Fuck it. I walk in between Donnie and his mother. "Hello, we haven't met yet, but I'm Nova, Donnie's girlfriend." I lie.

"Excuse me?" The Dominics said in unison, Donnie included.

I turn and face Donnie. "You can't hide me from your mother forever, she deserves to know. I love you and you love me." I dramatically proclaim.

"You know what? You're right." Donnie played along. "I'm so sorry. Mother you can clearly see the reason I don't want to meet with Chiara. Are you really going to stand in the way of my happiness?"

She looked at her son sadly, "Well, no. I just want you to be happy. If she makes you happy then of course I understand, but your father won't." She walks away.

"Nova, a word." Romero growls darkly.

Sebastian laughs, "You're in trouble." He teases.

I glare at him before following Romero outside. We sit down and he sighs, "Nova...walk me through your thought process."

"Well, Donnie doesn't want to marry her, so I thought I would pretend to be his girlfriend to get him out of it."

"And how is that any of your business?" He barks, his temper losing more and more.

"He's my friend!" I growl, not backing down to the 'Ice King.'

"Who you love *so* much." His voice ever so sarcastic.

I blinked a couple of times. "Are you jealous that I said I loved Donnie?"

"This isn't about jealousy, which I'm *not*." Yeah right. "You have no say so in *Casa Rossa* matters. I've told you before that you knew nothing of our world and how it works. Marriage in the *Cassa Rossa* and other mob families are simply business deals and you just fucked one up. That hurts the family, if you were anyone else, I would put a bullet in your head and let you bleed out in front of the family to set an example." He growls as he stands up fixing his cufflinks.

"He's your cousin. Excuse me, if I want to see him happy, fucking *descarodo*. " I scoff, before running back inside.

"Hey!" Donnie yells swinging an arm around me. "Thanks for the save, but you shouldn't have done that. Now the triplets are going to plan my demise." He laughs but I know he's not joking.

"I did it because I heard you and Sam in your room. I went to get you and heard you guys..." I confess.

He smiles that Donnie smile. "I think your mistaken, Nova"

"Donnie my vagina was on fire, I definitely did not mis-hear shit. Who the fuck cares? This isn't 1412."

He sighed, "Nova, you cannot say anything to anyone."

"I won't. Trust me. I swear on my life, I'll carry it to my grave. It's your secret. "

"Thanks." He said, his voice seemed sad. I pulled him into a hug and rubbed his back. "It's okay. I'm here if you need me and I can keep up the girlfriend act anytime you need."

He hugged me back and kissed the top of my head. "Did we just become best friends?" He laughed.

"Yeah, I think we just did." We laugh pulling apart. "So, are you not into girls?"

"No, I still like tits in my face. Women are too hot to give up." His flirty upbeat personality returning.

"Great, because I got you so many big booty strippers and that would have been really awkward if you didn't like women."

He dies of laughter as we make our way to the dining hall to eat. I sat down next to Cami and Jameson. Romero picks up a glass and starts a speech. "Donnie, you have been one of the most loyal soldiers I could ever ask for. Your loyalty has never wavered over the years and for that, I thank you. That's why I decided to give you the position of *caporegime*." He states and everyone looks at Donnie in shock.

"*Grazie capo. Io non ti deluderò.* [**Thank you, Boss. I will not let you down.**] ".

"*Saluti.*" Romero raises his glass. His eyes locked on mine as if he were trying to tell me something.

"*Saluti.*" The rest of the family cheers. Yet, the way some of them are looking at Donnie, Romero hit the nerve of many men in the room who wanted Donnie's position. Romero had just made Donnie a captain and judging by Donnie's face, I don't think he's all that happy of taking the position.

After dinner everyone congratulated Donnie, but the fake smiles were extremely present. I pulled him to the side. "Big booty bitches time?" I whisper into his ear.

He looks at me with wide eyes and nods. "Yes. Let's get the fuck out of here before they poison my drink."

I run over to Sebastian and whisper in his ear about the strip club. He nods and we head out. The music is thumping, I get us a VIP spot since I'm play cousins with the manager, Lucy Sanchez.

"*Que lo que, mama?!* [**What up, girl?!**] "She greets kissing my cheek.

"*Es el cumpleaños de mi amigo, así que pensé que nos soltaríamos.* [**It's my friend's birthday, so I thought we should get loose.**]"

"*¿Y eso? Yo no te he visto en este vaina.* [**What's up with that? I haven't seen you in this place.**]"

"*Sabes que este es mi lugar favorito, pero tu hermanoito lo reclamó hace un tiempo.* [**You know this is my favorite spot, but your brother claimed it a while ago.**]"

"*¡Carajo! Ya tienen que acabar con esa mierda.* [**Hell! You guys need to stop this shit.**]"

"*Escucha, no está aquí. Así que no te preocupes y mueve tu nalgitas.* [**Listen, he's not here. So, don't worry and move that ass.**]" She says shaking her ass in my direction. I laugh as I drum up her ass. I give her another kiss on the cheek and reunite with everyone at the VIP section. It was Donnie, Donnie's brother Leo, Cami, Sebastian, and me.

One of Lucy's sister's Yenni strips here and well she is just breath taking beautiful and sexy as hell.

Yenni approaches us and I already talk to her beforehand. She looks over at Donnie then me and I nod. She looks right at Donnie.

"Mr. Dominic, please follow me." She orders sweetly.

"Yes Ma'am." He gets up to follow her. Donnie mouths to me 'Thank you.' I smiled big and waved him to his way.

I saw more familiar faces coming our way, Aki and Aubery Yu. Extremely hot twins I went to middle school with. "Look whose finally back." Aki and Aubery greets with a kiss to my cheeks.

"Hello loves." I greet. "My friends would love to see you guys' dance."

"Of course." They say in union.

The twins do their thing, and the dollars start falling. Good thing I brought them some big spenders. It was raining money for sure.

Sebastian pulled me on his lap. "When are you going to give me a lap dance, sweet?" He whispered into my ear. "Those doe eyes staring back at me, on your knees in front of me. In nothing but lace." I look back up back and up at him. My dark brown eyes staring back into his hazel ones. I scoff and turn back around.

"You always bend, sweet."

"No, I don't. I don't give in *that* easy. "

"Over my bed...over Ero's desk."

I roll my eyes and sarcastically laugh. "I'll sleep with you tonight, just sleep, but you need to read me a book."

He looks at me surprised, then sighs. "I want to fuck you until you beg me to stop, and you would rather me read to you?" He gives in, kissing me on my cheek. "Fine, I'll read you a story.

The night was just amazing. Donnie was extremely happy, more than his typically happy self. Yenni must have *really* showed him an enjoyable time. Jameson and Romero were not too happy we left them out of the fun, but they don't exactly strike me as strip club guys. Romero is too much about business to let himself relax and Jameson, well that one was on me.

"Come take a shower with me, sweet..." Sebastian calls out from his shower.

"You can't trick me fox. I'm staying in here." I shout from his bed with *The Cask of Amontillado*, a book by Edgar Allan Poe.

He chuckles and finishes his shower alone. He comes out in every girl's weakness, the grey sweatpants. Then plops on the bed next to me. He takes the book from my hand and pulls me in closer. Sebastian starts reading the book to me and then going in detail to explain some words that were out of my vernacular.

"So, this guy, Montresor, gets this guy, Fortunato, drunk and lures him to go into his underground tunnels where dead people are put, and then buries Fortunato alive?!" I shriek curiously.

He nods.

"But...why though? He never explains it. He's just saying he did something to him but never actually what. What if he's just crazy and Fortunato is not like that bad."

Sebastian laughs. "Honestly, my problem with the book is how he killed him. Burying someone alive doesn't do the job justice. You don't need those types of loose ends. If you're going to kill someone, just do it. Nothing too dramatic needed."

His words bring me back to earth where I remember what kind of person is lying next to me.

"What?" His laughter arose as he looks down at me.

I twiddle with my fingers. "What's it like?"

"What like?"

"Killing someone? How can you emotionally follow through? Is there ever a part of you that doesn't want to?"

Sebastian's eyes don't leave mine. With a straight answer he says, "No."

"Oh."

"Every kill is not done lightly. If any of us decide to kill it's with a solid reason, we think about the repercussions of each death. We weigh the pros and cons. Therefore, no. Every time we kill, we are 100% committed. You'll understand." His words a bit of a whisper at the end. His finger traces my cheeks and then play with the ends of my curls.

I rub my thump against his rock-hard biceps. He replies by pulling me even closer, where I can feel the heat of his neck on my face. I leave a trail of kisses, which forces those beautiful hazel eyes to close. I look at his tattoo on his neck and wondered why they all have the same tattoo. It was a phrase.

"*Guardami negli occhi del perdente.*" I say aloud, tracing the odds with my fingers. "What does it mean?"

"View me in the eyes of the loser."

Sebastian looks down a bit. "Why do you all have this tattoo?" I pause, "What's the meaning?"

"It's how we see the world. Everything not as black and white as it seems. Everyone can be a villain or hero depending on who's telling the story. Life is about perspective."

Sebastian

The strong dark gaze wanted to burn through me. Deciding when we should finally come clean to Nova was feeling further and further away. At this point, we can't let her go. Especially to that expired mobster. She has all of us breaking rules that we'd never think to break before. What she did at the party was extremely dumb and will blow back on us. The family still thinks Ero is not fit to lead but fuck them.

Hearing Nova say she loved Donnie, even as a lie, had my body burning with a hefty fury I tried my best to hide. Did I want her to say it to me? I've never wanted a woman to love me before. I've always had women who fell in love with me and gave me good sex, but those women never lit me up like Nova. Not just in bed, but on a regular day to day and fuck, it was messing me up. She sees right through my smooth demeanor and still plays to challenge me at every turn.

Nova was already asleep. I could tell by her light snoring. It made me chuckle.

"*Resta con me, volpe.* [**Stay with me, fox.**]" I whisper.

Jameson

I break the door open in Valeria's apartment. It's completely empty. Fuck...Ero is going to kill him. I look around and there is a note tapped to the window.

I knew Ero would have you kill me. He can really hold a grudge, huh? I'm not your enemy, don't turn me into one.
-Xoxo Valeria

Chapter 14

Nova

Today was the day I was meeting up with the Crespo's and honestly, I don't know what to expect, but I felt in spirit that I was not leaving happy by any means.

"What are we doing to your hair, babe?" Dani asks, as she combs through my hair.

"A blow out sounds good." I answer.

"Aunty Nova, what are you doing?" Bo asks pulling on my hand. I pull him up on my lap and let him play with my phone.

"I'm getting my hair straightened."

"Like mine?" His dark brown eyes looking up at me, then back to the phone.

"Uh, yeah basically, but them I'm going to crimp it a little."

He looks up from the phone again, "What's crimp?"

"When you make your hair wavy."

"Oh." Bo acknowledges as he lengthens the end of his word. Bo was so damn cute, he really made me wonder what it would be like to have a child. Bo was definitely in his own class. I remember growing up with J.L and wondering if our kids would play together. J.L teaching my kids Mandarin and me teaching Bo Spanish. It brings home the reality of it all.

"Can we eat after, Aunty Nova?"

"Yeah, then I'm taking you to your grandma's."

After a two-hour hair session, I took Bo to a breakfast shop nearby. Now knowing he was full and ready to pass out I took him to J.L mom's house, a.k.a Aunty Junie.

"*Tā yǐjīng shuìzhele?* [**He's asleep already?**]" She asked in Mandarin.

"*Shì de, tā chīle hěnduō, xiànzài tā yǐjīng shuìzhele.* [**Yes, he ate a lot and now he has gone to sleep.**]" I answer back. After my Mami died, Aunty Junie and Uncle James took me in and raised me alongside J.L.

"*Nǐ kàn qǐlái hěn shòu, yīdìng yào chī.* [**You look thin, make sure you eat.**]" She comments. I laugh it off and pass Bo to her.

"Trust me my ass is eating all the time." I retort.

"Just making sure, I can't watch over you babies anymore."

"We are not babies." I whine.

"Whatever, you guys are *my* babies. I don't care how big your boobies get." Aunty Junie was always so damn funny. She had J.L young like my mom, so she was always a very cool, but overprotective parent.

I kissed Bo and Aunty Junie goodbye and went to finish getting ready for the Crespo party. The penthouse was empty, not to my surprise. Romero, Jameson, and Sebastian said they would be at the gym around this time.

I went to my room and changed into the green romper and wedges I had left on the dresser. My hair usually goes down my back when it's curly, but straight made me look like Rapunzel. My hair was down to my knees. I pull my hair back in a high ponytail, just to keep me from sitting on it.

Santino sent a car for me, and it took me to a house. Not a crazy mansion, but a big house, with an abundance of land.

"This way, Ms. Corzo." The man said as he opened my door.

Santino was waiting for me at the door. "Hey, did you eat yet?" He greeted. We exchanged cheek kisses.

"I ate this morning, but I'm still a bit hungry." I admitted. Santino and I walk inside, and I can't help but think people are watching me. Having so many people looking at me makes me nauseous, but not as much as the man standing at the end of the stairs, Daniel Crespo.

Sebastian

Shot takes a swing at me, but by luck I manage to dodge him. Shot really is the best fighter between the three of us. Romero was hitting a punching bag for the past two hours. Something must be eating at him.

"What's wrong Ero?" I ask. Jumping out the ring Leaning against the ropes of the rings.

"We still don't know whose pulling these fucking strings to that fucking attack. Also, Crespo wants us to just give him Nova." Ero answers, hitting the bag even harder.

"First off, we would never let Crespo get her. Case closed on that one. Shot and I are looking for Valeria. We will find her; she knows something, and we *will* get it out of her."

I look over at Shot and he is leaning against the ropes across from me. He looks deep in thought again. "I'll find her." Shot promises.

Out of all of us, Shot is the hardest to read. He's usually quiet or casually joking with us. He never showed us if he was angry or sad. Even as children it was the same. He only shows you if he decides to which is not often, but he's not trying to be cool about it, that's just how he is. Since Nova has been around, he smiles more, we all do. Even Romero has been able to relax around Nova at times. She'd been able to slightly take out the stick up his ass.

Nova

Next to Crespo was his wife, Sana. Seeing them took away my hunger immediately. I don't think I would have been able to choke it down. My breathing had slowed but my heart was thumping.

"You, okay?" Santino asked.

"Fine, let's get this over with." I say. He leads me into a room, and I see a new face, it's Elias.

"Hey Nova, I'm Elias." He greeted.

"Hi." I greet back.

We all sat down at a long table. Everyone was so quiet it was deafening.

"What would you like to know, Nova?" Crespo asked. His hands intertwined as he rested his chin on them.

"Why did you kill my mother?" I bluntly asked.

"I didn't kill her, but in a sense, I do blame myself for not being more careful."

I glared. "Then who did?"

"Beatrice Dominic, Servino Dominic's wife."

"That makes no sense." I huff.

He cleared his throat. "You'll understand soon enough. Your mother and I met when we were kids. At the time, the Crespo family and the Dominic family were close. Servino was a good friend of mine. I started my relationship with your mother when we were fourteen. We got pregnant with you at fifteen. I made sure to keep it a secret from my father by having you at a distance. I was waiting to take over *La Fiamma* in order to bring you and your mother back safely. The night I decided to kill my father, I left your mother with Servino, believing she would be safe. I told her to leave you with someone just in case things went wrong for any reason. After I killed my father, I went to get your mother and Servino told me that his wife had killed her. That he couldn't give me her body because he didn't want this to fall back on his wife. That is what started the war between us." His words left me at a loss. The Dominic's mother killed my mother, but why?

"Why would she kill her?"

"Beatrice never was diagnosed, but anyone with eyes could tell she suffered from depression and was schizophrenic. She would talk to people who were dead. Sleep all day, but sometimes be extremely happy. If the Dominic family had gotten the help she needed. I don't blame Beatrice, she was sick. I blame her husband who cared more about his status then the welfare of his wife."

My heart felt like it stopped. I felt sick to my stomach. I didn't know if he was lying of course. "So why tell me now?"

"Your mother never wanted this life for you or for herself. She told me that she wanted you to be raised normal. I've been watching your life growing up every step of the way. Clearing a path for you to achieve a normal life with no issues. Then you fell in with *Casa Rossa*, I honestly couldn't believe it. It was the most ironic thing to happen. I couldn't believe it when I heard that Romero Dominic had claimed you as his."

"We're not together." I say, taking in a breath to calm me down.

"Doesn't matter. There is now a target on your head. He should have known better." Crespo growled but regain composure quick.

"So, what now?" *What is his endgame?*

He leans back in his chair. "It's time to come home."

I laugh darkly, "Home?!"

"Romero doesn't care about you. He told me himself. He

has put a target on your head for being associated with him. I am your father; I will protect you no matter what. He will not."

"Why should I believe you?"

"Because he knows who killed your mother and he never told you."

"You're lying. You don't know that." I'm getting angrier by the second.

He shrugs. "Maybe your right. Go ask him." He runs his fingers through his hair. "When you figure out that I'm not lying. You're welcome to come home. You put your friends at risk being around them, like Jia."

"How do you know what about J.L?" My voice stern.

"Like I said, I have been with you every step of the way. Just like I know that the *Casa Rossa* was attacked, and they are looking for who's responsible."

"You know who did it?"

"No, but I'll find them and kill them."

"Why would you care about someone hurting the Dominic's?"

He sighed. "I don't. I care that you were in a hospital for three weeks." *He knew?* "One day I hope you realize that I have loved you your entire life, and that being away from you and your mother killed me, all those years. I could have chosen to be selfish and keep you with me knowing it wasn't safe. I gave you a chance to live a good normal life, like your mother wanted. I tried..."

All this information had me turned around. I couldn't tell fact from fiction. I noticed the Sana had not looked at me once since I was in the room. "I need air." I felt like I was going to suffocate in that room. I got up and ran out the door to the nearest bathroom. I just felt sick to my stomach. Did the Dominic's know who killed my mother and kept it from me to use me? Has everything been a lie from the start?

I threw up my guts in the bathroom. I felt sick, dizzy even. It was too much; it was all just too much to hear. What had my life become?

A knock had come to the door. "Nova? Are you okay?" Santino voice calls out.

"I don't feel well, I think I'm just going to leave for the day." I call out from the bathroom floor. When I come out, he is there waiting for me. He helped me to the car that dropped me off.

When I enter the penthouse. Jameson and Sebastian are gone, but Romero is sitting at the dining table. "You're late for dinner. Where were you?" He asks.

Before I answer I hit him with a question. "Do you know who killed my mother?"

Romero puts his phone down and looks up at me. His eyes slightly more expressive than usual. "You saw him, didn't you?" By his voice I could tell he was trying not to get angry.

Tears form in my eyes. "You knew this whole time?!" I screamed.

He gets up from the table and walks closer to me. "We we're going to tell you."

"*We?*" I scoff. "All of you, huh?"

"We we're waiting for the right time to tell you."

"When?!" I step closer to him. "When I was in jail?! Or dead somewhere?! Killing someone who didn't do anything but care for my mom?!"

"Listen!" He growled.

"Fuck you! You had all the time to tell me, but you used me. You guys see me as disposable. I'm done. Deals off, I'm leaving."

160

Romero grabs my hand. "Fucking listen to me!" The anger still surging through me, but I stop. "At first I didn't know who you were when we made the deal. "

"When did you know?" I press.

"The day we left Camila's shop."

I shake my head, "That was months ago..."

"Once I found out. I didn't want a thing to do with you, but I couldn't stay away. None of us could. We are so fucking attached to you. I don't know what it is, but it's there. You are not disposable to us." He professed.

That sick feeling in my stomach was back and then everything went black.

Romero

Nova looks at me with her beautiful brown eyes filled with so much sadness and anger. She held her head and started to sway. I caught her before she fell.

"Nova?" I ask.

No reply.

"Nova?" I said a bit louder.

No reply.

"Fuck, Nova! Please wake up!" I shout, shaking her slightly. I run to the elevator with Nova in my arms. I rush to the hospital with Nova passed out in the back. Once I get there, I get her to the ER. They take her and I wait.

I take out my phone and text my brothers.

Nova passed out. She's in the ER and she knows everything. I'll take care of her. Find Valeria.

-Ero

About an hour in Dr. Moretti tells me to follow her and

Nova still unconscious.

"What's wrong with her?" I ask. My eyes stuck to her.

"Nothing, she's just producing more blood. This happens in pregnant women to accommodate the baby. The blood flow made her dizzy. Her iron levels were a bit low as well."

Baby? Pregnant? Nova is pregnant with one of our babies. This baby really has intresting timing. Nova wants to chew our heads off right now. The last thing we need is a baby.

"I want an ultrasound done. Soon as possible." I order.

"Of course, Mr. Dominic." She left the room, leaving me with Nova.

I rub my thumb against her forehead. "I didn't want you to find out this way. I'm sorry." I leave a chase kiss on her lips before looking at my text.

We have her.

-Shot

I called Donnie to keep her for us, so Bash and Shot can meet me here at the hospital. About an hour later they were by her side.

"What's wrong with her?" Shot asked, worry wrapped in his voice. The collar of his shirt had blood on it.

"She's pregnant." I state.

Their eyes are widened, and they look right at me as if they had seen a ghost. "Who's is it?" They ask in unison.

"I don't know yet." I growl. Not wanting to go through a bunch of questions I didn't know. I begin to pace through the room.

Sebastian smiles at Nova. Does he think the baby is his? And what if it is? What if it's mine. Are any of us ready to be fathers? My mind has completely combusted. Will Nova leave us if she finds out? Her mother didn't want to bring her child into this life, and I doubt Nova does either. Fuck, what the fuck do I do?

Nova

I open my eyes and I see Jameson and Sebastian sleeping at my side. Romero is still awake and staring right at me with those dark eyes.

"Your iron levels are low. You need to eat. Jameson got you broccoli cheese soup." He orders. The sweetness from his plea yesterday was gone. I'm still mad at him, them, but I was too emotional to hear him out. I didn't speak to him. I just ate my soup and he stared at me.

"Good morning, Ms. Corzo. I'm here to run just a few tests. I'm also doing an ultrasound just so we can all have a look at the baby and just check the health." Dr. Moretti greeted.

Baby?

What baby?

Whose baby?

From the shock in my face, she could tell she made a mistake. "I am so sorry, Ms. Corzo. I thought you knew. Congratulations." Her smile becoming a bit nervous.

I couldn't believe that I was pregnant. I was on the pill, every time I slept with them. I mean I knew it's not a hundred percent effective, but fuck. Am I really pregnant right now?!

After running a few tests. She concluded that I was fine. Now she started to do the ultrasound. "Oh." She started.

"What?" We all asked.

"Your baby has some siblings." She laughed.

"Siblings? Like plural?" I stuttered.

"Yup. You are having triplets Ms. Corzo." She explained.

"How soon can we get a paternity test." Jameson asked.

The doctor looked at her board. "Well, Ms. Corzo is just about four weeks. When she's about eight weeks, come back and we can start the test.

"That long? Fuck." Sebastian groaned. His hand slid to my belly and rubbed it, which relaxed me a bit. Jameson was holding my hand and listening carefully to Dr. Moretti explain the health of the babies. I'm still mad at them for lying, but I can honestly feel that on some level they care.

"Should I schedule you to come back in four weeks?" She asks.

"Yes. We will all be here." Romero answered for me. Dr. Moretti nodded and headed out the room. "You two, get out." Romero ordered Sebastian and Jameson. They listen and once again I am left alone with Romero.

"What?" I ask, but there is no anger in my voice this time.

"We were going to tell you. We just didn't know how. I knew once we told you, we would lose you and so we selfishly prolonged telling you. "

"So, you were going to still let me kill Crespo?"

"At first, we were, but then we came to our senses and realized we could never do that to you."

"Then what's the point of our deal? You had no use for me then."

Romero grabbed my hand. "Like I said, we got attached." He chuckled. "Honestly, I think since the moment we met there was an attraction that made us all want to keep you near us. First it was sexual of course, but it's more now. I don't know what to call it, but all I know is we want you to stay with us."

"What if the baby isn't yours? Will you be upset?" I ask.

"Slightly, but I'll love my niece or nephew just the same." He answered honestly.

"How did you know about my mom? Did your dad tell

you?"

"No, I was there." My heart almost stopped.

"My mother was in a manic state and tried to kill herself, your mother realized it and tried to calm her down. When my father told your mother to run, it made my mother nervous, and she shot her. She seemed surprised, like she hadn't meant to. Then she shot herself in the head."

I lifted his hand and kissed it. "I'm so sorry you had to see that. Was it just you there?"

"No Sebastian had followed me and saw as well. The only one who wasn't there was Shot. He didn't know about your mother until we told him after you were shot. "

So, Jameson wasn't lying to me from the start. I squeezed his thumb with my hand. "Thank you, for finally being honest with me, 'Ice King.'

I didn't mean for that to slip out. He instantly glared at me, "Enough of that stupid fucking nickname." He growls. Just like that Romero is back to being Romero.

I glare back, ripping my hand from his, but he just smiles. He leans in and kisses my cheek.

"*Se solo sapessi il posto che hai nel mio cuore.*" He whispers into my ear. Again, my Italian isn't the best. He said something about his heart, I think.

"Triplets? Jeez this is crazy." I sigh.

"The penthouse will be too small; we need to buy a house."

"A house?" I blink.

"The kids are going to want to play outside. Therefore, we need a house with lots of land. We are going to have to beef up security. I'm sure Camilla and J.L are going to want to help you pick out a house."

A lightbulb came to my head. "Oh my god I have to tell J.L she's going to be an aunty!" Before I dial, I stop myself. "No, I have to make the surprise cute." I gush.

"Your emotions are changing so quickly; I can't keep up."

"Me either." I laugh sheepishly. I wanted to kill him just yesterday and now all I feel is joy that I'm going to be a mother.

Chapter 15

Nova

I honestly feel like Jameson has gotten even worst about my diet since I fainted. It's not my fault I'm eating for four.

I called Santino and explained to him the reason I felt sick, I didn't tell him about the pregnancy though. The Dominics don't like the idea of me talking to any of the Crespo's, but I deserve to have a relationship with my brothers if I can.

Today we find out who the father of my children is, and I am extremely nervous. I mean, either way it doesn't really matter, but I still feel this weirdness I can't shake.

"So, what did you want to tell me?"

I take out a box with three little white baby booties. She looks at it for a few seconds. "Wait...no... your fucking lying!" She squeals. She gets up and hugs me tightly. "I'm an aunty?!"

I squeeze back. "You are going to be an aunty to three."

"Three...?" She asks shocked as she pulls away from me.

"Three." I restate.

"Umm, who's the daddy? Is it that guy from the hospital?"

"Maybe." I nervously laugh, scratching the back of my head.

"Maybe? You had another secret boyfriend?" She narrows her eyes at me.

"So, I haven't been completely honest with you these past months. You remember Jameson is they guy you saw me with at the hospital. He and his brothers are triplets and I have been living with them and sleeping with them. So, now I'm pregnant with triplets too and today I'm going to find out which one is the father."

The look on her face told me everything. "Nova...Nova...Nova." She sounded like a mother who was trying to deal with her out of control teenage daughter. "Tsk, tsk, tsk." She flicked me on the head.

"I realize what I'm doing is crazy, but it weirdly works." I try and smile to make the situation seem better.

"You are insane, and you used to be the calmer one of us two. I'm honestly surprised, but I mean. Hey if it makes you happy."

If it makes me happy? Do the Dominics make me happy? I mean, am I going to move into a house and raise my kids with mobsters? I don't really see myself playing house forever. I wanted to be a lawyer. Maybe this is a sign I should finish my schooling. I mean I have kids to think about now. Not that I think any of the Dominic's would be deadbeats, but I need to have my own future set up just in case.

Several Hours Later

"Ms. Corzo, the babies are in perfect condition. All your levels are where they need to be. I trust Mr. Jameson is responsible for your good health" She giggles.

"Please don't compliment him, it makes him worse. He's been shoving that rabbit food down my throat. How he has muscle on his body I'll never know." I roll my eyes.

"That's because I eat good proteins and work out, *tesoro*." Jameson explains, his fingers slightly pinching my cheeks.

"So, who's the daddy?" J.L asked bluntly. I smack her arm. "Ow."

Dr. Moretti nods. "Did you want me to read the results aloud Ms. Corzo?"

I nod and she smiles, "You all are." She speaks.

"What? That's impossible." I laugh.

"Yeah, there's no way." J.L snickers.

Dr. Moretti looks them over again. "The results are correct."

"How?" Romero interjects.

Dr. Moretti clears her throat. "It's a phenomenon called Superfecundation. It's when the eggs are fertilized by different fathers. This, while rare, can happen when a woman is ovulating more than once and having intercourse with more than one man around the same time."

It's got to be mistake that's just impossible right? "So, you're saying that all three of these men has fathered one child inside me."

"Correct Ms. Corzo." She confirms.

"Great, I'm in my twenties, unmarried with three baby daddies." I sneer quietly to myself. I think Sebastian heard me because he rubs my belly and leaves a kiss on my forehead.

My head is still spinning from the news. I mean does this make my children cousins? Half siblings or full siblings because the Dominic's are identical. I'm eight weeks now and I'm starting to show now.

"Hey Doc, is sex safe for Nova?" Sebastian asked.

She nods, "Of course. Sex is safe to do while pregnant, just make sure your careful." She answers.

Are they thinking of having sex with me pregnant like this? As rough as they are? I shake my head at the circus in this room.

J.L hugged me goodbye as I got into the car with the Dominic's. "Are we going home?" I ask.

The moon was full today and I was watching it from the pool. I didn't want to think about what I've been pushing out of my head. If the babies are boys, will they be forced to be Made Men? I don't want that for my sons. I want them to be normal and grow up to be anything they want, preferably lawyers, but whatever.

I kick my feet in the pool and look at the moon once again.

"What are you doing out here?" Jameson asks coming outside.

"It's warm outside. It feels good. Pools warm to." I say swaying my feet. He smiles and takes off his shirt revealing his beautifully toned body. He takes off his pants as well, leaving him in boxer briefs and jumps in. I try to block the water from splashing me. He walks over to me and stands In between my legs. His large hands making their way to my shirt and pull it off me. I look down at my growing belly.

"I'm going to get so big." I laugh.

He kisses my stomach, "I can't wait."

"Yeah right." I scoff. "Once I get bigger, you guys won't even look my way." I roll my eyes.

He continues kissing upward until he reaches my nipple. His long tongue licking and teasing. A few moans escape my mouth. "I will never stop wanting to be inside you. I-" He wanted to say something, but he stopped himself before he could.

"You?"

He ignores me and continues to lick my sensitive nipples. The feeling is erotic, sensational, just over all mind blowing. His light eyes, seem darker in this lighting and it sends a chill down my body. A chill that makes me want to devour him. His finger is reaching down to my sex where a finger is slipped in.

"Jameson..." I moan. I could feel Jameson smile as his lips

land on my neck, then crosses over to my lips.

"You know, you never call us by our nicknames. Why?" He asks hovering his lips over mine.

"I like your names." I breathe, squirming under his touch. "Did you want me to call you guys by your nicknames?"

He kisses me even deeper. "Call me whatever you want, *Tesoro*."

"Maybe to keep some distance between us." I confess pulling away from his kiss.

He looks at me confused. "What do you mean?"

"I don't know. You guys do a lot of things that are a bit misleading you know. Any normal girl would start developing feelings for you guys. So maybe I don't want to feel that closeness by calling you guys by your nicknames."

"You think I'm misleading you?"

"Maybe. The day of the pool party you told me all you want is me, but what does that mean?"

He fills the gap between our bodies and wraps his arms around me. His forehead leaning against mine. "I'm sorry, I should have been clear. I like you Nova and I don't want to be with anyone else but you. That's where I'm at."

"I like you to." I smile widely. "But I also like Sebastian and sometimes even Romero. You all give me these butterflies I haven't felt before." His fingers start to move again.

"I give you butterflies huh?" His sweet smile returns.

"You do." I answer. Hardly able to say anything with his fingers going in and out of me. "Fuck!" I shout. Have I become more sensitive to his touch or it's just him.

I reach down and feel his rock-hard cock. "You're so hard. I can fix that." I purr into his ear.

By his panting I can tell he is tired of holding back.

"Come closer." He orders. I scoot closer to the edge of the pool and slowly his length enters me slowly. This makes me laugh. "What?" He laughs back.

"I'm pregnant, but I'm not breakable. Don't be so gentle." He didn't need any more pleas. He quickly entered me and began to pump into me at a steady pace.

"I'm not doing this because I think your breakable. I wanted to tease you." He smiles through his aroused face. His curls look so sexy dripping with water. I grab his face with one hand, while the other held up my body.

"Your curls are so beautiful." I cooed into his ear. Grabbing onto his soft curls.

This prompts him to fuck me even harder. "Fuck!" He shouted. "You feel so good inside and out. That's my favorite thing about you. You can make me feel so fucking good without even touching me."

"I mean it!" I say a bit loudly due to his thrust, making my voice hit a couple of octaves. "I love your sweetness, your curls, your protectiveness. I love it all, I love-" I stop myself. What the fuck was I about to say.

"*Tesoro!*" He pants loudly into my ear as he cums. He breaths deeply for a couple of seconds before cupping my face. "Don't leave, I know your scared. I promise you we will never leave you. You don't know how much you mean to us. At this point, you are one of us. Our children are Dominics, you are basically a Dominic now."

Tears pour from my eyes. "I want to stay, but I don't want my children to live the life of the *Casa Rossa* if I'm being truthful. I want them to be free to be happy and live their lives. I see how stressed-out Romero is being *capo, I* don't want that for my son or if we have a daughter, I don't want her to be given away to some guy for more power."

He runs his fingers through his wet curls and sighs, "I can

promise you that I will make sure that *our* child will grow up as normal as possible. I can't speak for Ero's and Bash's children. I'm sure Bash may have no problem with what you want but Ero might be a different story."

"I need to talk to them soon."

Sebastian

Valeria is tied to a chair; she looks incredibly bored. Despite having an abundance of freshly made cuts. The sound of her crimson blood dripping to the ground.

"Valeria, how long are we going to play this game? I don't want to kill you. You have too much talent to just kill off, but if I have to, I will." I growl. I hate when Ero decides it's a promising idea for me to step in. Donnie is fine taking care of her.

"You know I won't talk." She growls back, spitting up the blood on the floor.

The fun part of being me is my memory is a long one. If I recall the reason Valeria stays in New York is for her sibling, she's hiding somewhere. If memory serves, the child is living with someone under a fake alias. I text Donnie to find me that address as quick as possible.

"How much is your loyalty worth? I just need a name Valeria." She remains silent looking away from me. She really isn't a snitch, which I respect. But dying for a client is not like dying for family. Therefore, she's an idiot to die for someone who means nothing to her.

"Bad for business to talk." She laughs.

"You won't have a business if your dead. So, what's the point? It's not honorable at all."

She is quiet once again. I'm getting the feeling there's a little more to the story here.

Next Day

Nova

I look in my phone for a list of baby names. I want the sex to be a surprise, but with everything going on I might want to know early. Jameson's arms were wrapped around my waist. His wavy curls a mess. I get on top of his and bend down to kiss his lips.

"Wake me up like this every day from now on." He mumbles. He opens his eyes revealing those beautiful greens. He slaps my thigh and chuckles slightly when I hit him back.

"Stop." I whine.

He smiles but frowns quickly when I get off him. "I heard your baby names." He confesses.

"You did?! What do you think?"

"Athens was nice, I don't like Luca." His honesty gave me some clarity about the names. I nod my head and go back into my phone. "Is Athens for a boy?" He asks.

"I don't know yet, I like it for a boy or girl. Trying to keep the names unisex because I want the sex to be a surprise. What do you think?"

"I don't care, whatever you want, *tesoro*."

I laugh sheepishly, "What do you think the baby will be?"

"To be honest, I'm fine with either, but having a little girl would be fun. I remember how cute Lola was as a baby. There are way too many men in this family, girls would be a good change." I smile at his reply.

"I love you." The words slip from my mouth without warning. It just came out so naturally.

"Fuck!" Jameson growled. My eyes widen and my heart feels like someone just popped it. Jameson notices the shock in my face and freaks out a bit. "Oh, *tesoro*, I just wanted to say it first. I knew I should have said it last night." He whined, crossing his arms.

I laugh at his more childish side coming through. "I love you, Jameson" I repeat. He looks at me softly and pushes me down carefully, hovering on top of me. His lips crash into mine. "I love you too, *tesoro*. I love you so fucking much."

"I may love them to, would you still love me if I did?" I say, wanting to be transparent.

"Of course. I'm passed trying to keep you to myself, my brothers will never give you up." He says, rolling his eyes at the last part.

"I don't know if I love them, but I know I love you." I say, playing with his curls.

"Find out, *tesoro*." He stops hovering over me and gets up off the bed. "I'm going to make breakfast." With that he is gone.

I then leave my room and go into the living room, where Sebastian is reading a book, not to my surprise. "Whatcha reading?" I ask plopping down on the couch.

"Baby book." He says quickly. I then see that there is a stack of books next to him.

1. **How to Stop Losing Your Sh*t with Your Kids: Effective Strategies for Stress**
2. **The New Father: A Dad's Guide to the First Year**
3. **Childhood Schizophrenia**
4. **Childhood Depression**
5. **Encyclopedia of Infant and Early Childhood Development**

Sebastian must be really worried about being a dad. "Hey, are you worried about the baby?"

"No, the baby will be fine. I've never had one before, therefore I want to learn as much as I can. Our father wasn't exactly nurturing, and I want to make sure I'm not making the same stupid mistake. As you know our mother was extremely ill and no one noticed or cared to do anything about it. Any of us could pass down those genes to our children." Sebastian explained.

That's right. He was there when his mother killed herself. He was too young to understand that she was mentally ill, that's not his fault for not knowing.

"It's better to see any signs as early as possible." His eyes not taking

"Bash, it's not your fault you know. You were a little kid."

He snickers "Trust me I know. My father was the problem. I need to make sure I don't make any mistakes he did, sweet."

I trace his cheek, "As long as we try and be involved parents, we will be fine. Our kids won't be perfect, I mean look at me. I was valedictorian of my class and I'm now pregnant with the babies of three different men, who happen to also be brothers. So, I'm not exactly perfect." I rant. He smiles at my tenacity to cheer him up.

He kisses my cheek, "You *are* perfect, but thank you nonetheless, sweet."

He went back to reading and I leaned into his neck relaxing. His other hand was rubbing my head.

Without warning Donnie loud ass comes through the elevator yelling, "You traitors! Why was I not informed that I had three new cousins on the way!"

"Quiet! You loudmouth." Sebastian growls.

I snicker. "Donnie, I swear I was going to tell you." I whined.

"Romero is being so damn weird about who gets to know. Blah blah blah."

He narrows his eyes. "Then why the fuck does Cami know?!"

176

"She's dating my best friend."

He sits on the couch next to us. "Fine" His smile returns, and he looks at my belly. "So, what is it? Boys or girls? Or both?" He asks.

"Don't know yet."

"Let's make bets." Donnie 's idea makes my eyes gleam.

"Yes! Ok I bet that it will be two girls and one boy." I write down on a paper. I push it to Donnie.

"I bet it's all boys. Dominics make boys." He grins smugly.

I roll my eyes, "Don't you have a sister?" I retort.

"A fluke." He rolls his eyes. I can't imagine growing up with brothers.

I look over at Sebastian, "Sebastian?" I nudge.

He looks at me, then the paper. "Two boys, one girl."

"What do we win?" Donnie inquires.

I shrug, "Bragging rights?"

"Nah, Winner gets to name one of the babies."

"Are you insane? No." Sebastian growls.

"Fine I'll think of something else." Donnie grumbles to himself. I honestly don't think it's that bad if Donnie did win. I'm sure he won't give our kid a dumb name, but Sebastian has the right idea.

I get up from the couch and see what Romero thinks about the bet. Like always he's in his office. He looks up almost immediately.

"Are you okay?" He asked. That's been his favorite question for me.

I walk closer to his side. "Yeah, I'm fine. What about you?"

He smiles slightly. "I'm fine."

"Well, we were making a bet on what the sex of the babies will be. Any guesses?"

He cocks his head to the side. "All boys." He answers.

I roll my eyes. "Donnie said the same thing."

"Dominic's make males."

I laugh sarcastically. "You both have sisters." I point out once more.

"Mostly male, I meant." He retracts. Romero seems to be extremely focused these days especially with me being pregnant. He hasn't even gotten his usual haircut. His hair has completely grown out, his undercut was gone. He looks even more like Sebastian and Jameson.

"Hey Romero?" I start, my fingers pushing his hair out of his face.

"Hm?"

"Can I wash your hair for you?"

He looked surprised at my question. Before closing his laptop and getting up. He gestures me to walk out the door. We end up in his bathroom and I sit outside the tub. Romero his stripping and my eyes wander over his perfectly sculpted body. No matter how many times I see them naked it always feels like the first time.

Romero gets into the once it had filled up. "Why the sudden need to wash my hair?" He asks. I wet his hair with water then lather with shampoo.

"You're usually so methodical about haircuts, so I realize something must be going on. I wanted to help you relax. When you washed my hair for me, it felt so good and relaxing."

A smile appears on his lips. "Thank you, Nova."

"So, what's got you so stressed?" I ask. As I continue to massage his head. A small groan leaves his mouth, which brings me to press my lips together.

"Some old ghosts."

"Ghosts?"

"Deals my father made when we were children. I ended the deals months ago and now they aren't happy."

I rinse the shampoo out of his hair. "What deal?"

He sighs, "My father made an arrangement for the three of us. Marriage arrangements."

My eyes widen at his words, "Marriage?" I say quietly.

He turns his head to look at me. "We never accepted it, my father did. I had been meaning to decline the offer for some time but too much came up. When I finally did, they felt I was disrespecting them and now I have another enemy I need to keep us safe from."

"Why deny their request?"

He looked annoyed at my statement. "You." He answers.

I raise a brow at him, "I'm just the mother of your child. That shouldn't stop you. Like you said marriage is a business in this family." I say with my head looking towards my feet.

He took a long pause before he took his wet fingers and lifted my head. "If I give a woman my name, it will be you, Nova." His eyes burned into mine. Like it was his promise to me that we would be together. My heart tightened, was this his confession?

He turns around and lets me finish conditioning his hair. I don't know why but I get up and get into the tub. Romero opens his eyes and looks at me in confusion. "What are you doing?" He asks wrapping his arms around me.

"We have 15 minutes in this tub before I have to get out. Baby safety and all." I say nuzzling up into his neck. "I just want you to hold me."

"That wasn't a proposal." He clearly states.

STEPHANIE PEREZ

I nod, "I know. No marrying outsiders." I laugh weakly.

He didn't say anything.

Nothing.

Romero

"I know. No marrying outsiders." She laughed but I could hear the sadness in her voice. I want to tell her that it didn't matter. She was a Dominic with or without a ring on her finger. At this point, I cannot live without her. I have never felt affection from someone like this. She may irritate me, but fuck she was perfect for me, for *us*. I want to give her and the children a perfect life if I can, but living this life is anything but perfect. How can I promise her the world, when I have a million different people wanting to end us all. I want to be able to make her mine completely, knowing I could keep her entirely safe. How can you tell the woman you love that? So, I didn't, I hugged her tightly in my arms and hoped this was enough for now.

After the bath she lied down on my bed. I moved her slightly wet curls out of her face and watched as she moved trying to get comfortable. I rubbed her belly until she fell asleep.

"Once I eliminate those who threaten us, I will make you mine." I softly whispered.

She suddenly smiled, "I'm already yours." She whispered back. I was shocked and embarrassed for making such a declaration. "You don't have to say it. I feel the love you have for me." She put her hand on my chest and rubbed it slightly.

I nod. I will tell her one day. Just not today. Not until I've earned the right.

Chapter 16

Nova

Cami and J.L kidnapped me and took me to baby clothing stores. At this point, I am still in my first trimester, and they already have made me look at a hundred fucking cribs. When it comes to shopping, I feel like a six-year-old kid who just wants to go home, but their mom wants to look at the same shirt for an hour.

"Guys, I think we have seen enough cribs, bibs and whatever else babies need. At this point, I need a bottle and a nap." I whine.

"Hey, it's bad enough you won't find out the sex, let us have this. We are excited for you." Cami exclaims.

J.L nods in agreement. "I can't wait to meet them. I know they are going to be so damn cute." J.L coos. I feel her excitement, I remember when Bo was born, and I was an aunt for the first time. Seeing J.L become a mother was just magical. It really is something to be excited for, but it was hard for me because I was nauseous all the damn time. Dr. Moretti said it happen more frequently in mothers carrying more than one baby.

I decided to meet up with Santino, feeling bad about what had happened before. We met up and a little Cuban bakery nearby. Romero is probably going to get on my case about this, but I can't just ignore someone who did nothing wrong to me, who happens to be my brother.

"Are you...?" Santino treads lightly looking at my stomach.

"Pregnant? Yes. Sorry I didn't tell you. The Dominics and the Crespo's are...well you know."

Santino nods and then smiles. "I get it. I won't tell Dad if you want me to keep your secret."

"It's fine, I'm sure he knows. He got my medical records last time. This time won't be any different, I'm sure." I roll my eyes.

Santino laughs and sips his espresso.

I eye his espresso hungrily. "Fuck, I miss coffee."

"I'm sure you can have a little."

"Technically, but it's still bad for the babies. "

"That's unfortunate. I don't think I could handle going off coffee."

Suddenly, I hear screaming and glasses shattered. Santino pulls me on the ground and hovers above me. His men are nearby shooting back. People are scrambling like ants. Santino helps me crawl to the back of the shop.

"Are you okay?" He asked frantically.

"I'm fine." I answer truthfully.

I look at his white shirt and there is red blood running down his arm. "You're shot! We need to go to a hospital!"

He shakes his head. "No, take me home. Elias is a doctor, take me home." I find a rag and put it on the wound, but the blood keeps coming out. His men take us into the car, and I keep applying pressure to the wound until we make it to the house. Seeing the blood drip down was making me nauseous and I really felt like I would pass out.

Arriving at the Crespo home, Elias was waiting with, what I assume is a medical bag. Elias tells me to sit down on the couch. My hands were coated with Santino's blood. Crespo rushed down the stairs. "What the hell happened?!" He growls.

"He'll live." Elias says trying to take out the bullet.

Crespo's eyes go to me. He goes off somewhere and comes back with a rag. He cleans the blood off my hands. "Are you okay?" He asks, his voice is gentle, as is his touch.

"Yeah, I'm fine." I try to hide the fear in my voice.

Crespo rubs my palm with his thumb. "He's fine, don't worry."

"You don't know that."

He smiles at me. "I have strong kids. Trust me." I don't know why, but it made me smile to hear him say that. His eyes go to my stomach, he smiles but it seems...sad? "Congratulations." He gave me his best smile before tending back to Santino.

Why is he upset about my pregnancy? Is it because he knows it's a Dominic? I mean I wouldn't blame him. If he loved my mother as much as he claims he did, I wouldn't be the happiest either. He wasn't rude about it though. Is he trying to be nice for my sake? Is he willing to put away his hatred for their family for me? Can I really have two families between the Crespo's and Dominic's, or will I start a war? It feels like I'm making everything worse.

Jameson

Donnie had informed Valeria that if she didn't talk it would affect that child, she's keeping hidden in Queens. We found the location, and I guess we went ahead and went supervillain. The child was collected and put in a safe house until Valeria wanted to speak.

"Arlene Flynn. Ero's fiancé, she was the one who was behind the shooting. That fucking *gringa* bitch, from the Irish mob"

"Why, Ero rejected the proposal after the shooting."

"Did you forget? Ero claimed that girl in public, everyone

knows he claimed her. He put a target on her back."

"Why miss the shot?"

"We were friend's once. I still have loyalty to you. I would have never missed that shot. Are you crazy?" She growls.

"Thank you." I thank before leaving her in that room. I'll try to get Ero to take back his kill order. She proved her value, and he'll understand.

I go to Club Red where Ero is carrying on a meeting with other *Casa Rossa* members. I take a seat next to Ero.

"Arlene Flynn." Ero scoffs at the name.

"She was on my list from the beginning, but it didn't make sense since I rejected the proposal after the shooting. Then I thought about claiming Nova and what a spiteful bitch Arlene is. How our father thought I could make it work with her is beyond me." He scoffs once more.

"Do you think she acted alone?"

"Could be. Her father is said to be a brute with no brain. He's known for his violence, so I wouldn't put it past him."

"More hot-headed than you?" I joke.

"Watch it, little brother. I would hate for your tongue to go missing." He growls.

Ero's phone suddenly rings, and Nova's name is on the screen. "How is baby shopping going?" He answers teasingly, knowing Nova hates shopping for lengthy periods of time. His smile fades and he get up. "I'm coming, now...no I don't care! Are you okay?" His voice is beyond anger, and he walks outside the room. I get up immediately and follow.

"What's wrong?" I ask. My heart being out of my chest.

"Nova, come home now or I swear I'll go get you myself!" He snarls. Ero hangs up almost immediately after. She's with Crespo's family, isn't she? Why else would he be so angry.

"Where is she?" I ask again.

"She went to a café with Santino, and then shots were fired. He was shot protecting her and now she is at the Crespo house. I'm so fucking mad; I don't know where to start." He growls. "Why does she need them when she has us?"

I understand Ero's anger. Are we not enough for her? We sound like children fighting over our favorite toy, but he doesn't realize that's she is not just a *thing* we can keep to ourselves, eventually we have to share her with the fucking Crespo's if we want to keep her in our lives. If Ero can't play nice, we will lose her sooner than he thinks.

Nova

I look at my phone in anger. He is such a temperamental child sometimes. I know he hates the Crespo's, but Santino could have died taking that bullet to protect me. I don't give a fuck if he's mad, I know he has every right, but his temper is ridiculous.

You better calm the fuck down and check your fucking tone! I'm going to stay here tonight and make sure Santino is okay. If you come here, I will never speak to you again. *Descarado* Ice King...

-Nova

I'm sorry. I will calm down, but you must understand why I'm pissed off. Come home please. I will not be able to sleep with you somewhere else.

-Romero

I'm staying here. I want to make sure Santino doesn't die from protecting me. It's the least I can do. I'll leave early in the morning.

-Nova

Nova, please do not stay there. I don't trust them.

185

-Romero

Romero, he just took a bullet for me. Are you serious? What else does he need to do? Die?!"

-Nova

Fine. Be home quickly in the morning. You will definitely get a punishment once your home.

-Romero

I smile at the text and roll my eyes at the same time. He so fucking annoying and pisses me off like crazy, but I still love this overdramatic hot head.

Whatever, Ice King.

-Nova

"Nova, come." Sana calls out to me. She seems more relaxed now, even with her son having a bullet in his arm. She must be used to this, I guess. "You can stay here, in this room." She gestured towards this light green room. There were little white giraffes painted on the top.

"Was this a nursery?" I ask.

"Yes, it was yours. You loved giraffes as a child. Daniel would sleep in this room with you. He never wanted to leave your side." She smiles.

How can a married woman let her husband's mistress's daughter have a room? "Did it ever bother you, my mom and Crespo's relationship? I know you have an arranged marriage, but still he was your husband."

She inhales, her smile still on her face. "My marriage to Daniel is not one of love, but it is a partnership. My father gave me away to a man he barely knew because it raised his status and gave him more power. This isn't like those romantic novels, some girls get lucky and make it work, but I don't feel anything for Daniel but friendship. Your mother and Daniel's relationship never bothered me, honestly, I was extremely supportive of their

186

relationship."

"Yet, you had children with him?"

"I didn't have a choice, we both didn't. His father noticed that I wasn't pregnant and believed that I was no longer useful. It was more of a turkey base situation for the kids. We have never had sex. Funny enough the children were enough for me. I never was the girl who wanted to be married and have kids. I would be happy raising my kids alone."

"So why stay married after everything? His dad is dead right?"

"I would be given to another man. With Daniel I can do whatever I want with no restrictions. Once Daniel killed his father, I was going to leave, but after her death Daniel was a mess. I don't think I had ever seen him cry before. He never got closure, since we don't know where Servino put your mother's body. So, I stayed to make sure he didn't kill himself. Especially when he wanted to honor your mother's wish that you would not grow up in a mafioso household."

It brings tears to my eyes. Where is my mother's body? Did he just toss her somewhere? To think of my mothers' body being treated so disrespectfully angers the hell out of me. I tried to clear my head by looking at a couple photo albums I found. It was my baby book, and other album filled with pictures of my mom and Crespo before I was born. My mami looked so young. Her hair was long, which I don't think I had ever seen before. Growing up her hair was always short curls. She said she hated dealing with so much hair and honestly, I'm getting to that point myself.

Crespo was so young as well. From the year, they were about fourteen, maybe fifteen, in these pictures. Crespo had his arms wrapped around her and she was laughing. There was another one of Crespo drinking a cup of something. You could see his smirk as he looked into the lens. I think my mom took this. Another one of them falling asleep together on a couch. It brought a smile to my face. I wonder what life would have been like if we were all raised together.

Crespo's and Dominics were friends before if their mother never killed mine. I would have still met the Dominics at some point, right?

Sebastian

I noticed that Nova wasn't home, and neither was Shot or Ero. Why the fuck is everyone not home? I left not wanting to be in an empty household. I meet up with a friend of mine from my school days, Marcus McKnight. He had gone on to be a successful football player, I'm still jealous. He was a great kid in school. Never got into any trouble, grew up in a faith-based family. His parents were loving and supportive. Married his high school sweetheart. Kid hit the fucking jackpot of life.

"How are you, brother?" He asked taking a swig of his bourbon.

I look to the sky then at him. "I'm great, I'm going to be a dad."

His eyes widen and he shakes me with excitement. "God bless, that is amazing. I'm so happy for you, man!" He was completely ecstatic.

My friendship with Marcus was perfect because he didn't know the truth about my mafia background. I could just be a person around him, not a mobster. "Me to, but I'm scared."

"Wrong girl?" He narrows.

"No, definitely the right girl. I love her to death." I confess.

Marcus smirks, "Who are you right now? This can't be the same man." He laughed, but I know it was because he was proud. "If you truly love this woman, you better make an honest woman out of her."

"I just might." I answer. My brother would be pissed if

I ask her to marry me. I laugh thinking about the look of their faces. Who knows what I'll do.

Nova

I snuck over to Santino's room to check on him. He was sleeping, his arm had been wrapped. I sat on the floor next to his bed.

"Worried?" A voice says at the foot of the door.

"Hey Elias. Yeah, is he okay?" I ask, looking back at Santino.

"Our brother is a lot tougher than he acts. You think someone so sensitive would be a bitch but he's ruthless. Trust me, big sis." Elias reassures. His voice sound like Crespo's, even his laugh, even looks the most like him too. Santino looks like his mom, but he had the same eyes as me.

"I'm sure you guys have guessed that my children are Dominics. I want you guys in my life. I want to know you guys, but with Crespo's hatred for them and them him, do you think it's possible?"

"I'm not sure." He answers honestly.

My phone blows up with texts from the Dominics.

Did you eat? How do you feel?

-Jameson

What are you doing? Why aren't you home, sweet?

-Sebastian

Call me. I cannot sleep.

-Romero

Elias narrows. "Baby daddy?" He asks.

"Baby daddies."

"Ah" He nods and leaves the room. I also leave and go into

the room Sana showed me. I get a knock on the door and it's Sana. She gives me some clothes to sleep in and I thank her. I call Romero and put him on speaker.

"What's up, Ice King?" I shout.

"Stop calling me that." He growls. I snicker in response. "What are you doing?"

"Showering."

I can hear a low hum through the phone. I then get a video call from him two seconds later. "Why did you video call me? I'm not doing anything in this shower." I giggle.

"If you would just come home and ride me, we could stop this call now." He insists.

"Is that what you want? You want me to ride you?" I flirt. "So, beg me." My devious nature coming through.

"Excuse me?' He growls.

"You heard me. Beg me." I taunt once more.

He narrows his eyes at me. "Never." He is not backing down. I wouldn't expect any less from him.

"We'll see once I come home in the morning." I retort.

"We'll see." He chuckles. "Eat before you sleep. I'll be waiting for you in the morning. "Sometimes Romero would flash that sweet smile. It just fills my body with nothing but butterflies and warmth.

After ending the call, I found my way to the kitchen. Crespo was there eating ice cream. "Sweet tooth?" I say coming into the kitchen.

He chuckles, "My father hated sweets in the household. So, I have a bad habit of eating it in the middle of the night."

"That sucks." I commented. "Can I....?" I gesture to the ice cream pint.

"Of course. Feel free to eat whatever you want. You don't

have to ask." He insisted.

The ice cream was cookie dough. I took a scoop, put it into a cup, and ate some. I danced a bit as I ate it. We talked a bit more before we both went to sleep.

The next morning, I woke up and checked on Santino. He was asleep so I made some breakfast for the family. I gave Elias my number so that he could update on Santino.

Elias sent me back home in a car and it felt good to be home. I mean it was only one night, but this place was home for me, and I just wanted to continue sleeping here. I ran upstairs to Romero's room. He was sleeping soundly. I crawled on top, slowly, to not wake him.

"You really are a glutton for punishment." He laughs.

My eyes widen. "Do you all just pretend to sleep?" I growl.

His firm hand cups my ass and squeezes. "I waited all night for you." His dark green eyes burn into mine as he lifts his top half. I am facing him on his lap. My legs on either side of him and a little space for my pregnant belly.

He lays me down on my back and tears off my clothes. I am completely bare now and extremely wanting. I lift my body back onto his lap and kiss him deeply. I rub my wet heat over his cock but don't let it go in. "Beg me." I order.

He snickers, but his face tells me he is at his breaking point. His eyes are shut as he relishes the feeling of my pussy grinding against his cock. My teasing with always be a double edge sword because I can't help but moan and want to push his cock right inside me. "If I feel the need, I will fuck your ass if you want to keep your pussy from me."

"Beg me and you can have both." I get off his lap and switch over to licking his cock. My tongue ran up, down and over.

He grabs my hair and pushes my mouth down on his

cock. "Fuck, you suck me so well…" He praised.

"I'm glad." I moaned slightly. I stopped sucking suddenly, "My pussy feels way better though."

He smiles. "Yes, it does." Romero sets me on the bed and holds my arms above my head.

I narrow. "What are you doing?"

He answered me by shoving his dick inside my pussy. I moan from the sudden pressure. "You seem to forget your manners. Don't worry, I'll remind you." He whispered into my ear.

He continued to thrust consecutively. "Oh! Romero, yes!" I cried. "Fuck me harder…!"

"I didn't hear a please, bad girl, what did I say about manners?" He grunts out. Romero was just as lost in me as I was in him. Even through his teasing I knew he would grant me an orgasm if I gave into his little power trip.

"Let me cum please!" I beg. My voice completely breathless at this point.

"Not yet. You'll have to wait as punishment. No cumming." He orders.

As he fucks me harder and harder, I can feel his orgasm rising. With a couple more thrust, he empties himself in me. My body is still hot and impatiently waiting for him to let me cum. I get mad and push him down and hop on top of him. His thick glistening cock entering me.

"Fuck, Nova. You are relentless."

"You're one to talk." I say in a hushed tone.

I start my pace, but Romero grabs my hips and tries to set another pace. "Only I will allow you to cum. Don't forget, you're still on punishment." He growls as he slaps my ass.

I moan from the eroticism of it all. His hand knew the right about of strength to spank my ass. He rubbed my newly slapped behind while I rode. "Romero, please!" I cried once more.

"Who do you belong to?" He teased. Romero's cock going deeper and deeper.

"You!"

"Exactly." He growls. "I own every part of you inside and out and I'm getting tired of you fucking forgetting." I lick the bottom of his lips and he groans against me his usually so calm and collected demeanor has slipped away. "*Cazzo*, brat." He curses. I remember it meaning fuck.

"Cum now." He orders and I fall apart. I wet his cock completely with my cum. "All fours." He orders.

"Give me a minute to catch my breath." I whine. He slaps my ass even harder this time. Then rubs the same spot. It's so hot that I'm already dripping and waiting for him once more.

He slowly but surely enters my pussy from behind. His slow withdrawals were painfully hard for me because it felt amazing but the teasing itself made me want to scream. His slow lingering thrusts turned into blows quickly. I began screaming for him to fuck me even harder. I love Romero for his rough and teasing sex. He always wants to be in full control, but he should know I'll never just roll over for him completely in bed.

His hand was on my ass and the other on my belly. Even with Romero's roughness he was still making sure that the babies were always okay. Making sure not to go too far. "Comfortable?" He asks.

"Very. Please continue Romero." I beg.

"Once these babies are out. I will not be as gentle as I am now, Nova." He promised, the heat of his breath at the side of my ear

"I would never ask you to." I moaned. I reached back to press him closer, but he just held my hand to my side.

"Stay still." He growled.

"Or what?" I challenged

He smirked and took a handful of my hair. Pulling me back harshly to fuck me even deeper than before.

Chapter 17

Romero

Nova's smart mouth never ceased, and it costs her many punishments. Her body writhed as I continued to fuck her long and deeply. I had to control myself because she was pregnant, but it was fucking hard. Her deep brown eyes looked back at me desperately, hungrily and everything in between. I would never get enough of this brat. I want to punish and please her for the rest of my life.

"I-I want to suck you off again." She shuddered. Still shaking from her third orgasm.

"You want to taste yourself, Nova? To lick up all the cum you left on my cock?"

She smiled with satisfaction. My dirty girl was so precious. "Yes. I like the way I taste." She whispered.

I flipped her on her back and kissed her deeply. "I do to. Your pussy is so sweet." I groaned into her lips. "Just like these soft lips."

After a few more round of sex, Nova slept soundly next to me. I wanted to sleep next to her for the remainder of the day, but I had business to attend to. Donnie has been having issues with his men because of a rumor of his sexuality had been spreading. I was not a fool I know exactly who had been spreading it around.

I made my way to my uncle's home. "Hello Mr. Dominic, I will notify Mr. Angelo that you are here." His house cleaner, Sasha, greeted.

"Don't bother. He's in his office?"

She nods, "Yes sir."

I make my way up the stairs and open his office door. "Uncle, we are overdue for a chat." I say as I take a seat.

"Romero, it's not like you to come without calling." He states.

"Uncle, would you die for *Casa Rossa*?"

Without hesitation he answers, "Of course! Why would you even ask such a thing?"

"Then why did you tell Donnie's men about his interest in men?" I ask. He looked at me in shock, but I could tell he was not remorseful. "I could care less who Donnie fucks, but you intentionally want to sabotage him, which in turn hurts the family."

"I thought it would open your eyes to see no one will follow that fagot!" He growled. "After what he did, I can't even marry him off anymore! Trying to pass off that *scimmia* as his girl." He scoffed. Did I hear that correctly? What did he call Nova?! Growing up my father told me that my uncle's bigotry came from my grandfather. I would try to ignore it growing up.

Without thinking too long I took my knife and stabbed it into his palm, nailing him to his desk. He screamed in agony. "Romero, what has gotten into you?!" He screamed.

"That's the mother of my child, you're talking about." I confess. I didn't want anyone to know about her pregnancy for safety reasons but fuck it. Everyone was going to know. Everyone in this family better fucking respect her at all times.

I pull the knife out slowly so that he can feel the agonizing torment. "I apologize! I didn't know!" He whimpered like the pussy he was.

"Uncle, you disappoint me. Not just as a father but a Made Man. You let your jealousy of your own child, bring the family down and now you have disrespected the woman carrying my

196

child. How useful are you to me right now?"

He looked at me not sure if he should answer.

"The answer is not at all. Therefore, you serve no purpose in this family. You live because I allow you to." I growl. Bashing his head against the desk and shoving my gun under his chin. "I will grant you mercy on behalf of my cousins. Try it again and well...you understand."

He was still shaking, "Y-Yes. I understand, Boss."

I smile sarcastically, "Great, it was so nice to see you Uncle. I truly hope the next time we meet are under better circumstances." I say letting go of his head and putting my gun back in my holster.

Now that my uncle had remembered his place it was now time to see the men who dared defy me after I named Donnie a *capo*.

Donnie and his men were at our gym. Now I know not all his men were idiotic enough to disobey him or worse me, but there is always the few.

"Ero, what's up?" Donnie gleamed.

What people forget is that just because most of the time Donnie was a sweet person, they forget that he is a cold-blooded killer like the rest of us. It's time for these men to remember what kind of man Donnie is.

"I'm sure you know about what you father has done." I bluntly point out.

He laughs, "It's not true, you know that."

"I don't care if it's true or not, but what I will not tolerate is any of your men thinking that they don't have to follow your orders."

"I haven't had any issues yet, Ero."

"*Yet*. Remind them why I chose you as one of my captains.

There must be absolute loyalty."

Donnie nodded. "I know, Ero. Trust me, I would never allow any disloyalty in our family. I'll kill anyone who turns out to be disloyal in a second." He pauses with a laugh. "Not even their families will be able to find them."

I smile, "Good to hear." As much as I don't want to admit it, Donnie is my favorite cousin. His father is a stain on human society, so I have no idea how Donnie came to be such a sweet human being. Annoying as hell, but still good.

I get a text from Nova.

Where did you go, Ice King?

-Nova

I roll my eyes at that foolish nickname.

Business. How are you feeling?

-Ero

Fine, I'm a bit hungry, but I'm eating fruit, and I'm going to make a breakfast sandwich.

-Nova

You might be alone tonight, with soldiers around of course. Get Camila and A.J to keep you company.

-Ero

Where are you all going to be?

-Nova

Business.

-Ero

Still treating me like an outsider huh.

-Nova

I'm not.

-Ero

She didn't text back after that. Why can't she see that I don't want to bother her with gruesome details if I don't have to. She's pregnant and I want to make sure she is stress free. It's like she wants to be stressed out for no reason. My inquisitive little brat. I also need to find her an assistant to help her when we are not around.

Nova

Why does he keep shit from me? Like at this point it doesn't make sense. I'm tired of the 'alpha; I'll protect you' bullshit. Like I could help if he would trust me for five seconds. Fine I'll just go back to school then. I'm not going to sit here playing mafia baby mama to three mobsters. If I'm not allowed in their business, I'll focus on other things

A law book sits in front of me while I put my sandwich together. Since I've been here it seems that that's all I have been reading, aside from the times Sebastian reads to me and the babies.

I get on the phone with a few people regarding how quickly I can start law school. I took a year break, but honestly, I'm ready to move forward with my original dream. After the babies are born, I'll start school again, hopefully. I mean three newborns are going to be a challenge, but I have faith that I'll be fine.

A.J and Camila came over soon after and I told them about my plan. "I'm so excited for you! Of course, I'll babysit if you ever need."

"Me to!" Cami stated happily.

"Thanks guys. I really am going to need the help. I'm sure the Dominics will be great fathers, but three babies are still a lot." I whine jokingly.

"I still can't believe you're pregnant." J.L giggles.

"You and me both. But I'm happy. You know I always

wanted to give Bo a cousin. That boy gave me baby fever since you had him."

"Are you guys talking about me?" Bo's cute voice comes from the living room. He comes over to the kitchen and I sit him on the counter next to me.

"Yeah, cutie." I speak. "Are you excited to meet your cousins?"

He smiles brightly, "I can't wait to play with them! Did you name them Aunty Nova?"

"Not yet. I have so many names but I'm picky."

He started to hop in excitement. "How long until I meet them?"

"Well, I'm two months now...so give or take seven more months."

He slaps his cheeks, "That long?!" He gasps.

We laugh at his response. "Yup, that long." We all say.

"I can't believe you've been living in this penthouse. I don't think I've ever even been to one." A.J gasp.

I laugh, that was exactly how I felt when I was here. "Yeah, but they want to move us to a house. They said the penthouse is too small for the kids.

"Too small?" This is a five-bedroom penthouse!" A.J laughed.

"Trust me, I want to stay here to, but Romero is not budging. He sent me a couple homes he liked and told me to choose one."

I pull up the home listings. "13 bedrooms?! Why so many?" J.L asked.

"I have no fucking clue. But I mean, I'm sure I can come up with a few Ideas for the rooms. Plus, it's surrounded by grass. So, the kids can play. It has a pool too which is great. Also, it's on a lake so we can look at the water. I'm pretty sure he wants to buy so that he can remodel it. I doubt we will have 13 bedrooms. I mean we'll have seven or eight max and the others will be playrooms or offices. I mean I would be fine with four bedrooms. The kids could just share a room like the rest of us had to growing up." I explain.

"40 million dollars? How rich are the Dominics?"

I take a second, "I'm not sure." I mean I know their rich, but 40 million for a house is crazy. I've never asked because I never cared.

Romero

I wanted to pay a visit to the boss of the Irish mob, Alex Tavish. We had a deal with him and his mob to keep a safe distance. He is by no means a friend, just a sitting enemy that could strike at any time.

Alek wanted to meet at a club he didn't own, just for neutrality. "Why the visit, lads?" Alek asks, as he drinks from his glass.

"Your sister, Arlene Flynn took it upon herself to hire someone to shoot up our home." I bluntly explained.

"Sounds brutal, mate. My half-sister is a bit of a raging twit, but to do something so idiotic doesn't make much sense." He replied. His arrogant smile never leaving his face. "You know what? Why don't I get her over here now." He laughs. "I actually would love to see what she has to say." He whispered into a man's ear.

About thirty minutes later Arlene Flynn was standing before us. "What are you doing Alek?" She asked nervously.

"These fine lads say you try to kill them. If so, I would like to know if it's true. Because if it is, there is no punishment they could offer that will be worse than what I give you for making moves without my say so." His demeanor darkened.

STEPHANIE PEREZ

"I would never." She answered. Her head facing the floor.

"See lads, she's not done a thing. What makes you think it was my sister anyways?" He asks narrowing his eyes.

"Her hit girl gave her up. Valeria is many things, but she's not a liar." Jameson stepped in.

"If you believe it, why not take us to war?" Alek is borderline insane. He is insanely reckless, but he does not lie from what I have seen.

"I have no issues with you Alek, I just want your sister." I growl.

"What does Valeria look like?" A small smile appears on his manic lips. "Spanish girl, right? I distinctly remember her knocking on our door, pissed off. I'm not sure what it was about but I have this weird feeling that girl was Valeria. So, what have you really been up to, sister?" His mocking smile looking toward Arlene.

He lifted her head and smiled widely. Her nervous façade was gone. "Okay, you caught me." She was giggling. "I honestly didn't mean you any harm. I just wanted one of them to be mad enough to kill you." She growled looking and her brother. "You fucking demonic loon."

Alek snickers at his sister's confession, "You really are something else, las." He whispers darkly. His blue eyes almost looked black. "Well, you heard her lads. You can kill her if you want. I don't have any use for her. Consider this as amending our truce."

While I am going to put a bullet in her head for almost killing Nova and our children, it was interesting to see Alek's behavior towards his little sister. I'm not sure I could bring myself to kill my siblings.

"Collect her." I ordered.

My men did just that and we got up to leave.

Jameson put a bullet in her head and that was the end of that. Even with this threat gone, it still does not put me at ease with the rest of the enemies who come out to hurt our family once more.

Sebastian

Romero let me know the threat was averted. Valeria delivered on her intel; Romero still wants her dead though.

"Let me go, I gave you information." Valeria growled.

"What's to stop you from killing us next time? I mean you did this for money. Your too skilled to just let run around." I ask, a devilish smile gracing my lips. She smiles knowing full well that she would try to kill us if the check was big enough. I take my gun out and sigh. "Don't worry, I will make sure the boy is taken care of for the rest of his life, you can die knowing he will be fine. I will make this quick and easy." I reassure.

I bring the gun to her head, and she closes her eyes waiting for her fate. I pull the trigger and she dies instantly. Her body limps in the chair and I get the men to clean up the mess and take her body.

From what I remember, she didn't have any family aside from the boy. I'll have my assistant find him some parents to raise the boy, with a massive trust fund that he will have once he is an adult.

I got home after finishing up. There was blood on my shirt, and I wanted to get rid of it soon. Hopefully, I don't run into Nova and have her see me covered in blood. When I arrived, the place was quiet. One of our soldiers informed me that the girls had slept in Nova's room and that she was currently in Shot's room. Of course, she is in his room.

After my shower I went into Shot's room to check on Nova. She was lying down on her side since she can't lay on her belly anymore. Sometimes I couldn't even tell she was pregnant because she always wears oversized sweaters anyways. I'm sure a part of her closet is just a hoard of sweatshirts. I kiss her forehead and leave to find something to eat in the kitchen.

"Hey, fox." Nova's sluggish voice greets with a yawn.

"Did I wake you, sweet?" I internally slap myself for waking her.

She shakes her head. "I smelled food." She chuckles. She walks next to me, and I lift her on the counter. She takes a bite out of the sandwich I had just made.

"Bad, little fox." I say taking a bite out of the sandwich still in her hand. She sets it back on the plate and crosses her ankles.

"I've been meaning to talk to you about our baby." She starts.

"What about?" I get her a cup of water and she drinks it to speak clearer.

She crosses her arms. "I don't want our child in your family business. I don't want our kid to be a monster."

I'm sure she hasn't told Ero this and she won't like his reaction. I honestly don't care whether are children want to be in the business or not, but we are our fathers only sons who will carry on our name. I'm not sure I can guarantee her wish.

"I don't know if I can promise you that." I answer honestly.

Nova looks away from me and presses her lips to a fine line. I can see she is thinking deeply about my answer. She takes my sandwich and eats the rest in anger, but mostly hunger, I'm sure. I try to hide my smile.

"Why can't you promise me?" She glares.

"What if our son or hell even our daughter chooses to become part of the business?" He snickers.

"This isn't funny. I don't want my kids to be--" She stops herself.

"A criminal?" I cut her off. She sighs but can't look me in the eyes. "Weren't you going to kill your father not too long ago, sweet? A little hypocritical, don't you think?"

Nova looks me in the eye this time. "Yeah, your right. Who am I to judge? But I don't want that for my kids. Killing people instead of outsmarting them. That's what I should have done with Crespo from the beginning. Killing was the easy way out."

I scoff, "It's effective. So, you think we are taking the easy way out when we kill?"

"Yes." She answers bluntly.

"I'm sure I've told you before, but we don't kill lightly. We aren't some trigger-happy monsters. Is that what you think of us?" It's hard to make me angry, but Nova is being a bit difficult.

"I don't know what to think because you guys leave me out of everything, so I just assume the worst." That's fair. "All I know is, I've been shot at multiple times in the same year. I'm sitting here like a dear in headlights because I have no idea what's going on. I don't know who your enemies are, I don't know who I have to watch my back around. I'm a sitting duck, except now I have kids to worry about."

My lips press against hers softly. "I can promise you this, "I will never stop trying to protect you and our child. You and our baby are my top priority. I will always do my best to make sure you both are safe, even if it means I die in the process." I professed. As the words came out, while surprising, I meant every word. This little fox wormed her way into my heart, and I would protect her for the rest of my life.

She wraps her arms around my neck and pulls me closer. The sweet smell of her green apple shampoo fills my nose. "I get it." She says softly into my ear.

I wanted to tell her I had just killed Valeria, but I think it would be too much truthfulness for one day. She wanted to be included but I saw her face when Romero told Shot to kill Valeria. She says she's ready for the hard truths, but I don't think so. Not yet. Just remain the way you are my sweet, oblivious to the blood dripping from our hands....

Months Later...

Nova

I lay in a cold room with doctors, and the Dominic's swarm me. I'm in labor and it's extremely overwhelming. My body is covered with sweat and I can't stop crying. The pain is unbearable, and I feel like I might die. I might be really dramatic as a first-time mother but fuck it sure feels like my body is going to give out from this pain.

Three pallets of green eyes stare at me as they hold my hand, cleaning the sweat from my head. "It hurts." I whimper.

Reassuring words are whispered to me as the doctors try to get me to push. My vision gets hazy but seconds later I hear the first cry. Minutes later I hear another cry and then one more.

"Congratulations, three baby girls!" The doctor gleamed.

"Girls?" The Dominic's said in unison. Which worried me for a second, but the smiles on their faces put all my worries to bed quickly.

"Eris, Rhea, Selene. My three little goddesses." I said as I hold one to my chest. Jameson holds one and Sebastian holds the other. I look over at Romero and he takes her from me.

"You're amazing." Romero whispers to me as he rocks my daughter in his arms. "Thank you."

After the babies were cleaned off. They were taken for tests, which was hard because the Dominics didn't want to give them up.

I slept throughout the day. I was so damn tired, but so happy to meet my little princesses. After my nap I got to meet all of them without being on the verge of sleep.

"Ok, baby Eris belongs to Romero, Rhea is Jameson's, and Selene is Sebastian's." Dr. Moretti explained.

All the babies were different in appearance. One interesting thing was they all had the same shade of green as their dads. Eris was already proving to be an interesting baby; her dark green eyes were wide open as she looked at J.L. Selene and Rhea were fast asleep in their father's arms. Donnie was scratching at the door to get in, but Romero kept him out like a bad dog. Eventually we let him in, and he could already tell who belonged to who. He noticed their eye color first.

Cami was so mad that she couldn't be there since she had been stuck in Italy. We video chatted and she got to see them that way. She was showing us all the custom Italian clothes she was going to bring for the newborns.

Once we brought them home, Romero had hired two nannies, Carlotta and Ava who were their nannies as children. That was the only reason I allowed the nannies. I mean I don't want strangers watching my kids, but because the Dominics can vouch for them, it makes me feel better. Plus, J.L and Cami will help occasionally as well. These kids will be super smothered.

Chapter 18

Nova

We moved from the penthouse into this new house, three months before the babies were born. The babies were all in one nursery. Cami, J.L and I decorated it. It had royal blue and white walls, white furniture with pink accents and cute little stuffed animals on shelves.

The Dominics slept in the nursery for the first few weeks. I didn't know they'd be so hands on, especially Romero. Carlotta and Ava had to kick them out so they could do their jobs. It was like two angry aunties disciplining their nephews. I'm fairly sure Ava threw her sandal at them at least twice a week. She reminded me of Aunty J, J. L's mom, throwing sandals at us when we were bad.

The babies started to have even more differences as they grew. Rhea and Eris had my brown skin tone with wavy hair. while Selene has olive skin with curly hair. They all had such nice lashes, I'm sure they got from their fathers, because without eyelash extensions, I look like a dying baby bird.

The children were a little different in personality. Eris was already giggling and laughing, Rhea was getting there, but just mostly looked around at things curiously, and Selene giggles, but it's hard to get her there. So far, she likes to be held the most and she rocks her body a lot.

In my spare time, I have been trying to condition them to start saying mama. I know it's going to be a while before they talk, but I'm trying to get them too as early if I can.

Romero was walking toward the room; I could tell because he was shouting in Italian. I walked outside and whisper, "Your daughter is sleeping. Stop being so fucking loud."

He says something else and ends the call.

"What happened?" I ask.

"My legal businesses are becoming harder for no fucking reason. There's someone trying to contest my father's will."

"Why?"

"The legal business where we make the *clean* money are now being contested. My father left it to us as a means to clean our dirty money. Without it it's going to get tougher to clean our money."

"But who could contest your dad's will. What did it say?"

"I need to read the fine print again. My father was not one to make mistakes when it came to business, especially if it was damning to *Casa Rossa*."

Romero sits down on a nearby chair, and I wrap my arms around him and rub his back to try to calm him down. Romero's temper was only tolerable in the bedroom. We haven't had sex due to my body still healing from giving birth. Romero without sex is twenty-four-hour Ice King. A lot moodier and easier to piss off, I didn't realize that was possible.

After I fully healed, I held off on sex because I was a bit self-conscious of my post-birth body. The Dominic's didn't understand why I was self-conscious because they still wanted me like three hungry wolves. The babies were an effective way to keep their mind off the four months without sex.

Romero's hands wandered but then he immediately stopped himself. He suddenly picked me up and threw me over his shoulder. "W-What are you doing?!" I stammer in a hushed whisper.

"Bed" He stated.

"I'm not tired." I growled. He ignores me and brings me to my room. He sets me down on the bed and brings a chair in front of the bed and sits on it. "What are you doing?"

"Strip." He orders.

"I'm not ready for anyone to touch me yet." I say, crossing my legs and fidgeting on my bed.

He smirks, "I won't be touching you." I raise a brow to him. "I want to see you touch yourself."

I could feel the heat rush to my face. I'm not a saint I've definitely masturbated before, but never in front of someone. "I can't do that!" I tense up.

"It wasn't a suggestion. Either you do or I will." Her dark green eyes become much darker with every word. "Everything about you is sexy, there's no other woman who compares, yet you won't let me touch you."

"You're just horny." I scoff, pushing my hair out of my face.

"I am. I'm so fucking horny. All I want to do is fuck you till you can't move. I want to leave marks all over that perfect skin. Watch you swallow my cum, mouth or pussy, but I'm restraining myself because I want you to remember how perfect you are to us." His words are his version of sweet, but I feel them just the same.

I roll my eyes and he smirks. "What?" My eyes narrowing.

"Brat." He chuckles. "Strip, I won't ask again." His voice dripping with dominance.

Romero

Nova's big brown eyes stare me down in defiance and it takes everything in me to not tie her hands behind her back and put her over my knee. To have her curls fisted in my hand as she takes my entire cock into my mouth. I'm hard just thinking about what those brown eyes do to me.

She slowly starts to strip. First, she takes off her shirt, revealing her perfectly round swollen breasts. Her nipples were perked up beautifully. She hated wearing bras which was strange since she complained about her heavy breasts, but I don't mind the easy access. Next, came her shorts that revealed her blue lace thong. My first thought was to pull on it until it rubbed against her clit.

She leans back on a pillow for support on her back to be more comfortable. Her fingers move the lace aside but don't take them off. Her fingers then spread the lips of her cunt apart. I hear her exhale and it is like a vibration sent straight to my cock. With two fingers she enters herself. Sweet little moans follow.

"Good girl." I praise. "Go deeper. I want to see your cream on those fingers." She slips three fingers into her pussy, while her other hand plays with one of her breasts. It's enough to make me cum here and now. It's hard trying to keep it together for her sake. This is not about me, it's for her. I want her to own her body again.

"Romero, touch me..." She pouts. My little brat is always wanting more, huh?

"You heard my rules. No touching from me. Now follow them and keep shoving those pretty fingers in, until I can't see them." I tease.

"Oh, fuck!" She moans. She uses her thumb to rub her clit, while her fingers go in and out of her quickly.

"Keep going. Don't stop." I order, watching her knowing her small fingers may get the job done but in no way is that the same as when I fuck her with my own.

"I'm so close."

"No cumming without permission." She tries to glare but she's too overcome with her own pleasure to even try. I get up and hover over her. I kiss her lips and her moans vibrate my body. "Ask me."

"Can I cum please?" She begs in between kissing me.

I pull away and grab her face with one hand. "Such good manners. Cum, brat." I order.

She sucks in a breath and gasps as she cums. I grab her hand and lick her cream off her fingers. She watches me, rubbing her legs together. Her sweet taste was heaven. It had been so long since I've been able to taste her sweet juices. I hold her legs still and licked the cream from her pussy directly. My tongue plunges into her, licking up the sweet cream that's left.

"I wish you could see through my eyes. How beautiful you look with your legs spread apart for me. Your eyes, an enchanting daze and such kissable swollen lips." After I lick her clean completely, I whisper into her ear, "I let you have the first orgasm but the next one is mine."

I move away from the bed and head towards the door. "You're leaving?" She pants.

"I told you, this was about you. I need to take a cold shower before I fuck you raw. I know you're not on birth control yet, but I don't mind more kids." I confess.

Our babies are beautiful, those little princesses, take after a beautiful queen. Eris has my eyes and wavy hair, but everything else her mother. I was so scared to be a father, but once I got to hold her for the first time, I had known true fear. I would watch the world burn, if it meant she stayed as perfect as she is now.

Now that I have a child. Keeping these legal businesses have become even more important than ever. I see what Nova meant when she didn't want the children in the life. Before she was born, I didn't understand, but now I rather leave *Cassa Rosa* in another Dominics's hands. If Eris decides she wants to take over, fine, but if she doesn't, I want to be able to leave her something else. The mobster in me wants to turn her into a boss who can't be challenged by anyone, who kills, if necessary, but the father in me wants to keep her in the light. I've only been a parent for four months and I already want to pull my hair out. Fuck, I know it will not get easier from here, but I can try to make the path easier for her.

Nova

The Ice King left me wanting yesterday and I had to take a cold shower to return all the brain cells I lost when Romero licked my pussy and fingers clean. I smile at his sweet gesture to help me with my self-confidence though. The Ice King isn't so icy about thirty percent of the time.

Sebastian had been on a call on the patio for some time. I didn't realize what part Sebastian played in the family until now. Romero was the boss, Jameson the enforcer, and Sebastian ran the majority of the legal businesses. He never was that guy, the serious businessman type but after the babies were born, he spent more time going to his office in Dominic Tower. I always wondered why Romero was the only one with an office at home at the penthouse.

I walk over to him with some food. He notices my presents and smiles. He wraps up his conversation quickly and gets up from the seat. He takes the plate from my hand and sets it down.

"I felt like I haven't seen you, sweet." He says pulling me close.

"Yeah, school has been taking up my time..." I reply.

His hazel eyes look up and down. "You seemed flushed, sweet. Dreaming of me?" I roll my eyes trying to get out of his grip. "I have to visit Dominic Tower tomorrow. We could go out to dinner afterwards." He suggests.

"Dinner?"

"Yes, so we can...reconnect." His devilish smirk tells me everything he's thinking. His arms wrap tighter around me, constricting my movements even more. Pushing so close to him I can hear his heartbeat. The steady beat of his heart is like a soothing lullaby.

"I don't think any of you have ever taken me on a proper date." I laugh. Should I count when Jameson and I went to get pizza?

He looks like he's thinking back. "Shit, I guess we haven't been taking diligent care of you, huh sweet?" He looks apologetic as he kisses the top of my head.

"Not at all." I playfully scoff. I look up and give him a peck on his lips. He narrows his eyes as if it weren't enough to satisfy his hunger.

"Such a chaste kiss? I guess I haven't earned a kiss filled with your passion? It's fine, sweet. Save those lips for better use tomorrow." His devilish smirk returns as he kisses the crook of my neck. A small gasp escapes my lips. He chuckles into my skin and kisses it a few more times before his phone rings. I push him away to stop the heat gathering in my panties. "I'll see you tomorrow around three."

"Okay, I'll meet you there. I've never been to Dominic Tower before. It would be nice to see it."

"Okay." He nods. "Thank you for the food." He thanks before taking the call.

I'm left to my studies, while the babies are being watched by their nannies. I try my best to spend most of the day with the babies if I can. Is it weird to want to spend every moment with your kids? No, right? I feel like if I leave them for even one day, I'll have a panic attack. Maybe that will stop when they get old enough to talk back. I laugh out loud at the thought.

"What's so funny, *tesoro*?" Jameson's voice says from coming into the study.

"Motherhood." I laugh. "I'm having a bit of separation anxiety." I admit.

"You? Did you forget we all slept in the nursery for the first couple of weeks? Trust me, I think you're at a healthy place with the babies. We on the other hand are crazy." He snickers, rubbing the bridge of his nose.

"Yeah, boys sure are clingy, huh?" I tease.

He walks up behind me and rubs my head softly. "How's school?"

"Read ten chapters on allegations and then I have a paper to write on government structure." I explain.

He groans. "Sounds boring, but I'm happy that you're finally in school."

"Me to and it's not boring. I'm surprised you guys don't learn about the law system."

"That's what we have lawyers for, *tesoro*." I shake my head and rest it on the desk. He kisses the back of my neck. "I'll leave you to your homework. I'm going to check on the babies. To-night, come sleep with me."

I lift my head and look back at him. "Ok." I answer. He leaves the room and I'm left with the yearning in between my legs, but school is an amazing distraction.

The Next Day

I look up at the tall building in front of me. The reception-ist looks at me with a perfect smile and I let her know Sebastian is expecting me. She lets me up to the top floor and there is a nice waiting area. I sit and text Sebastian that I'm here.

Meetings done, sweet. I'll be out soon.

-Sebastian

I see there's some refreshments and get a drink while I wait. I stand not liking to sit for too long. I see a bunch of people walking down the hall. They must be from the meeting. Out of the crowd one person stands out. He's incredibly handsome. He's wearing a dark blue suit; he was clean cut. He had a low fade hairstyle that complimented him well. He was slightly darker than me with dark brown eyes. I wonder who he was, definitely someone important the way he carried himself. He looked at the girl who came to add to the refreshments and she dropped the bottles of water. He smiled and kept walking. I got up to help her.

"Thank you. I'm a mess." She nervously laughed.

"Nah, you're fine." I reassure her.

"Are you waiting for Mr. Dominic?"

I nod. "Yeah, I am."

"Are you, his girlfriend?" She smiles sweetly. How do I answer this? I'm not his girlfriend. I'm the mother of his child who he has sex with from time to time, but not a girlfriend.

I sigh, "No, I'm family." I answer. That seems safe. I mean I am family, it's not a lie.

"I was hoping he got himself a girlfriend. The only girl I've ever seen visit him was this blonde girl, she was pretty. She looked like a real-life Cinderella." She exclaimed. Wait...I feel like I've said the same thing about the girl I met when I visited Sunny. Her name was Gia.

Did Sebastian and Gia hook up? Are they still hooking up? I mean if they are I can't be upset. I'm not their girlfriend and they are all free to do whatever they want. Especially since I've put them on the pussy ban for four months.

It doesn't matter. I am going to enjoy tonight and not make this a big deal. I hear more steps walk down the hall and it's Sebastian. He's holding his suit jacket over his shoulder looking like a model as always.

He grabs my hand, interlocking our fingers. He brings my hand up to his lips and kisses it. "You look beautiful, sweet." His hazel gaze analyzing me. I looked over at the girl and she looked at me with a shocked face as if she fucked up. I smile to reassure her she's fine.

"Thanks, you look great, as always." I return the compliment.

Sebastian and I took a car to Columbus Circle, where we stopped in front of a restaurant called *Teo's*.

Sebastian held my hand the whole time until we were seated. The inside was super upscale and fancy. I'm a picky eater so I hoped they had something on the menu I liked. I picked up my menu and every time I looked up Sebastian was looking at me like he was about to laugh.

"The fuck is so funny, Sebastian?" I narrow.

"Don't worry, I made sure they have chicken tenders." He teases. I roll my eyes, annoyed that he knows that's what I want. I swear I have the pallet of a five-year-old.

Sebastian calls over the waiter and orders himself a drink and then looks over at me. "Water is good." I answer. I try not to drink anything but water when I eat because juice fills me up. We order some calamari to start. Then continue on with the evening.

"So, what was the meeting about?"

"Legend Brooks, he has a building right next to us and is trying to take Dominic Tower. At first, he tried to buy us out, but we would not let it happen. So now, he's contesting our father's will."

"I think I may have saw him. Dark blue suit, extremely good looking?"

He glares at me. "If you say so. I've only ever heard good things from this guy. When he sat in the meeting room, he was respectful and charismatic, but the whole time I felt like his eyes were telling me he would slit my throat and drink my blood to get Dominic Tower. It's kind of fun playing this game with him." He chuckles darkly.

Fuck, why is it coming back? My stupid jealous thoughts

about Gia. Ignore it damn it. Leave it alone, it doesn't fucking matter. He's giving you his time now and that's all that matters.

Sebastian looks at me questionably. "What's wrong, sweet?' He asked. His finger's pulling on mine.

"In the spirit of communicational skills, I wanted to ask if--okay, it's not a big deal or anything, but are you and Gia like still a thing?" My words coming out of my mouth so quickly I doubt he heard me.

"Gia and I were never a 'thing' we slept together from time to time, but that stopped over a year ago." He yawned.

"Really? Have you seen her lately?"

"Only when I see Sunny. She used to come to my office when I needed to get off."

"Oh ok...cool." I try and act like it didn't bother me, but it does, and it shouldn't. Romero's right I am a brat.

Sebastian grips my finger. "Sweet, I mean it. I haven't touched her since I touched you. You ruined me for other women. I can't get it up for anyone, but you." His laugher brings me a bit of peace. "Why do you think I've been in the office so much? I need a distraction or else I'll gobble you up. My hand is not enough." He whines.

I giggle at his dramatics. "Well, let's see how the night goes and maybe I'll give you a treat."

"Treat? No, this fox is ravenous, appetizers aren't going to be enough, sweet. One taste and I'll become feral." I got up and gave him a lasting kiss. Sebastian seemed to want to speed up dinner after that kiss. "I hope you're all healed up, sweet. You aren't getting away from me tonight. I'm going to taste every part of my dessert. I hope you have no plans tomorrow. "I knew his words held weight. The Dominics don't make threats.

I lay my head on his shoulder and he kisses me gently the whole ride home. Our smiles never leaving our faces. Getting home Sebastian went straight for the nursery. He looked over his daughter and nieces. Now that I think about it, the Dominics are identical, does that mean all the kids are technically theirs? Are my kids' full siblings? Cousins? Half siblings? Family gatherings are going to be interesting.

"I can't tell if she's really cute or she's just my kid." Sebastian laughs holding Selene in his arms. "I love you and mommy so much, Selene." Did he just...say he loves me? "We are always going to be there for you. You come from a strong family." He finishes.

"You what?" I say as he puts Selene down in her crib.

"You're going to make me say it, huh?" He snickers. "Nope, I'll decide, sweet."

I make a hmphed sound and kiss my baby's goodnight before leaving the nursery. Sebastian picks me up bridal style and rushes me down the hall into his room.

Chapter 19

Nova

"Finally, the fox has caught his prey. What delectable prey indeed. I don't even know we're to start." He sets me down on his bed and rips off my dress, not takes off, rips.

"Hey! You crazy fox!" I growl, sitting in red lace panties and a matching lace bra to match.

He stands closer to the bed and picks me up, so my legs are wrapped around him. He sits down on the bed with me in his lap and I lick my lips. His mouth deep into my neck and shoulders. At this point Sebastian would tease and taunt me, but he was taking his time with my body.

I lean in for a kiss when he comes up from my neck. He dives into the kiss with no hesitation. Pulling me close with one hand on my back and the other in my hair. His tongue dancing in mine, the sweet rich taste of wine still on him. His hand left my hair and lowered to the back of my neck. His grip was firm, but not painful. I could feel his erection through his pants and the fact that he was still fully dressed, was weirdly attractive, but I was getting impatient. I grab his belt buckle and undo it carefully.

"Impatient, sweet?" He teases, breaking our kiss.

"Very..." I breathe into his neck. He sneakily takes off the last of my bra and panties.

I move my head back up and match his gaze. "It seems my prey is more of a predator." He teases tugging on my hair. I arch my back a bit to rub myself over his erection. He exhales and his eyes clench slightly. I then take it a step further; I stick my hand into his dress pants and rub down his length. His pained expression makes me smile that I now have the upper hand. Once his erection is pulled out fully, I hover over it; letting him feel my heat.

Sebastian's hands are now at my side trying to push me down on his length, but I don't let him. "Condom, remember?" I glare.

He narrows his eyes and lightly leaves a kiss on my lips. "Sorry, sweet, but fuck no." He laughs.

"I'm not on birth control, you want another baby?"

He smiles, "Yes I do." His thump traces my lips. "I'll pull out, sweet. Even if I had condoms, which we don't ever since we started fucking you, I don't want anything between us. I'm addicted at this point. I want to feel your skin against mine, condoms just won't do." My head was telling me this was a bad idea, but my pussy was louder and said it should be fine.

I could feel his tip rubbing against my entrance. My legs grew weak, and they give out, letting Sebastian push me down deep onto his cock. "Fuck, sweet. How did I manage to go months without being inside you." He groans. All the Dominic's were vocal in bed, and I found that most attractive. Hearing them moan and groan when they were inside me filled me with satisfaction.

He grabs a hold of my hair to make it easier to push me deeper and deeper on to his cock in the angle he prefers. I can't even speak, the only thing that comes out is my whimpers.

"No words for me, sweet?" He struggles to get his words out. He picks me up, his length sliding out of me and dispelling my trance.

He lays me on the bed on my back. "Missionary- "Before I could speak, he pulls my legs until I'm at the edge of the bed. He spreads my legs wide and enters me harshly but his strokes after a bit slower. His hand snakes around my neck and squeezes.

Sebastian

Watching Nova so ready and open for me, makes me primal. Without much thinking I wrap my hand around her neck and choke her enough to make it easier for me to thrash into her. I squeeze a bit harder to see if she gives me a reaction and she does.

"Are you trying to kill me, fox?" She mocks. Her words stuttered in mid ecstasy. I loosen my grip on her neck but continue to go deeper into her. I'm like a horny teenager who is about to bust for the first time and it's embarrassing. If I came now, she would never let me live it down. I stop my thrusts and remove my hand from her neck. I hover over her with my dick still firmly in her. I lean down to kiss her plump lips. This was to keep me from cumming, but the way her tongue is moving right now is bringing me to the brink. Her hands lift, running through my hair and the other caressing my cheek and jaw.

"Trying to make me cum early, sweet?" I groan into her mouth.

"Maybe." She laughed, but the strain told me she was close herself.

I return her laugh. "I promise I won't cum in your pussy but be ready to swallow me. I will cum inside you any other way I can." I pant into her ear. My thrusts continue and I lift her legs high, holding them together. She was already squeezing me, but this angle was really working in my favor.

"Sebastian!" My name sounding incredible from her lips. Her nails digging into my hips. She clenches onto me, and I know she's ready to milk me.

"Let go, sweet. That's it." I growl. She belts out a scream and I know she has reached her climax. I can feel her all over my cock, but I continue to reach mine. Her pussy is super sore, but it just adds to my pleasure. When I'm close, I let go of her legs. "On your knees." I order. She follows it swiftly. She takes my length into her mouth and within seconds I cum, spilling into her mouth. I open my eyes and glance down at her licking her lips and after swallowing me. She looks so beautiful with her curls a messy poof. "Get on something soon. You know how much I love seeing my cum slide out of you."

She lies back on the bed exhausted, and I follow as I lay next to her. She looks at me as if she is waiting for me to say something, but I smirk and play with her hair. "You're annoying." She rolls her eyes turning her back to me.

I laugh at her tantrum. Pulling her close to me and stroking her back until she falls asleep. Trust me, sweet, I love you.

Jameson

Gregory has been killed by the Russian's so now we have no fucking spy. Ero is not going to like this. The Russian's haven't made any effort to attack just yet and so I assume that they don't know who he was spying for. Then again, they are in Miami right now, so what point to come start a war in New York. This life can really be exhausting sometimes.

I look down at my daughter, Rhea. "You and mama make it worth it." I say to her. She smiles at me, as if she understood my words. I take a bottle from next to me and place it in Rhea's lips. Nova isn't too keen on using the bottles, but she can't be around 24/7. Rhea is super calm once she eats though. She might be the fussiest out of the three. Rhea's eyes a reflection of mine when I look into them. Some days she looks just like Nova and other's she looks like me. Every time I hold her it pains me to let her go. A tangible representation of the love Nova and I share for each other.

"I'm sorry I can't be here all day with you, *principessa*. Daddy has to make sure the silly Russians don't think they can enter our territory without me slicing their necks. Then there's the Irish's boss who might be an actual psychopath." I ramble. Rhea looks at me with wide eyes as she continues to drink her milk.

"Let's keep this between us?" I whisper to her. She blinks at me with her big eyes and then closes them. I take out her bottle and put her back into her crib. I call Romero to meet up with him.

We sit in the back booth of our club. "What's going on?" Ero asks.

"Gregory is dead. Our direct line to the Russians is gone." I bluntly reply.

He slams his bourbon on the table. "Fuck, what else? I swear everyone is trying my patience. First, the fact that I can't kill Crespo, then the fucking Irish prick's psychotic sister, now this fucking asshole wants our fucking building." He growls running his fingers through his hair. "It's like the second we stopped dropping heads, the world went to shit. Bash says Brooks won't budge, of course he has no standing to our building so hopefully he goes away quietly. Or better he doesn't, and I cut him down."

I smile, "Yeah, life would be so much easier if all of our enemies would just die, but they're like cockroaches, you have to kill them yourself. Preferable with a hammer- "

"Or a chainsaw." Ero inputs.

"Just give the word and he's gone. What could he even want with our building. He's a millionaire with his own business. What use is trying to take ours?"

"No clue, all I know is that cat is on his last life, so he better use it wisely." He puts on his coat.

"You just got here, Ero. You don't come around that much anymore. Don't leave just yet." Harmony purrs taking a seat next to Ero.

"I'm spoken for. So is he." Ero answers coolly standing up. "Let's go." He says and I stand up and walk out of the club with him.

"Where are we going?" I ask.

"Meeting." He answers.

Romero

For a while now I have been trying to figure out what my father did with Nova's mothers' body for the past year. My father did not leave any clues to where he may have put her if she is even still in this country. I contacted Nova's grandmother in Cuba, but she had no memory of her daughter even being dead. That was not a fun conversation. She did mention about a child Nova. I remember Nova saying her grandmother had dementia, but I did not realize to what extent.

"Did my father ever ask you to help him transport a body into Cuba?" I ask Matanza sitting across from me.

"He had me transport a lot of shit, but Cuba I would remember. He never asked me to send anything over there, especially a body." He says taking a slow drag on his cigar. He could be lying. If my father swore him to secrecy, he would take it to the grave, which means there is a high chance he buried her in Cuba. Although, why put so much work in for one body? It makes more sense that she is in the states.

I blow out the smoke from mine and look down at my watch. It was already two in the morning. Nova and the babies are sleeping.

Nova

I wake up with Sebastian's arms wrapped around me. I turn around and cuddle into his chest. His fingers and tangled in my hair.

"Sweet." He starts. His eyes still closed.

Mine are also closed as I ask, "Yes?"

"Let's take a weekend trip to Italy at the end of the month." He suggests.

"Aren't the babies too young to fly?"

He breaths in. "We'll check in with their pediatrician. But do you want to go?"

"Of course, that's amazing. I've never been outside the country before. I've never even been on a plane."

"What, you've never been on a plane?" His eyes open slightly. I nod and he yawns turning on his back. I mimic his contagious yawn and lay my head for a couple more seconds before getting up from the bed.

"I'm going to check on the kids." I yawn stretching out my arms.

Suddenly his hand stops me. "Hold on. I'll come."

We spent our mornings feeding and bathing the babies. Romero and Jameson were still sleeping when we checked.

Sebastian read to the children. They really seemed to really listen when he spoke. All the children were like that with the Dominics. A natural love that increased every day.

Carlotta and Ava took over for the time Sebastian had to return to the office and I had to do some schoolwork.

I needed to run to the store for a few items. The Dominics I have an assistant go get my stuff, but that's just too extra. We already have *two* nannies I am more than capable to get my own stuff. I did have a big change since the shooting though, two bodyguards around me and a car always following me. I want to say the Dominic's are being over the top but honestly who knows these days after everything that happened.

I enter a couple baby stores looking for new bottles, toys etc. "Ms. Corzo. Let me hold that for you." Vince says from behind me.

"Thank you." I smile passing him my bags.

"Nova?" A familiar voice calls out and I see Donnie in his amazing Lamborghini truck. He finds a parking spot and joins me on the sidewalk. He greeted me with two cheek kisses. "Did the demonic trinity let you out?" He laughed. I flip him the bird and we continue walking down the strip. "Shopping for baby stuff?

"Yeah, they are growing so fast I need new clothes for them already."

"Ah."

He looks at the stores coming up. "Let's go in here. I need a new suit." He says and we go into the store.

"Hello, welcome to Mashiro." A woman welcomes us in.

"Babe, get the car started for me.?" A voice says. I look over and see *him*, Jacob Hernandez, my ex-boyfriend who cheated on me with one...no eight different girls.

He looks over at me and makes eye contact. "Who's that?" Donnie asks.

"Cheating ex who turned out to be an unbearable narcissist once he got drafted." I explained.

"To war?" He laughed.

"I fucking wish." I snickered. "But no, Basketball."

Jacob smiles and walks up to me with an unfamiliar girl on his arm until she walks out the door. "Nova, how long has it been?" He greets brightly. Vince and Louis get in front of me and block his way. "Whoa, what's with the security?" He laughs awkwardly.

"Ms. Corzo?" Vince looks at me waiting for an order.

"It's okay Vince." I smile. Vince and Louis move out of the way but Vince glares at Jacob.

"Damn you got security? You famous or something now?" He jokes.

"Can we not do this? Act like we left off on good terms."

He ignores me and looks at Donnie, "Boyfriend?"

"Doesn't matter." I answer.

"So, no. You know I tried to find you at the club, but you stop working there. I thought we could talk. I wanted to apologize about how we ended things. You were such a great girlfriend and I treated you like shit once I got a bit of money and fame. I was stupid and I apologize. Seriously, I fucked up." I could not tell if he was sincere, but it's been three years and the past was the past.

"Thanks." The word trying not to escape the confines of my mouth. I'm sure the look on my face told him the conversation was done. In that moment I truly hoped he meant what he had said.

"This was unnecessarily dramatic." Donnie stated.

"Yeah. So how about that suit?"

Jameson

"Listen, I don't have all day. I ask a question you answer, it's really simple." I groan. Jeri's blood dripping from my fingers. "Come on, I have shit to do."

"I don't know anything, Shot. Your father never talked about the girl you're describing. Plus, your father only killed one woman before and that was to set a tone." Jeri winced.

"My father is dead. You answer to us now. Are you not a loyal soldier? If not, I have no use for you."

"I have been loyal since before you were born, Shot. Plus, you should be asking Sunny. You know how chummy they were. Even after the breakup, they were always close. Best of friends, of course I don't think he cheated but he only told his secrets to her."

How stupid, I didn't even think about Sunny. He's right, Sunny was more of his right hand than anyone. He must have told her something.

I call Sunny and schedule to meet with her later in the day. If Sunny hated anything, it was unannounced visits.

Later in the day I make my way to see Sunny. She brings me to her office, and I sit in the chair adjacent from her. "What's going on? You aren't one for last minute discussions." She smirks.

"My mother killed Nova's mother and I want to know what my father did with the body. So, I'm asking you if you know anything."

She looked at me with wide eyes. "What?"

"You didn't know?"

"Of course not. That poor girl. I'm surprised she would want to be anywhere near you, knowin' what she does." She huffed. "You know your father gave me a safe to hold for him many years ago and I didn't know why so I just left it. I never peaked and now I have a sick feeling in my stomach." She trembled. I had never seen Sunny like this. She was the most put together person I knew.

"Where is it, Sunny. I'll take it." My hand covers hers to calm her a bit.

Sunny shows me where it is, and I take it off her hands. The safe seems light, but honestly, I wouldn't put anything past my father right now. I try a couple of passwords, until I realize that it's our birthday.

It opens and all that is sitting there is a book. I flip through it until I find a page with writing. There're coordinates with a note.

Sunny, Crespo will never stop trying to kill us all. That's fine, we can hold him off. If we cannot for any reason. Use this as leverage against him. These are the coordinates to fine his girl. Pass this on to my sons if I have died. Don't let him hurt my children.

-S. D

Is she alive? Or is he just fucking with Crespo. Nova won't be happy if we keep this from her. We're going to have to tell her.

Nova

Jameson came through the office and greeted me with a loving kiss. *"Tesoro, I* have to tell you something. You said you wanted complete honesty, but you have to be ready for it."

I looked at him with concern, "What's wrong, are you sick? Are you okay?" I frantically asked. Goosebumps all over my arms.

"It's about your mom. I think we all need to be here for this. Bash and Ero should be here soon."

An hour later Romero and Sebastian make their entrances and we all meet up in the living room. We all look at Jameson waiting for Jameson to talk. "Spit it out, Shot." Romero growls.

"I went to see Sunny. Our father gave her a safe for insurance. She never opened it. I decided to take it and inside was a note from our father." Jameson explains, handing the note to Romero. Romero then reads it aloud and we all look in utter shock about what we just heard. Is my mother alive? No, there's no way she would be alive.... right? I can't even let myself believe that she is alive, I just can't.

"You don't think..." Sebastian starts.

"No, I don't. Your dad is fucking with us. These coordinates are probably where he buried her." I say quietly.

"We can check it out. You do not have to go, baby." Romero gently coos. He's never called me that before.

"No, I want to see where she is. I want to say goodbye. I never got to." I try to hold it together, but tears start to call from my face. Romero wipes away my tears and pulls me to his lap. I buried my face in his neck. He rubs my back, trying to soothe me.

I'm not making a sound, but my tears are defiantly waterfalling. "God, I hate crying. It's so fucking annoying. How do you guys do it?" I laugh darkly.

"What do you mean?"

"I never see you guys' cry." I mumble.

I feel another hand on my back. "We get sad too, *tesoro*, we are just used to loss. This life is filled with it. I think I went to forty funerals in the span of a year. I can't even tell you about the number for all the years I've been alive. This shit is routine for us." Jameson says, his hand moving to rub my neck.

"What about when I die?" I ask. Both Romero and Jameson's movements stop.

"Don't ever say that again." Jameson voice was stern. I move my head to see his face and he looks mad. I don't think Jameson has ever been mad at me before. "I didn't cry, but I saw my life flash when you got shot. You mean so much to us, even if we are not the most vocal about it. I don't think I could handle it if you died."

"He's right, little fox." Sebastian groans. "I don't think either of us would know what to do if you died, you've given us so much, in such a brief time. Don't ever fucking die on us. It's us until the end of time, you hear me."

Romero remained silent but hugged me. I know Romero is a hot head, who's not the best with his feelings, but I feel his love, even without the actual words. His arms wrap around me tightly and his head goes into my neck. "Brat." He manages to say. Romero is a walking contradiction sometimes. Most of the time he's a know-it-all who has a plan for everything, but when we talk about our feelings, he can't come up with a single thing to say.

"Donnie can hold it down here, while we find her. We should all go together." Sebastian suggests. My phone starts to ring in my pocket, and I know it's Donnie by the ringtone. Is he a warlock or something?

"Yo." I answer.

"Hey, you free? I wanted to pass by and see my cousins. Hopefully, I don't bump into your ex again. That dude was really creepy, like some stalker type." He laughs.

Romero snatches my phone. "What ex?" He growls into the phone.

"Oh, my bad. Did not know you were there, boss. Yeah, Nova's ex ran into us yesterday when she was shopping. He was all sappy, that little fucker. Apologizing to her and shit, I know his type, he isn't sorry. Probably wanted to get a hit of Nova one last time. I can understand." He teased.

"Donnie, you fucking traitor." I growl.

"Listen babe, we're still best friends, but he's my boss and will shoot me for not telling him. You can see my issue. Love you though." He says smoothly.

"Fine." I grunt. I can't be mad at Donnie. He's literal sunshine.

"You weren't going to tell us, what a bad girl you are." Sebastian sneers

"I was. I just didn't think it was important, he's a fucking loser who will end up unhappy. A malicious personality like that, only attracts more bullshit. Fuck his apology. I don't know why people think women have to just suck it up and be the bigger person. Fuck that and fuck him. I'm not mad anymore, but I won't forget." I growl. This sudden anger really had me on a roll. "And you know what? We need to establish something. I want to know something."

"What?" All three said in unison.

"Am I the only one that you guys are with. Not just sex but dating wise too."

"Yes, sweet. You're the only want I want." Sebastian confesses. "Who else is going to love your big forehead."

"You think I could deal with *two* brats?" Romero growls. "Just one is enough."

Jameson leans in and kisses me to Romeo's annoyance. "I love you, *tesoro*, I've already told you. I can't wait to give you, my name." Jameson's sweet words touch something warm in my heart.

"*Our* name." Romero huffed.

"Ok, good to know." I smile, resting my head on Romero's shoulder.

"I'm still on the phone. This is really uncomfortable." Donnie whispers through the phone.

Chapter 20

J.L

"We need a girl's night out. Nova, you have been stuck in this house with school and babies. They won't die if you're not there for a couple of hours. They have two nannies, security up the ass and I'm sure Sebastian and Romero said he would be home. You got that first mom separation anxiety. Look I've been there, remember when Bo was born, I never wanted to leave him. I don't think I went out until he was one. It's been almost five months. Going out for one night does not make you a bad mom." I lecture. Nova looks at me nodding but I know she still doesn't want to leave them, especially at night. I'm surprised she let the triplets convince her to get nannies.

"Okay, okay you win. I'll go out with you guys. Peer pressure much?" She glares, but her eyes quickly soften. "Where are we even going?"

"Blue light, it's a new club. I went with Cami the other day and it was such a great vibe in there." I swoon falling onto Nova's incredible bed. Her room is super spacious, she's living like an actual princess. This room is so cozy and warm, I wouldn't be surprised if the triplets fight to sleep in here. This whole new life Nova has is just out of this world, but so is mine. Cami is such a refreshing change. She really makes me feel like I'm in a fairy tale as cheesy as that sounds. After a year together, I really feel like I'm in love. Cami is God sent; I'm convinced.

Bo was in the nursery playing with his new cousins. Those girls are going to have such an overprotective cousin forever. He really adores them. In times like this I wish I had given him a sibling; he is such a social child he could have used one. I can't imagine not having Nova, she's such a great sister to me. Helping raise Bo. No matter if she had work or school back then. Even now with her own kids, she still will take Bo whenever. It does help that she loves him so damn much.

"So, what are we wearing?" I nudge.

"I'm going to wear a white strapless top with a matching white skirt." She proposes. I look at the outfit and damn that is going to look amazing with her curvy figure.

After my indecisive ass couldn't pick for an hour, she picked out one and forced it on me, but it looked amazing so I can't complain. The club was full. Everything look like they were in their own world, which was great. So many nice booths. Everything is just so perfect and new. We make our way to the bar and order.

"Whiskey sour." I order.

"Crown apple with cranberry juice please." Nova orders.

"Whiskey is the drink tonight, huh?" The bartender says.

I raise a bow to him with a smile, "Whiskey is always the drink." I laugh.

"Amazing. Well, you guys have fun. The night is just starting!" He exclaims. The club is just as amazing as I remember. Everyone who works here is so hospitable and you feel like they are part of the fun to.

No... no... no... why tonight of all nights is this idiot here?! Jacob fucking Hernandez is sitting at a booth in the corner. I try to lead Nova out of eye view, but it's too fucking late he sees us, but Nova hasn't noticed. I pull her into to the other side of the club.

"Why are we all the way over here?" She's very suspicious of me at this point.

"The lightings better. I want to get some pictures of you in that fit."

"Well, get good ones. I really got to pee." She whines crossing her legs. The bathroom is closer to us than him so hopefully she doesn't see him.

We make our way to the bathroom, and I try to rush her in. I wait for her to finish washing her hands and try and flee, but like the fucking snake that he is, he slithers though the people and makes his way to us before I can get Nova to other location.

"Nova!" He yells running up to us.

I glare harshly. "What the fuck do you want?" I growl, standing a step-in front.

"J.L chill out. I just wanted to say 'hi'."

"Why?"

"Because we were all friend's once. Shit, the past is in the past. It's not high school anymore." He growls

"You're right, we are grown. So, why do you feel the need to talk to us. You're a famous basketball player, right? We dulled your shine for too long. Those were your words, right?"

Jacob looked over at Nova. "You're right the past is the past, so it lets leave it there. Let's move on." She says with the utmost class she can muster.

Nova

"Were such a great couple, Nova. With time we can be that again." He pleads. I almost choke on my drink. J.L decides to go back to the bar saying that she can't listen to him sober.

"Jacob, we are *done*. I can't make this any clearer." I sigh.

"Why because you're with someone?" He huffs. This fucking guy doesn't understand shit.

"Me being single or not is not why I don't want to be

with you. I've outgrown you. I'm not the same puppy dog who showed up to every game, even though your ass sat on that damn bench for the first fucking year!" I annunciate loudly.

He looks at me with so much confusion. It really baffles me how I ever stayed so loyal to a complete and utter narcissistic idiot. His sweetness made up for the fact that he was the biggest waste of space of all time. Once that sweetness was gone, I realize that he had nothing to offer me, but emptiness. I don't like the idea of bashing your ex because at some point I cared deeply for him but when that same guy tells you that you mean nothing to him and that he could do so much better because he was going to be a huge star. Then admits that he has been cheating on me with girls that are on his level and that I would never be able to measure up. Just the memory of it makes my blood boil.

"All these girls are the same. They just want my money and to bring up their own status. I realize this is my karma, but I have learned my lesson. If you give me another chance you would be able to see that I've changed."

"No." I go to walk away but he grabs my arm. I glare, "Let go before I embarrass you." I threaten. He doesn't let go but I try to yank my arm out of his grasp. I stick my acrylics into his arm, and he winced, letting go almost immediately. I take my first step to get away from him and I hear a loud sound. I see Jacob's body slamming against the wall of the club and people starting to stare. Jameson Is choking the life out of Jacob right now.

"I'm going to enjoy making you suffer "Jameson growls, his grip getting tighter and tighter. I can see the light going out of Jacob eyes.

"Don't do this here, too many eyes. "I whisper in Jameson's ear. He lets go of Jacob and he falls to the floor. The manager of the club comes up to Jameson and apologizes. Jameson tells him to bring Jacob to the back.

Jameson turns to me and look at my arm. "Did he hurt you, *tesoro*?" His voice is soft and concerned.

"Nah." I say but now it did hurt a bit. I may despise Jacob, but I don't want Jameson to kill him. I remember what he did to the pastor for slapping one of Sunny's girls. "Don't kill him." I plead.

Jameson's soft gaze tightens. "As you wish." He leans in and kisses my lips.

I pull away with narrowed eyes. "Why did you come?" I ask curiously.

"J.L called me because she said she was going to stab him, and she can't go to jail." He laughed.

"Well, there goes the night." I laugh sadly.

Jameson takes my hand and leads me to the dance floor. I smile as we dance together. He spins me round and holds me close.

Jameson

Nova dances in front of me with her ass pressed up against me. My hands are resting on her hips as they sway. The lights illuminate her beautiful dark eyes. The joy in her voice as she whispers sweet nothings into my ear is perfect.

I had brought Cami with me to keep J.L company. I could see them sitting in the booth wrapped up each other. My thoughts were the same, wanting to be wrapped up in Nova. "Follow me." I say into her ear. I guide her to the back and down the hall to the room. This new club belonged to a friend of mine. I got to see it before it opened and there is a room with a two-way mirror. I step into the room where you can't see into the other room but the other can see into ours. Little does Nova know that insect is going to figure out firsthand who she belongs to. I had told my security to tie him to a chair with duct tape. The room was set up like a meeting room.

"What are we doing in here, Jameson?" She asks jumping on top of the table in front of the huge mirror. Her legs crossed bugging me because that skirt hugged her hips perfectly.

I walk over her, towering her with my height and leaning down to her glossy plumb lips. "On your stomach, ass in the air." I order. She quickly complies and gets into position. Her skirt is making her legs press together which is perfect. I poke her panties with a finger. "So wet. For him? "I tease but the joke makes me annoyed at the thought.

"Fuck no." She growls. "Just you, I want you so badly, J." Nova begs. I'm a little taken back by her shortening my name. Her small hand reaching for me behind her back. I grab her hand and kiss it.

"*Tesoro*, you're so cute." I chuckle. My tongue licks her drenched fabric. She twitches from my touch.

I move my hands under her shirt and rub her erect nipples. Circling them with my thumbs. Nova lets out a moan and buries her head into her arms. I keep in mind that he is still watching everything that I'm doing to her. I'm trying my best not to let him see too much of her perfect body. Nova is a perfect distraction, I almost forgot that he was on the other side.

Pulling her panties down, I leave them at her ankles. I stick my tongue inside of her wet and needy pussy. Her body reacts almost immediately. Her legs rubbing together, her head lifting from her arms to cry out from the sensation. Nova was such a beautiful girl to look at and seeing her overcome with arousal was just the fucking cherry on top. "How bad do you want it? "I ask, still deep in her pussy.

"Badly, I need you right now. I want you to fill me up. I want to feel your lips all over me, as your dick fucks me." She orders. Nova's words have me on the brink. I could never deny her anything. The words of the woman I love became law to me. Whatever she wanted from me she would get. I mean especially when she asked so nicely.

"How could I ever deny you? "I pull down my zipper, releasing my bulging erection. I rubbed myself against her entrance whining to tease my girl just a little bit. She was so slick that I thought I would just slide into her.

"Waiting for an invitation?" She jokes. I chuckle at her eagerness to have my cock shoved into her heat. Nova was always impatient in the bedroom. She can never wait; she hates to be teased.

I remove my dick from her entrance and stick a couple fingers into her. Teasing her canal for the time being. While my fingers go in and out of her, I kiss the insides of her thighs.

She suddenly stands up and my fingers slide out. "What's wrong, *tesoro*?" Worried that I had done something wrong.

She goes on her tippy toes and kisses me deeply. "Let me ride you."

Her hands move to my chest, and I lay down on the table. She gets on top of me and lowers herself onto my throbbing cock. I can feel her slick cunt as I enter her. Her walls are clenching tightly.

"Fuck! It's been so long since you've been inside me. God, I feel so fucking good. "She exclaims. She pulls up her skirt so she can have better movement. She starts bouncing on my dick. I could see her big round tits bouncing along with the movements. Even though they were covered it was still fucking hot. Nova didn't need to be naked to be the hottest girl in the room. Her essence alone just pours pheromones.

She leans down to kiss me, while she continues to bounce. The mix of her kiss and her slick cunt was enough to make me frantic. My hands were firmly on her perfect round ass. My grip on her ass was harsh to guide her more of my pace. I wanted to be deep inside of her, to get lost in Nova. It wasn't too hard. "So, fucking perfect. You better be careful I might put another baby in here this year."

"You better not, I'll fucking kill you." She laughs through her moans. "Maybe in a couple years. "

My laugh is strained as I get close to cumming. Nova on

top, was such a quick way to get me to cum. I let her ride me for a little longer and try my hardest not to cum myself.

"Yes..yes..yes…so good." She mutters to herself.

"Cum, *tesoro*, cum on my dick." I growl.

She lets out a scream and coats me with her sweet cum. She shakes in place for a bit before falling onto my chest. I pat her head and let her relax for a minute before I put her back on her stomach to fuck her ass. I won't be mean and fuck her sore pussy.

I rub her back a bit. "It's okay, relax." I can feel her body relax. I give her my jacket to lay her head on. I rub her cum into her ass and coat my dick with it one more time. I enter her a bit at a time. It had been a long while since we had done this. "Tell me if you want me to stop."

She puts up a thumbs up which is all her tired body can manage. "So cute." I gleam. Slowly inch by inch I go deeper into her until I'm all the way in. Being inside feels like a vise. Nova is gripping me with all her strength. She starts to tense up and the small moans are audible.

"It doesn't hurt. You can keep going. I want you to cum in my ass." She says breathless.

With that, I plunge myself into her. Feeling the amazing tightness of her asshole. Loving the pleasure that I was bringing her. I pounded into her over and over until her cries became louder. The sweet harmony of her moans filling my ears.

"Oh, fuck! That's it, right there! Cum inside me. Don't waste a drop!" She cries.

With one last pump I stilled inside her. My hot load taking up space in her small hole. Her body finally gave out. I kissed her lips. "Come on, we have to get home and kiss our daughter goodnight. Don't fall asleep." I snickered.

"I'm not sleeping. I'm catching my breath." She mumbles. "I can barely move." She whines.

"And we wouldn't want that..." I joke. She slaps my arm as she jumps off the desk and lowers her skirt. "I'll meet you in the car."

She nods and leaves the room. I look into the mirror and smirk. Walking through the connecting door, I see him there glaring at me with a hard on. "Enjoy the show?" I ask removing the tape from his mouth.

"Are you going to kill me?" His body shaking angrily. Does he want me to kill him?

"I wanted to, but my girl said I couldn't. So today is your lucky day..." I smile mockingly.

Even with my statement he still glares at me. "What if she decides that she wants to be with me? Do you think because you have a kid together, she'll stay with you? "

So, this is the delusion that Nova was dealing with. This guy really won't let her go. I can understand where he's coming from, except I realized quickly that she deserved the world and that I would give it to her. There is nothing that could keep me from Nova now.

"No, she'll stay with me because she knows her worth. She knows that I will love her after death and lastly, she can't live on this earth without my cum dripping out of her. God, she really does have the prettiest expressions when she cums." I snicker. "Like I said, this is your lucky day. Don't lose your last life. "

"Fuck you!" He shouts.

I promised Nova I won't kill him but...

I release him from his bonds, and he gets up quickly. He tries to throw a punch, but I dodge it and he falls to the floor. I put my foot on his chest and keep him down. "Which hand did you grab her with?"

"Get off me, *mamagüevo*!"

"I should break both to be sure." My foot lift from his chest and stomps on his hand, then the other. He rolls on the floor crying in agony. It was music to my ears. He will take this as a lesson. How generous am I to give him such a lesson?

I left the room and met up with Nova in the car. She was completely knocked out. I lifted her head from the seat and lay her head on my lap. Stroking the long strands of her curls. Her body was still hot from our session. It brought a smile to my face to see the small smile on her face as she slept. Didn't she say that she wasn't going to fall asleep?

Chapter 21

Nova

The coordinates left for my mother were right here in New York which gave me chills. Has my mother been here the whole time? Buried in an unmarked grave. The thought brought me to tears. I wanted to tell myself I was prepared, but was I?

The Dominic's and I arrived at an old mansion. "Where are we?" I ask.

"Our family home." Sebastian answered, his voice filled with distain.

This is where she was killed.

Romero held my hand the whole car ride. Honestly, I needed him to because I didn't know what we were going to walk into. The car stopped and I took a deep breath. When we entered the house, it looked old but well-kept as if someone were still here taking care of it.

Loud steps can be heard down the hall, which makes me step closer to Romero. Is this place fucking haunted?

"You must be Mr. Dominic's children." A voice says from the top of the stairs. We turn to see a man in a white coat. A doctor? "I am Dr. Ismat, — "

Before he could finish introducing himself. Romero snapped, "Where is the woman? "

The doctor wore a nervous smile. "Oh, you must be talking about Ms. Ramira. Follow me."

I brace myself for the worst as the doctor was leading us to the backyard. Is that where they buried her, in the backyard like some pet?

Chills ran down my spine as I see my mother's body laying down on a lounge chair. Her body isn't moving, she's so still.

"Is that her?" I ask cautiously.

The doctor saw the horror in my face. "Oh no, she's very much alive I am so sorry. She's just taking a little nap right now; she tends to do that when it's sunny outside. So, let me give you the rundown. Servino brought her to me after she had been shot in the chest, when she fell from her gunshot wound, she had hit her head and that caused brain swelling. We were forced to put her in a coma. She was in a medically induced coma for a couple of weeks. When she woke up certain pieces of her life were missing. It's been a couple of years and she is finally healed completely from the gunshot wound and her brain inconsistencies. "The doctor reassured. "She is still having complications but it's not from lack of physical healing, the rest is mental."

"So why is she still here? Why would he want to start a war with Crespo if she's fine now?"

"Servino was very paranoid that Crespo would retaliate for the accident. So, he told him that she died and kept her here to heal until the moment presented itself to bargain her back."

I ran over to my mother and shook her slightly. *"Mami?"* I try to say but I can barely get it out through choked tears. I don't know how to react in this instant, my mother is alive. There's too many emotions and I don't know which one I feel the most.

Her eyes opened slowly. Her breathing became frantic, and she wouldn't turn her head to look at me. I grabbed her hand and she held it tighter. Tears start pouring from her eyes. "Mi niña." She greeted me through tears.

"Yeah, *Mami* it's me."

She hesitated but hugs me tightly. I can feel her head rubbing the top of my head. It felt like I was that little kid who had lost her mother. All I wanted to do was stay in my mother's arms forever. She hugged be for several minutes before looking behind me and seeing the triplets.

"Are you, *her* sons?" She asked the Dominics.

"Yes, I'm Jameson and these are my brothers Sebastian and Romero. Our father has past, you don't have to stay here anymore. We made peace with Crespo after our children were born." Jameson explained.

"Our?" She narrows her eyes at me.

I smile nervously. My mother didn't want me in this life, so telling her I have three children with three mobsters is definitely going to get me a massive punishment.

"You know about Danny?" Her tone was low. I almost laughed hearing her call him that.

"Yeah, he and I have been working through a lot this past year. He tells me stories of when you guys were young." My voice filled with whimsy. She smiles as if she is remembering her life with him and honestly it brings the biggest smile on my face. It makes me think once more of the life we could have had.

After explaining everything that led up to the point of finding her and how I had three kids by three men, we took her home with us. She fawned over the kids immediately. This whole situation still had me in shock. It seemed like any moment from now I was going to wake up and this all would be a dream. My mother is alive in front of me, I'm living out my passion going back to school, I'm a new mother and I'm in love.

"Do you want to see him?" I ask my mother as she rocks Rhea.

"What if he's moved on?" She sucks in a breath.

"*Mami*, you should hear how he talks about you. He still in love with you. Even after all these years." I reassure her. After giving him a chance, we really bonded. He loves my mom; I don't think he'll ever be able to move on from her.

"I'm surprised he was so open with you. He wasn't always that way with me. I had to force him to tell me his feelings." Her laughter filled the air.

"Yeah, I can see that. He wasn't the most open before. We worked our way there." I laugh. I call Crespo and tell him that I'll be over soon.

Arriving at Crespo's home with my mother was surreal. When I opened the front door Elias was there with a shocked expression. "Dad! Come quick!" He yells. Crespo comes down in a hurry.

"What is going on!" He yells but cuts himself off quickly as his eyes land on my mother. "*Cara mia.*"

"You know it's rude to stare." My mother joked.

He rushed down the stairs so quickly I thought he might trip and die. He pulled my mother into a kiss and while in the moment I thought it was cute, it wore off quickly. It's so weird watching your parents kiss, blah.

"*Ti aspetto da una vita amore mio.* **[I have been waiting for you for a lifetime my love]**." He said something in Italian but I'm not too clear on it. "Please tell me you're staying here." His words pleading.

I rolled my eyes, "Um no, *Mami* is staying with me." I growl, pulling her closer to me.

Crespo glares at me and I glare back which insights laughter in my mother. "I'll stay here with your papa, you already have a full home, but if you need me to be there I will. I'm not going anywhere *mi bebe* I promise. Nothing could ever separate us again. I'm still young, only thirty-nine. "

"Thirty-nine-year-old grandmother." Crespo jokes.

"Forty-year-old *abuelo*!" She growls.

This small scene in front of me somehow made up for all these lost years. My mother and father reunited to continue their love for each other was priceless. Crespo held my mother tightly in his arms as if he would never let her out of his sight ever again. I spent the rest of the day and most of the night with them. It was hard to leave my mom there, but I knew that she would be all right.

When I called J.L and her mom about it, they couldn't believe it. Obviously, I had to lie a bit since they don't know about the whole mafioso family dynamic.

When I made it back home, Romero is in the kitchen with food on the island. I hop on the counter, and he kisses my lips. "What's all this?" My feet dangling as I wait for his answer.

"With everything going on, I am sure you forgot to eat." He answers serving me a plate. A smile rose to my lips because this is the Romero that only *I* get to see and it's so fucking sweet. Truth is, I haven't eaten all day. Adrenaline will really make you forget anything necessary for a prolonged period. I think the shock hasn't worn off and I just forgot.

"Thanks."

He looked up at me then went back to eating. "Let's take a bath." He suggests.

"You hate baths." I point out.

"But *you* like them." He protests. He really is trying to be nice to me today. I haven't heard the word brat come out of his mouth once. My mother returns from the dead and Romero is being sweet to me, I must be in a parallel universe. "Also, I need to brush out your hair today."

"I'm thinking of cutting it. It's just too long."

Romero looks up as if he's thinking and then looks back at me. "Short hair would look nice on you to." His devilish smirk appearing. "But I also like it long. I don't mind taking care of your hair for you. It's nice when I wrap it around my wrist when I have you on all fours."

I feel the heat rush through my body. My adrenaline is spiking once again. At this point, I need an ice bath to calm me down from the insanity that is today.

After a bath, I followed Romero into his giant closet. His closet filled with his expensive pristine suits. I'm convinced he was born with a suit on. He has some casual clothes but it's like 10% of his wardrobe.

He puts on some boxer briefs and pulls me onto his lap as he sits on the small couch in the room. I trace my fingers down his tattoos. "Are you going to get more?" I ask referring to his already many tats.

"Maybe. Why?"

"I think I want to get one."

He smirks, "Can I pick out your first tattoo?"

"No way. What would you even put?"

He snickers "Nothing bad, do you trust me?"

"Yes." I answer truthfully. "But Sebastian and Jameson have to approve it. I know Jameson will be the voice of reason."

He nods, "Fine."

My fingers linger on his neck. "I wonder what I should put there?"

"My neck? That's where you want it?"

"Yeah, so everyone can see." I laugh maniacally.

"Marking your territory, brat?" He taunts. His hand caressing the small of my back.

I push his wet hair back, then pull on the ends. "Brat? What happened to 'baby'."

He snorts the cutest raspy laugh. It makes me smile and pull him close to me. Romero's laugh dies down and he pulls me into a heartfelt kiss. His forehead leaned against mine and we closed our eyes. His breath became a bit unsteady for some reason. His fingers lock into my hair and rub circles with his thumb.

"I love you, Nova Corzo. Until today, I did not feel worthy enough to tell you. I could not tell you I loved you until I was able to give you peace. My family, I included, have taken so much from you. I could not forgive myself for letting you believe Crespo killed your mother, when you found out, it broke something in me because at that point I had fallen so fucking hard for you. I knew that I had no right to tell you I loved you until I was able to give you closure about your mother. I needed to fix what we broke." His words were so honest I was in shock. There was also a strain on his voice, as if he were on the brink of tears one fell from his eyes of course. did not think Romero would ever cry in front of me, but I defiantly tried my hardest to not cry at his declaration.

"I love you, Romero. I love all the facets of you. The parts of yourself you save for me and the tyrant. I love every part of you. Even if I didn't find my mother or know what happened to her, it would have not stopped me from loving you. I'm not angry with you anymore, I know that you truly care for me, even when you didn't say it." I stare into his dark green eyes and kiss him once more. "But I'm happy you did."

And for the first time that night, Romero, and I made indescribable love through the night.

I woke the next day to babies giggling. Their room was in the same hall as ours for safety. Donnie said he was visiting this morning. I went into the nursery and saw Donnie and...Lola. The Dominic's younger sister with the bad attitude. I haven't seen her since the babies were born. She doesn't seem to like me.

"Hello." She greets flatly.

I give her my best smile, "Hey, Lola. Glad you could come. You know if you ever want to come over feel free to drop by."

Her stone-cold stare doesn't waver. If Romero is the Ice King, then this is the Ice Princess. Her face only lights up when she looks over at the kids.

"Lola, are you free today? Donnie and I are going to a café with the kids, so they can get out a bit. Want to come with us?" I offer.

She looks back up at me and nods slightly. "Sure." She answers. I wasn't expecting it, but I'm happy that she said yes. She's my children's aunt and the sister of the men I love, I want to have some kind of relationship with her.

Romero wakes up shortly after and I explain to him that we will be gone for the morning. He looks at me nervously and then back at her sister Before kissing me goodbye. The three of us and the kids ended up at a nice outdoor restaurant. The kids were distracted by their stuffed animals, and we all sat and talked for a bit. Lola wasn't the most expressive, but she did join in our conversations. At one point Donnie got up from the table so that the two of us could be alone.

"Hey Lola, I hope I haven't done anything to offend you. I really want to get to know you if I can." I start.

"You haven't, I just don't know anything about you. I was surprised when I first saw you, I could not believe that my brothers had allowed a woman around the family. It had never happened before, so I was suspicious of you. Then rumor started to circulate that my brothers were sharing a woman, so I didn't think much of you. I wondered what kind of woman could steal the hearts of my brothers. You have to admit it is a weird situation. After spending some time with you today I realize that I should not have judged you without knowing you. This whole situation is very weird. I mean if you make them happy then, fine." She monologues.

I didn't really know what to say to that. I mean yeah, the situation between us all is not exactly the norm, but it works for us and we're happy. I can understand where she's coming from, I feel like I'd be overprotective of my siblings to.

"I meant what I said, I really would like it if you would come over. Or we can go visit you as well. You're their aunt, which makes you an important person in my life as well. I hope that we get to know more of each other throughout these years."

She smiles and I do the same in return.

...

Weeks later I realize the triplet's birthday was coming up. We didn't really get to celebrate last year because they wouldn't tell me the date because they wanted me to relax when I was pregnant. Only those triplets would be born in October.

I've been on the phone with Donnie for weeks planning a birthday surprise. Donnie suggested we do it in Italy since it got delayed due to my fear of leaving my mother, but my father has been overprotective and has many bodyguards for her. So, I feel a *bit* better leaving.

I want the triplets to have a calm relaxing birthday. So, we're going to fly out to Italy, stay in a villa with the kids, Cami, J.L, and Lola. I wanted Donnie to go but, he needed to make sure that territories were being protected while the triplets were away. They think that we're going for some dumb reason Donnie made up, which is good because I want them to be surprised. They still don't know that I have found out their birthday, so this should be fun.

When we land in Italy, I am just excited to even be here. I've never left the states before, so all of this was so breathtaking. The amount of culture here was amazing. The streets were so different from America. I mean you see it in the movies, but in real life it doesn't hold a candle. After a day of J.L and I being the biggest tourist ever, we got back to the Villa and got a good night's sleep. In the morning, I woke up super early so that I could cook breakfast for everyone. I didn't let Jameson do one thing, because I knew he would want to cook like the parent he is. Cami, J.L and Lola helped me with the kids so that they would be as quiet as possible, therefore, the triplets could sleep in.

When breakfast is ready, I jumped on all their beds, I regret waking Romero up this way because he gave me a punishment that morning. I could barely walk to the kitchen afterwards. I made all their favorites. Sebastian was like me, so he likes brown sugar bacon, pancakes and toast, Romero Egg whites and bacon on toast with black coffee, while Jameson liked avocado toast with an egg and turkey bacon.

"Why the amazing breakfast, sweet?" Sebastian observes, taking a bite of bacon.

"I cook for you at home all the time. Spoiled brats." My attempt at avoiding the answer. Jameson smirks and I glare not wanting him to catch on.

"I've been meaning to ask you guys, what part of Italy is your family from?" I ask taking a piece of bacon from my plate.

"Originally? Sicily but our mother's family came from Campania. She was American born like us though." Jameson answers.

"Hmm." I nod.

Sebastian clears his throat. "Don't forget, sweet. We are going somewhere alone this morning. Dress comfortably."

"Ok." I finished my food, I jumped into the shower and picked out a nice airy dress with cute sandals.

Sebastian informed me that we had to take the plane to Sicily because the car ride was way too long. I wondered where Sebastian would be taking me. We had an hour ride on this plane ride. I was laying on the bed in the back trying to fall asleep.

"Sweet, sleeping is not how you pass the time." He purred into my ear. His hand sliding up my legs, then ass. He lifted my dress and tugged at my panties. "You know what I just realized;

you've never had sex on a plane."

I blush and look away. "Who says I want to?"

"Oh, sweet." He chuckles pushing a finger into me. I clench immediately. "How can you lie to me? What were you thinking about in here all by yourself?"

I keep looking away from him. I wasn't thinking of anything until he came around me. If he didn't always drip fucking sex appeal, I wouldn't get so fucking horny.

"Collecting all your firsts, fills me with such joy." He mumbles pulling my panties off and tossing them next to me.

Sebastian's tongue runs along my folds teasingly. I can feel his smirk as he starts fucking me with his tongue and fingers. My moans start to come out more rapidly as his fingers move with so much vigor. My hands grab his hair pushing where I want it.

"Only you, Nova. Fuck, you are so beautiful. No shame to fall apart in front of me, sweet." He grunts. "Such an honest body. I couldn't have asked for a better scene in front of me right now."

I arch a bit from the sensations and his words. "Sebastian..we're going to get caught."

"I hope so." His eyes focused on mine as he lifts his head. "Do you want to get caught? Shot has turned you into a little exhibitionist, hasn't he, sweet? Did you like it when he fucked you at the pool, in front of so many eyes. Or do you like the act of almost getting caught?"

Have I become so kinky? I can't lie and say that I don't like either because I was completely turned on when Jameson had me on his lap and fucked me until his cum filled me. It was a euphoric experience that I wouldn't mind being in the middle of that again.

"Nothing to confess to, sweet? That's okay. I'll get rid of

your modesty soon enough." His lips hum against me.

"Deviant." I growled.

"Shot is better than me because I couldn't let anyone else see you. Other than my brothers of course. Your body is for our eyes only. Same goes for us, we belong only to you, sweet." He moves up my body till he reaches my lips. Our lips slowly coming together and then apart. My arms wrapped around his neck pulling his closer.

He laughs suddenly into my lips. "What?" I giggle.

"I'm trying not to let my full weight on you. If you pull me down, I'm going to squash you, sweet." He chuckles kissing my forehead.

The attendant knocks on the door to let us know we are about to land.

Chapter 22

Nova

Sebastian gripped my hand rather tightly as he walked with me. I didn't know where he was bringing me, but wherever it is it was something that made him nervous. I finally noticed that we were at a cemetery. The cemetery reminded me of the ones that are in Louisiana where they are above ground. He leads me to two graves that are decorated very beautifully. On the grave, it reads the names Servino Dominic, and the one right next door is Beatrice Dominic. These are his parent's graves, why would he bring me here?

"I know you're probably wondering why I would bring you here. I doubt you want to be at the graves of the woman who almost killed your mother and the man that held your mother as a bargaining chip." He breaths in deeply. "When I visit my parent's graves, I would speak to them in Italian, but I want you to hear what I have to say. "

I rubbed his back to ease his tension. "Mother...father... this is Nova. She is the mother of your grandchildren. We have three girls that are beautiful and healthy. That bring so much happiness into the Dominic family. Nova is Daniel Crespo's daughter and I know what you're thinking, 'this is a bad idea,' but it's the best thing that ever happened to us. I am going to spend the rest of my life beside this woman, and I just wanted you guys to know. We are going to be better family now that we have Nova. Mom, I never got a chance to tell you that I was sorry. I should've realized or someone should've realized that you were going through something you didn't understand and if anybody had cared to help you, you'd still be alive right now. I won't make the same mistake with our children, if they happen to have the same need for help as you did." He finishes.

He turns to me and smiles through teary eyes. "I love you, Sebastian." Both my hands holding his face.

His hands lay on top of mine. "I love you, little fox. I love so much Nova."

"Are you crying?" I tease. Kissing him on lips as I snicker.

"Keep teasing me, sweet. I'll make sure you're sore for a week. I've always gone soft on you. Maybe Ero's right, punishment is the only way you learn." He jokes and leans back into the kiss.

After the trip to the cemetery, he took me out to a genuinely lovely place for lunch before we were turned on the plane back to the Villa.

I hold Selene in my arms, Rhea in Cami's and Eris is thriving in her cute baby walker. Full of giggles and energy as Jameson gives her a toy.

"*È questo il tuo giocattolo preferito?* [**Is this your favorite toy?**]" Jameson playfully said something to Eris. Something about the toy I'm sure, I really need to learn more Italian.

"*Vamos cojer el cake* [**Let's get the cake.**]" I whispered in Spanish to Selene as I bounce her on my lap. I pass her onto Sebastian and run into the kitchen. I get the cake out and put twenty-four candles and bring it into the living room.

The girls help me sing and the triplets smile widely at the surprise. I place it on the coffee table and the babies' eyes light up. The triplets blow out their candles and we start the celebrations with some music.

Jameson pulls me into his lap and kisses me cheek. "The day is not over; we still have to open presents." I gleam.

I go get three boxes and pass them out. Jameson opens his gift and its new combat knives, for Sebastian new dark literature and Romero a watch I designed.

I then had to move the cake before the little three messed it up. I put them in their highchairs and let them attack pieces of cake.

Romero comes up behind me and wraps his arms around my waist as I wash some dishes. "How nice of you to spoil us today." His hand lifts my dress and rubs my inner thigh. I exhale, a reaction of his gentle touch. "Cami and J.L are going out on a date. The kids are going to sleep soon. So that leaves us. You did good today, deserving of a reward."

I back up and rub against him slightly making him hiss in my ear. "Yeah?" I challenged.

"But this reward is also for us. We all have something we want from you." His cool breath on my neck.

"What is it?"

He dries my hand with a nearby rag and locks my hand with his. "Follow me."

Out of the corner of my eye I see Jameson and Sebastian taking the kids to the baby room. I follow Romero to the master bathroom and on the bed is an outfit. An emerald, green lace lingerie with black stockings.

"Don't be nervous. Put it on, this color looks perfect on you. I remember the first time you wore that emerald dress." His gently removes my dress and lets it fall to the ground. "You looked so beautiful and sexy I don't know how I let you out the door without leaving my trail of cum inside you, so that no matter who you saw at that party you would think of me. "

I don't speak just try to control my breathing and put on the lingerie. His dark gaze set on me as I sat in the bed in the attire, he had picked out for me. His lips connected with mine and I wrapped my hand around the back of his strong neck.

"Starting without us, little brother?" Sebastian teases.

"I'm glad it fits, *tesoro*." Jameson's smooth voice entering the room.

"Wait, all of you? Last time this happened, I got pregnant with triplets. I don't think I'm up for that again." I laugh nervously walking backwards, away from them. I felt like a rabbit surrounded by deadly wolves ready to devour me. Sebastian sat behind me and loosened his tie and quickly tied my wrist with them to my front.

"Any tighter and you break my wrists." I growled at Sebastian.

"Can't risk you escaping, you know how sneaking foxes can be, little fox."

"Said the fox to the fox." I scoffed. He smirks and pushes my curls out of my face. He ties my hair into a ponytail going down my back.

"Perfect, now we can see those pretty doe eyes of yours. You look more like a doe now being tied up.

"Do I? You know how hard a doe can kick?" I joke. I feel a hard tug on my ponytail that makes me fall on my back.

"Tsk, tsk, tsk. What will we do about that smart mouth of hers?" Sebastian sighs.

"The possibilities are endless." Jameson comments. "So,

let's make the most of it."

I was on my back thanks to Sebastian yanking my damn hair. Jameson starts by tracing my nipple with his thumb. His finger was warm and gentle. He crawled on top of me and began to lick my nipples. Suddenly I could feel liquid running down my breast.

My fucking breastmilk was coming to out! What a way to kill the fucking mood.

"Sweet." Jameson comments as he starts to lick up my milk. "I didn't think it would taste so sweet." He continues to lick my nipple until it's clean.

Romeo looks over me, I'm guessing to Sebastian, smirking. "Let's all have a taste."

Jameson moves over and now Sebastian and Romero have taken one nipple and each mouth. They lick gently until they can taste some of my milk.

"Taste kind of like a latte." Sebastian chuckles.

"It does a bit." Romeo agrees.

"Quit that! It's so embarrassing." I whine, trying to cover my breasts.

Romeo takes a rag and cleans me of any milk. "Very well. We'll leave your tits alone...for now."

Sebastian runs hand on my side it was over the fabric I was wearing, but I could still feel his warm hands. He sat there and waited his turn, but by the expression I was saying he was ready to attack at any moment.

Romero spread my legs and rubbed his thumb to the lips

of my pussy. He didn't enter it, just rubbed the outside. This put me in a frenzy, he was the king of teasing and that was never fun for me. I guess I'm a lot like Sebastian, I just can't wait. Romero reach down with his mouth and begin to lick at my canal. Slow strokes continued for a few minutes. I tried to reach for him, to press him down deeper into me, but Sebastian was holding my hands hostage. It wasn't enough that he tied my wrists together, he was holding my hands on top of my head. So, I had to sit there, and squirm is he filled me with endless ecstasy. I could feel my climax reaching. They all had such a talented tongue; I didn't know if I was going to be able to hold out for much longer.

"You're going to cum soon I can taste it. You're completely soaked." Romero snickers, his tongue still working its magic.

"No way, I'm going to outlast you all." I challenged.

Jameson raises a brow. "We'll see."

"Ignore her, little brother. Her body tells a different story. Dirty brat is sopping wet, she will come soon enough. Wouldn't you?" Romero taunts. He has the right of it though. I'm so close I will not be able to hold out.

"L-Let me touch you." I beg. Romero stops and looks up. He unties the tie from my wrists, surprisingly.

"What do you have planned?"

I get up from the bed, stand on my tippy toes, and kiss Romero. I push him on the bed. I strip him of his pants and underwear. His cock was fully erect and had a bit of precum. I hover over his cock facing the opposite direction, reverse cowgirl. I slowly slip him into me, and I gasp from the warm feeling.

"Jameson, Sebastian, stand in front of me." I ordered and they listened.

I had them strip of their clothing so that I could suck one off and give the other a hand job. I blew Jameson first as I bounced on his brother's dick and stroked the other with my hand.

"Take me deeper, *tesoro*." Jameson moaned. I did what he said, and it make me choke, but I know that just made him hornier.

Romero started to speed up almost as if I wasn't giving him enough attention. My jealous Ice King pushed deeper into me as I bounced.

My hand stroked Sebastian's cock and played slightly with his balls. He gripped my hair and pulled it back, making me release Jameson's cock from my mouth. "Sweet, turn around." He ordered. I slipped from Romero's cock to turn around. I laid a top Romero as his cock poked at me entrance. "I want to see if we can fit two of our cocks into your cunt. I'm sure we can."

My eyes turn wide, but I wasn't opposed to the idea. How would that feel? Would they follow through? I look to Romero, and he smiles and pulls me into a kiss. He enters me once again and fucks me.

"Bash, what are you waiting for? Her pussy could use another cock." Romeo groaned in between kisses. I brace myself for Sebastian's cock to join Romero's inside me. I thought they were kidding but I know better to not believe a Dominic.

"Fuck...this feels weird..." I moan. The start moving in unison and my moans get exponentially louder.

"How does it feel now, sweet?" Sebastian groans into my shoulder.

"Good...so good...you're both rubbing against my walls

and it's like a double dose of pleasure." I cry.

"Fuck, you're suffocating us. Should we fill you up with our cum now?" Romeo growls.

Sebastian slaps my ass harshly as he continues to pump into me rising the heat level in my body. Sebastian takes his dick out of me slowly, leaving me feeling with a need to refill that space. I feel a warm liquid being rubbed into the hole of my ass.

"*Tesoro*, I'm going to need you relax." Jameson's soft voice echoing in my ear as the tip of his cock aims at my hole. His hands grip my hips, while Romero's hands were pulling my ass cheeks apart. Even with what I assume is lube, Jameson was struggling to fit all the way into my ass. "Why wouldn't you let me in?" He laughed.

"My ass isn't the problem, shrink your dick." I joke until Romero pulls my head back down to him, slipping his tongue into my mouth. It must have been the medicine I needed to have Jameson enter me because seconds later he slipped right in. That pressure consumed me once again. Cries left my body as they drove into me.

"Are you letting them stretch you out, sweet? How does it feel?" Sebastian cooed stroking his own cock as he watched from the side.

"Amazing! The three of you are so perfectly made for me!" I try to say though a series of moans. "I love you all with all my heart."

"Heart and pussy." Romero corrected. "We love you to, brat." His lips returned to mine. The way Sebastian and Jameson shifted; they must be surprised that he said it back. It was quickly ignored though, and they continued.

Jameson

I swear I was leaving indentations on Nova's skin. The way I was holding on to her as I fucked her. Ero and I had been putting holes and other rips all along the green lingerie she had on. It looks amazing on her, but her body is even better to look at. Romero and I continued our efforts. She really was trying to last with us, and she might just beat us.

"I'm...gonna cum. I-I can't wait anymore! Fuck!" She came and I could feel the shakiness in her body. The sweet sound of her moans fluttering around. I followed soon after in defeat and filled her ass with my cum. I slipped out of her, and she laid on Romero for a second as he stroked her hair. She slowly got up and put her attention onto Bash. She got on her knees and took his cock in her mouth. His hands fisted into her hair, pushing her deeper and deeper. You could tell she was trying her best not to gag, but that's the best part.

"Sweet, you're so cute. Trying not to choke." Bash teases. "Funny thing is, I want you to."

She flipped him the bird and we all chuckle. Her stokes becomes faster and within seconds he cums into her mouth. His cum fall down her lips but she licks it all up. He pulls her in for kiss. "You're good girl, sweet. You swallowed all my cum, didn't you?"

"Of course, she did." I chime in.

"Did you forget about me, brat." Romero says pulling on her pony tail harshly. She went to smack him, but he grabbed her hand.

"Pull my hair again and I'll leave more marks than tattoos can cover." She threatens as her hands twitch with anger. Bash was right she was a little fox.

"Promise?" He retorts with a wicked smile.

Romero

I remember a time when Nova would have pretended, she didn't want the three of us and now she takes us all with no issue. Nova, my first real love and mother to my child. I could not ask for a more perfect girl. This was not the reward we were giving Nova; this was more for us. I wanted to get some family portraits done. Nova always complains that our home feels empty without pictures. I've never cared about stuff like that, but if it's what she wants.

I wrapped Nova's hair around my hand and had her lay against the pillow I front of her so that I could get a better angle of her pussy. I loved fucking Nova's pussy from behind, while pulling on her long hair. She pretends she hates us pulling on her hair, but she loves the pain from it. My little masochist loves to have her ass slapped, hair pulled, and pussy brutally fucked.

I entered her quickly, not giving her any warning. She was so warm and soaked. "Ready to cum again? Let's cum together this time." I whisper into her ear. She nods her head slightly.

I start to pump into her getting starry eyed with just the feel of her. Nova's soft skin, her smell, the way her body pressed against me, was just the ultimate experience. Being with Nova will never grow tiring. This beautiful woman before me is always surprising me with her as a person and how she makes me feel as well. Listen to me being so fucking sappy, it's making me sick.

Nova cries out every time I push deeper into her when I pull her hair back. "Even when you cry, you're still so desirable.

Nova cries out every time I push deeper into her when I pull her hair back to match my strokes… "You're so pretty when you cry out like that." I say into her neck when I lean over.

"Don't ease up! Fuck me until I can't stand..." She whimpered.

"Such a dirty mouth. Fine, if that's what you want." I say kissing her flushed neck. Her whole body was flushed. I left a few red marks on her supple ass. She looked like an art piece of *my* creation. I was going to cum any second. "Cum, now." I growl spilling into her.

Her shakes returned and I knew she had came once again. She tried to muffle the scream begging to escape her mouth. "Fuck..." She mutters.

Nova

I was still on my stomach trying to catch my breath. I could feel Romero's hand rubbing my back. A smile appears on my face as I turn to them.

"What, sweet?" Sebastian narrows with a smile.

"If this is what my future looks like, I'm going to have a very happy life..." I hummed. I watch the Dominic's get dressed and then I hear the babies crying loudly. The three of them run out the door quickly and I follow behind after throwing on clothes and getting a gun. I run to the baby room and Romero has a man up against the wall.

"Stay with the kids!" Romero shouts after me. I ran to the nursery and settled the babies.

Suddenly I get a hard smack to the side of my head, and I fall to the ground. The gun is still in my hand. I open my eye and without hesitation I shoot the gun till the bullets are gone. I hear noises and footsteps come into the room. Jameson is at my side, and he is saying something to me, but my head is dizzy from the hit.

"I'm fine, my head just hurts. Check on the babies." They we're wailing because of the loud sounds of gun fire, I'm sure. Sebastian came to side and carried me off the floor. "What's happening." I ask drowsily.

"We got careless. We're back in Italy not everyone it's too fond of us. We might have to cut the trip short, sweet. I'm sorry." Sebastian apologizes. "But the rest are gone. Romero and I killed him, and you killed his partner. Romero is chewing out security."

"He's dead?" Through all the confusion, I had just realized that I had killed someone for the first time, but I didn't feel any guilt. Is there something with me?

"He could have hurt our children. Don't you dare pity that garbage. You protected the family, I'm proud of you." He nuzzled against me, bring his head on top of mine.

Chapter 23

Nova

I was quiet the rest of trip. I told Sebastian that killing someone was an easy way out but then I killed someone. I'm such a hypocrite. Is this how they felt when they killed someone? I felt like I didn't have a choice but to kill him. I now realize was Sebastian was trying to tell me before.

My three little sister ones slept on the bed with me the whole trip back. I just wanted them close as possible. I feared last night being the last time I saw them. I could see the worried expressions of their faces as they looked at me, but those looks faded, and they went back to their aloof structure.

"Finally, home." Sebastian sighed with Selene and Eris in his arms. I carried Rhea in mine and set her down in her crib, Sebastian followed and did the same with the Selene and Eris.

I walked to the kitchen and sat on the island with a drink in my hand. The Dominic's stayed close by and waited for me to speak. "What the hell did I do?" I whispered into my cup.

"Officially became one of us. Your first kill. I didn't want this for you, but now you understand." Jameson starts.

"I just killed another person. I didn't even hesitate. I- "

"And you shouldn't have. If you would have our kids would be dead or worse. This might happen again, and you need to understand that. I'm not going to sugar coat it for you. You're one of us so I'm going to speak to you, frankly." Romero cut in.

I look over at Romero and I can see that worry on his face again. "I'm not going anywhere. I knew the risks and I chose to stay. I meant what I said, I love you three and you are my future." I reassure. "But I'm going to need time to come to terms about what I've done."

Sebastian walked up and kissed my forehead. "You are stronger than you think, sweet." He whispers into my ear. I wrap my arms around him and pull him closer. I bury my head into his chest. I still didn't feel bad about killing him but that feeling inside me that I had killed someone was still lingering.

Jameson rubs my back a bit and tells me he is going to check on the kids once more before going to sleep. I lift my head and Romero is leaning against the wall. "You should get some sleep." I say and then look at Sebastian, "You to."

"I'll sleep when you do." Romero answers coolly. His eyes are closed but he is waiting for an answer from me.

Sebastian brings me down from the island and I take the hand Romero offers me. his lips press against the top of my head as he leads me to his room where I drift into sleep.

Two Months Later

The Dominics were super sweet to me and understood that I needed time to myself for these last two months. Busy with their own lives, I got to see them only for a bit, while I focused on my studies. My phone vibrated with a text.

**Tattoo day, sweet. Don't chicken out.
-Sebastian**

I'm doing it. I already accepted. What are you guys thinking?

-Nova

It's a surprise, unless you're going to tell us what tattoo your giving us?
-Sebastian

Be smart about it.
-Romero

I put a lot of thought into it.
-Nova

Can't what you mark us with.
-Jameson

For their tattoos I wanted it to reflect how I saw them. I wondered if they were thinking of the same thing.

"*¡Bebe! ¿Por qué dejas estas luces encendidas?* [**Baby, why are you leaving all these light on?!**]" My mother yelled from the hall. She had been staying here while I work through my murder mishap. Jameson loves her around because he hasn't had to cook. Romero and she don't get along the best, two alphas don't mix well, but Sebastian is fine with her, but he keeps his distances. I guess seeing my mom doesn't bring him the best memories.

My mom comes in with Selene on her hip. "*Bebe*, come help me put up the tree together. It's the babies first Christmas. I get up almost immediately, I loved decorating the tree during Christmas and baking that was also fun to do.

"What are we doing with the tree?" Jameson's voice comes through the hall. He sees the girls playing on their mat in the living room and heads to play with them.

"Are we opening our presents on Christmas eve?" I sound like little kid every time my mom's around.

"You can't do that, *tesoro*." Jameson chuckles.

"Yes, we can. We always opened our presents the day before. It's tradition." I gleamed.

"A tradition in how to make you stop crying. Nova screamed and cried until I let her open her presents." My mother explained.

"She's *always* been a brat. Good to know." Romero voice suddenly coming into frame.

"Says the guy who throws a fit because the ends of his shirt wouldn't fold into his suit jacket. Try again, Ice King." I scoff.

"Well, I know what naughty fox is getting coal for Christmas." Sebastian says coming in from the hall next.

"Yes, we do." I retort, staring right at him. He just gives me his charming smile and walks over to kiss me.

Sebastian pulls away and looks at his phone. "D.J and Astra should be here soon for our tattoos, sweet. Can't wait to leave our mark."

"Tattoo?" My mom asks curiously. I forgot to tell her.

"Yeah, I thought I'd get one." I smile innocently at her.

"Okay." She drags out before opening boxes full of tree lights.

Sebastian's phone goes off and he gets up. "They're here."

Sebastian leaves and then comes back with a woman that looked about my mother's age and the other looked similar to her. "Nova, this is D.J and Astra, they are really skilled tattoo artist. They have done my tattoos and a lot of the other people in the family." Sebastian explains.

"Well after twenty years, I better be good." She laughs. She comes up and shakes my hand. "Nice to meet you Nova. Do you know what you're going to put on these three?"

"Yes." I walked closer to her and whispered in her ear what I wanted so the Dominic's couldn't hear.

For Sebastian, a quote from our favorite author saying "There is no exquisite beauty...without some strangeness in the proportion" going across his side. For Romero, a crown dripping with water and Jameson a two headed skeleton; to show the Greek tale of how humans came to be before they were split apart.

"Why did you choose this?" Jameson asks looking at the sketch. I wrap my arms around his neck and lean on his back.

"Well, in Greek Mythology they said that humans were made with four arms, four legs, and two heads, but Zeus decided to slit them in half so they would have to find their other halves." I explained. "You are my first real love, and I am so happy to have found you."

"What about mine, sweet?" Sebastian asks looking down at his sketch.

"You taught me that love is sticking around even when it's not perfect, you are a living version of "in sickness and health." I know no matter what you will always love me, even when I'm old and can't remember you, I know you'll always help me remind me." I turn my head to Romeo and look happily into those dark greens. "Lastly, my Ice King. Your tattoo is a symbol of the part of you I get to keep to myself. Most of the time you are an Ice King guarding your kingdom, but then the ice melts away, and I get my soft-hearted king, who will make life easier for me, because he genuinely wants to. You taught me that love takes time and patience."

Romero smiles and pats his lap. I let go of Jameson and sit on Romero's lap. He wraps his arms around me, and I lean back on him, while D.J starts on Jameson's tattoo. The tattoos didn't take as long as I thought since they were small tattoos. I was last and I was a bit scared to be honest.

"What is it?" I asked.

"A secret until it done, *tesoro*." Jameson says holding and kissing my hand.

"Almost done, hang in there." Astra says sweetly.

When she finally finished, I saw it in the mirror, and it was a book with the familiar saying the triplets had on their own bodies. "*Guardami negli occhi del perdente.*" Sebastian reads aloud.

"View me in the eyes of the loser, right? You guys all have the same one." I gleam.

"Now we match." Romero states.

I look over the tattoo of the book and it looks like it's flipping the page and there are three initials on the book of the pages; R.D, J.D, and S.D. "You branded me?" I growl.

"What the problem? Till death do us part, little fox." Sebastian snickered.

I glare at the demonic triplets I've saddled myself with.

Few Days Later

It was the night of Christmas Eve and we spent it with close family. J.L, Sebastian and Lola were on the floor playing with the girls. Donnie and his siblings were spread across the couch. The Crespo family and Dominics are cordial, but in no way are they spending holidays together, so I'll be over there with the girls for Christmas.

I lay into Romero's arms on the couch with a small blanket on me as I watch everyone enjoy the holiday. It feels like one of those hallmark movies in here, you know if hallmark made movies about the mafia.

"*Bebe,* time to open your gift." My mother says bringing a small box.

"It's from Shot, Bash and I." Romero says. I sit up and open the box. In the box, is three rings, the rings have a weird design on the band. I slip all three on my ring and they all fit perfectly to make the three emerald gems to line up as if it was one ring.

My eyes well up with tears. "It's beautiful. It's perfect, thank you guys."

Romero takes my hands and slips the ring off and slips it onto my ringer on the left hand. "Ready to be a Dominic?"

I laugh, "I can't marry all of you, that's not legal." I laugh.

"Legally yes, but we can change your surname." Romero chuckles. "A piece of paper doesn't dictate your place in this family."

I nuzzle up to him and smile, "You really want me to be a Dominic?"

"Of course!" Donnie gets up and sits next to me hugging me tightly, but Romero keeps pushing him off. "That means we're cousins. I love you cous."

I laugh at Donnie's antics and hug him back, but Romero puts a stop to that quickly by pulling Donnie back by his hair.

I smile widely before I try out my new name. "Nova Dominic."

About the Author

A Cuban, Florida girl with a useless bachelor's degree in Psychology, spends her free time writing out her passions onto paper. When she's not in school, trying not to fail out of every subject, she is spending time watching in insane amount of anime and playing every new Batman game that comes out.

Lets Talk!

I would love to talk to you guys and see how you feel about the book and if you guys would be intrested in any squeals?

Squeal Ideas

Donnie?

J.L x Camilia?

More of the triplet Dominics?

Socials

Insta: @sp_the_author